RALPH COMPTON
SNAKE OIL JUSTICE

A RALPH COMPTON WESTERN

Ralph Compton
Snake Oil Justice

Jackson Lowry

THORNDIKE PRESS
A part of Gale, a Cengage Company

Copyright © 2022 by The Estate of Ralph Compton.
The Sundown Riders.
Thorndike Press, a part of Gale, a Cengage Company.

Thorndike Press® Large Print Hardcover Western.
The text of this Large Print edition is unabridged.
Other aspects of the book may vary from the original edition.
Set in 16 pt. Plantin.

LIBRARY OF CONGRESS CIP DATA ON FILE.
CATALOGUING IN PUBLICATION FOR THIS BOOK
IS AVAILABLE FROM THE LIBRARY OF CONGRESS.

ISBN-13: 979-8-88578-492-4 (hardcover alk. paper)

Published in 2023 by arrangement with Berkley, an imprint of Penguin Publishing Group, a division of Penguin Random House, LLC.

Printed in Mexico
Print Number: 1   Print Year: 2023

THE IMMORTAL COWBOY

This is respectfully dedicated to the "American Cowboy." His was the saga sparked by the turmoil that followed the Civil War, and the passing of more than a century has by no means diminished the flame.

True, the old days and the old ways are but treasured memories, and the old trails have grown dim with the ravages of time, but the spirit of the cowboy lives on.

In my travels — to Texas, Oklahoma, Kansas, Nebraska, Colorado, Wyoming, New Mexico, and Arizona — I always find something that reminds me of the Old West. While I am walking these plains and mountains for the first time, there is this feeling that a part of me is eternal, that I have known these old trails before. I believe it is the undying spirit of the frontier calling me, through the mind's eye, to step back into time. What is the appeal of the Old West of the American frontier?

It has been epitomized by some as the dark and bloody period in American history. Its heroes — Crockett, Bowie, Hickok, Earp — have been reviled and criticized. Yet the Old West lives on, larger than life.

It has become a symbol of freedom, when there was always another mountain to climb and another river to cross; when a dispute between two men was settled not with expensive lawyers, but with fists, knives, or guns. Barbaric? Maybe. But some things never change. When the cowboy rode into the pages of American history, he left behind a legacy that lives within the hearts of us all.

— *Ralph Compton*

CHAPTER ONE

Every small West Texas town looked the same, but Jerome Frederick Kincannon, Professor of Potions and Apothecary Extraordinaire, still felt a thrill of what might be possible as he looked around the haphazard streets, his sharp coal-colored eyes missing nothing. There had been a crudely painted sign alongside the dusty road coming in proclaiming this desolate remnant to be Chagrin. Jerome figured it would be more like Jubilation if he found the men he had sought so hard for almost a year.

Leland Benjamin. Curtis Benjamin. Another gang member he had never heard named. And most of all — worst of all — Hank Benjamin. The leader of the notorious Benjamin gang, the man who had killed his wife and son in the most brutal fashion possible.

At the persistent memory, Jerome sucked in his breath and squinted, letting a small tear roll down his cheek. It left a muddy trail that immediately dried in the hot air. Where it caked, it began to pucker the skin.

"Marcie. Arthur."

He hastily turned his face and rubbed away the evidence of his caring against the padded shoulder of his trail-grimy pearl gray coat. Luckily, there wasn't anyone to see this small reminiscence being swept away. He had to sell his wagonload of potions, elixirs and vile concoctions to keep going with his search for men whose faces he had never seen and whom he knew only through the bloody trail they had left behind. Showing any weakness detracted from his credibility when he interrogated lawmen and citizens alike.

He snapped the reins and drove his medicine wagon through the middle of town, following a street that must have been laid out by following a drunk cow. There was a soul-numbing sameness to all these Texas towns because of the lack of water, the slow decay of the buildings and a palpable malaise caused by the Butterfield Stage Company running fewer and fewer coaches. The railroad had bypassed Chagrin and laid tracks some distance away to the north, through San Angelo. With cargo and people gathering around a distant depot, there wasn't any reason to come to a town like this.

With or without a railroad, from the dilapidated look of the place, he wasn't sure why anyone had ever wanted to live in Chagrin.

The simple desire of men and women to move on in search of the ever-elusive greener pastures was made easier by the very railroad that killed their town. They needed only to hop on a train and be halfway across the country in a few days. Only that easy escape wasn't offered by this town.

For his part, Jerome Kincannon knew what he sought in Chagrin and every other town that was its twin: revenge.

He reached the far end of the street in less than five minutes, struggled to turn his medicine wagon about and drove back. He pulled off the main street, edged around a dead horse drawing flies by the thousands and parked his wagon behind the single saloon in town. It spoke volumes that there was only one gin mill in the entire town and not a dozen or more. Chagrin was dead and refused to admit it.

Joints aching from long hours on the road, he climbed down from the driver's box and wrapped the reins around a convenient hitch post. Brushing dust from his clothing, he stepped into the street and repeated his trip from one end of Chagrin to the other, this time on foot. It hardly took longer for the circuit walking than it had driving.

Jerome tipped his hat to the few women he encountered, all of whom tried not to stare at him. He was a tall man, almost six feet in height, broad shoulders, thick chest and powerful hands that performed dexterously when he mixed his potions. He had grown up in Indian Territory near the Cherokee capital of Tahlequah, working hard on his family's farm until his parents and two brothers had died in a cholera epidemic. This had firmed his desire to do something to prevent such tragedies from happening to others, but he had quickly found he didn't have the stomach to be a doctor. This revelation had led him to apprentice himself with an apothecary, learning the trade at Fort Smith until old Mr. Poulin had died after imbibing one of his own experimental elixirs.

By then Jerome had saved enough to buy the business from the apothecary's widow — and he had met Marcie. He closed his eyes for a moment and pictured her perfectly: long blond hair flowing as the stiff Arkansas breeze pulled it back from her pale oval face. Bright eyes the color of the finest emeralds shone with life, and her every movement was fluid, graceful perfection. His callused hand moved to his cheek where she had so often caressed him.

"You all right, mister?"

"What's that?" Jerome opened his eyes.

The grassy meadow where Marcie had been running, so full of life, disappeared, replaced by heat and a fifty-foot-tall dust devil fitfully waggling its way down Chagrin's meandering main street.

"I said," the old man called, almost shouting as if Jerome were deaf, "are you feelin' fit? You wobbled a mite, and I don't often see folks standin' round with their eyes closed 'less they're afflicted with a touch of sunstroke." The old man pushed back the brim of his straw hat, looked up into the cloudless sky and squinted at the burning sun momentarily blocked by the miniature tornado of the dust devil. "Folks what ain't used to the sun and heat start doin' strange things."

"Like standing in the street with their eyes closed," Jerome said, grinning. "There's nothing to worry about, old-timer. I've spent the livelong day sitting on a hard wood seat, driving my rig into your fair town. I only need a few minutes to get my

11

legs under me."

"Oh," the old geezer said, spitting into the street. The dry dust engulfed the spittle and swallowed it, leaving behind only a small, hard clump. "That means you're some kind of peddler, don't it?" The man stepped back tugged his hat brim down and squinted even harder as he took in Jerome's clothing.

Jerome knew he had to appear prosperous to sell his elixir and he had spent a great deal of his money buying the cutaway gray coat, the brocade vest chased with gleaming gold threads, the once creased dress pants and the fine high-topped shoes, now sorely in need of a good shining. He tucked his thumbs into the armholes of his vest and struck a pose as if he had already lowered the stage at the rear of his wagon and spoke to a large crowd of curious citizens.

"I am none other than J. Frederick Kincannon, master apothecary and practitioner of medicinal arts thought lost long centuries ago. Many call me Professor of Potions. I learned my trade by palaver with the Cherokee medicine men, through intense study of ancient Sumerian tomes and at the feet of a man wiser than any human can reckon, none other than Dr. Severn Poulin."

"Poulin?"

The old man spat again, wiped his lips

with his sleeve, then fished out a cloth bag from his shirt pocket. Arthritic fingers working slowly, he pulled out an inch-long chaw of tobacco. He looked at it skeptically, then offered it silently to Jerome, who refused. Relieved but having done his neighborly duty, the man popped what remained of the plug into his mouth and began chewing with noisy gusto.

After the juice began seeping into his tongue and cheeks, the man said, "I knew a Poulin once. Over in New Braunfels. He was a card cheat. They upped and hanged him after they caught him with a second ace of spades."

"The Poulin to whom I refer was an honorable man versed in the most arcane of the healing professions."

"Do tell?" The old man spat, then asked, "Kin I ast you a question?"

"Please do."

"What the burnin' hell's a 'See Marian tome'? Anything like them marble graves they put aboveground over in New Orleans?"

Jerome almost laughed. Fighting to keep his composure, he said solemnly, "All will be explained when I bring around my medicine wagon to properly display my tonics, elixirs and other potions to cure what ails you."

"You can cure all that?" The old man looked skeptical.

Jerome hadn't mentioned what those maladies might have been, but he had his suspicion in a man of this age.

"I can, using my secret potions."

The old man looked him over again, then snorted. "If that don't beat all. Professor of Potions."

With that, he shuffled down the street, following the brown cloud left behind by the slowly weakening dust devil.

Stride long and confident, Jerome went from store to store, personally greeting the clerks and owners. Chagrin was no different from any other town. The folks were a mite suspicious to start, but they warmed to him when it was obvious he wasn't bringing trouble their direction. He made a show of keeping his coat pulled back so they could see he wasn't wearing a gun, but he also made certain no one saw the brace of knives hidden about his body like some tinhorn gambler.

"Good day, sir," Jerome said to a man in an apron busily sweeping out a small restaurant.

"You want somethin' to eat? I kin fix up a plate of stew. It's late for lunch, early for dinner, but you got a hungry look about you, and I aim to please."

"That's mighty kind of you," Jerome said.

"Fifteen cents. Fer twenty I'll throw in a cup of coffee."

"Better and better," Jerome said, going into the tiny establishment.

The serving space was hardly ten by ten. He settled down at the table by the only window and looked out. Hardly anyone was stirring. The late-afternoon summer heat was too oppressive, though like so many prairie dogs, heads occasionally popped into view as the citizens tried to catch sight of the stranger.

"You get many sightseers through Chagrin?"

"Nope, cain't say we do," the waiter said. "Not much to see in this part of Texas. Truth is, the town's dyin'. We's on the road from San Antonio to El Paso, but road agents have been plyin' their trade too aggressively fer anyone's likin'. Now and then we git a payroll rattlin' through fer one of the Army forts, but not often. And they don't stop. Can't blame them, though we serve the best beef stew in fifty miles." He winked broadly and added, "You're prob'ly thinkin' it's the only stew. You'd be right."

Jerome tried to keep his voice calm. "Road

15

agents, eh? These outlaws have a name?"

"Reckon they do, but I don't know 'em to call by their first names. They'd probably lie and give a summer name, anyhow."

The waiter chuckled at this. No outlaw would ride into a town like this and announce his presence by shouting out his real name unless he was a true desperado looking for a fight.

"Have you heard tell of the Benjamin gang?" Jerome watched the waiter's face reflected in the window, eager for any hint of recognition.

"Cain't say that I have. Why're you askin'? You don't look like no lawman to me, not that it's any of my business."

"I'm not a lawman. I came up from San Antone to sell my healing elixirs, but it's worrisome hearing all this about outlaws along the road. You ever catch the name of any of those owlhoots? It'd be a boon if I knew who to avoid."

Jerome poked at the stew on the plate dropped in front of him. A single hunk of beef floated in a sea of grease. Carrots and something green and lacy slowly drowned around the meat. The waiter grabbed a coffee cup and filled it, a little of the brown liquid sloshing out onto the checkered tabletop. Jerome never noticed. He intently stared at the man for any sign of recognition of the murdering swine he had chased across the entire state of Texas after getting on their trail along the Red River ten months back.

"Never heard none of their names, no, sir, and Benjamin wasn't among them that I didn't hear."

Jerome frowned, trying to decipher what the waiter meant and finally decided he had to look a little harder and travel a little farther to find the Benjamin clan. His shoulders slumped as he shoveled the food into his mouth, barely tasting it as it slid down his gullet. The coffee was hot and bitter, but it washed down the stew with its chunks of stringy meat and carrots boiled almost white.

"Thanks," Jerome said, counting out the money for the waiter.

"You huntin' fer desperadoes, you might ask over at the saloon. Somebody there's gotta know." The waiter gave a contemptuous snort. "They think they know ever'thing, at least."

"Is the marshal around? I need to purchase a vending permit."

"Waterin' Hole Number Three," the waiter answered. Seeing Jerome's confusion, he added, "That's the saloon. Don't know where the other two waterin' holes are, 'cept maybe in Jackass Morgan's head. They surely aren't in Chagrin and never have been."

"He the owner?"

"Is, and that moniker's chosen real good, too."

Jerome stepped into the street and almost staggered back a half step. He hadn't realized how hot it was in the late-day sun and how much even the dubious shelter provided by the restaurant cooled him down. Tugging at his derby hat to shade his face as much as possible with the narrow brim, he went down the street to the marshal's office, only to find it empty. After a quick look at the half dozen wanted posters nailed to the wall, he went back outside. Jerome heaved a deep sigh. None of the posters was for the Benjamin gang or any of its vicious members.

Jerome had spent the better part of a month after his house had been burned down and wife and son killed finding who might have been responsible. In spite of the crime happening in Judge Parker's jurisdiction, the "hanging judge" had not sent out any of his marshals to investigate. Too many deputies roamed through Indian Territory on other business to spare even one, the court clerk had said. Jerome had taken it upon himself to ask, to follow and to ask more questions, and finally he had found a barkeep north of the Red River who put a name to the men responsible for ruining Jerome's life. The bartender had accurately recounted what several men had said about their crimes.

Hank, Leland, Curtis and another un-named Benjamin relative. They would pay.

Settling his coat about his broad shoulders caused a new cloud of trail dust. Jerome strode down the street toward the saloon, cheerfully greeting men and women who poked their heads out of stores along the twisty street. He made a point of inviting them to his sales pitch later. He kept it sounding more neighborly than forceful, knowing he would draw them from curiosity as well as need to cure their aches and pains.

He stopped in front of the saloon's swinging doors, stared inside and was surprised to see that it was both larger and more elegant than it had any right being. A large stage with decent curtains stretched across the entire back of the saloon, with tables and chairs, mostly empty after a noonday rush, arrayed so every patron could get a decent view. *Or a view of the indecent,*

Jerome mused. The kind of performance that went on in such gin mills wasn't likely to be the least bit tasteful.

A full-sized Brunswick bar carried a sheen betraying long hours of diligent polishing. Gleaming brass spittoons placed at either end of the bar showed some attention to the needs of the patrons. None of this was what Jerome had expected in a town where the main street wandered about like a broke-back sidewinder.

"What you gawkin' at, mister?"

Jerome straightened when a bearded face was thrust up at his clean-shaven one. His eyes skipped from the truculent stare to the man's threadbare vest, where a marshal's badge, hammered out of a large Mexican silver ten-peso piece, hung precariously.

"Just the man I wanted to see," Jerome said.

"You got a problem?"

"Not at all, sir," Jerome said, wondering who had put the burr under the law dog's saddle. Even after Jerome had assured the marshal that there wasn't any trouble requiring his assistance, the man looked suspicious. "I sell patent medicines and need a vending permit."

"Twenty dollars. No scrip. Silver or gold coin," the marshal said flatly.

20

Jerome quickly calculated what he might sell versus such a hefty toll. He began fishing in his vest pockets to find the coins to pay the marshal. As he counted out the coins into the lawman's callused hand a few at a time, he asked, "I've come up from San Antonio and heard rumors of an outlaw gang the entire way. The Benjamin gang. You have any news about them?"

"Never heard the name," the marshal said, squinting nearsightedly as he stared at the coins Jerome had put into his hand. The mental effort of adding to cipher the total forced him to frown.

"Hank Benjamin's the name I heard most, but Leland and Curtis also got mentioned. Not favorably, either."

"That's it."

"You've heard of them?" Jerome stood a little straighter, towering over the lawman. "When? Where?"

"I meant the money. It's all there. You kin peddle your pizzen all you want. Till the end of the week. You want to sell past Sunday, you got to pony up more money." The marshal dropped the coins into the side pocket of his threadbare coat. "For a freewill donation, Parson Patterson'll let you say a few words to his congregation. Don't think on stayin' longer 'n that, though. Not without renewin' your license with me."

"Thanks," Jerome said, feeling as if he had fallen off a cliff.

For a brief instant, he had thought he had a decent trail to follow, but the marshal had meant something else by his statement. No posters, no knowledge of the Benjamin gang. So close, though. All the way up the road Jerome had heard the outlaws' names whispered with something approaching awe. His left hand touched a hidden knife along his right forearm. The leather sheath and substantial steel of the blade reassured him. One day he would find the Benjamins and they would die. Fast, slow, it didn't matter to him as long as they died for what they had done to his family.

Jerome looked back inside the saloon, saw the bartender idly wiping up spills on the long polished oak bar under a picture of a reclining naked woman that almost made Jerome blush. After giving the marshal such a large bribe to do business, he decided not to wet his whistle, after all. He needed to preserve what capital he had left and pre-pare for his first sales pitch.

Returning to his wagon, he dropped the stage, opened the rear double doors and climbed up. There was barely room for the single milking stool inside the cramped wagon, but Jerome maneuvered about from long experience. He settled onto the stool, took down his bottles and beakers and began mixing. He had learned the apothecary trade well. Precision, careful labeling and having everything he'd need close at hand before he began the current formulation speeded up the process. Every batch of elixir was different, but all the potions were potable. Jerome had no desire to poison his customers, but he always added a drop or two of nitric acid to give a mule's kick to the first sip. If the buyers didn't get that immediate jolt, they would never believe the medicine worked.

For all he knew, some of the potions actually did work. And if they didn't, their being a quarter alcohol by volume made the user feel a mite better afterward.

Satisfied with his afternoon's work in the close quarters, Jerome moved three cases of bottled potion to the rear of the wagon, closed the doors and drove around to a spot down the street from Waterin' Hole #3. There was no reason to compete with the tarantula juice sold there, but most of his customers were likely to be heading for the saloon. Jerome brushed off his coat, tossed his hat aside and ran a comb through his lank dark hair to make himself presentable.

He knew he cut quite a figure, tall and confident and handsome enough for the ladies to admire, but he had to look authoritative to make the men buy the two-dollars-a-bottle concoction.

He took his time positioning a stand and the garish advertising placard on the small stage. Satisfied a crowd could see the sign, he moved his cases to the proper spot where he could whip out bottles without stumbling over them as he moved about. Dramatic gestures were always necessary to capture the crowd's attention. There was a kind of mesmerism Jerome had developed when he bent and pointed and struck poses like some demented actor. He always felt the crowd responding to him, following his every word and always buying when he hit the proper crescendo.

Working as an apothecary had never been quite so exciting, but then there had not been the driving need to garner enough money to hunt down killers. Customers had come into Mr. Poulin's shop on their own. There hadn't been a need to go persuade them.

Jerome saw that a few of the townspeople he had spoken to earlier drifted closer, keeping their distance as if afraid and yet too curious to run off. He pretended he didn't notice them, but as their numbers grew, he estimated how much elixir he could sell. Three cases might not be enough for the town of Chagrin.

When a full two dozen people began edging closer, he went to the edge of the stage and loosed his bass call for one and all to come learn how their woes could be solved with a single bottle of his mighty potion. Jerome avoided naming himself to be a doctor but hinted at secret formulas and arcane rituals he had endured to gain the knowledge it took to brew his vile-tasting curative.

"What you say your name was, fella?" asked a well-dressed man in the front of the crowd, now numbering over forty.

"I am J. Frederick Kincannon, noted chemist and apothecary. Many among the crowned heads of Europe call me the Professor of Potions."

"You're not a doctor?"

"I make no such claim, sir. And even if I were, I could never match your expertise in this area." Jerome's quick dark eyes had spotted a stethoscope poking from the man's side pocket. "I am not an expert at auscultation and medical diagnosis as you are, Dr. — ?"

"Doc Felman," someone at the rear of the

crowd supplied. "He'll as soon take off your leg as your busted-up arm. He can't tell the difference!"

This produced a round of chuckles, but Jerome allowed himself only a small smile.

"You are well-liked, I see, Dr. Felman," he said. "I assure you I am not here to take away your business but to assist you. There are many days when you are inundated with patients, I am sure. My intent is to provide a miracle elixir to assuage the maladies assaulting your patients until they can reach your surgery for more comprehensive curative methods."

Jerome saw that most of the crowd had no idea what he was saying, but it sounded learned, and he thought the doctor actually followed his reasoning. He hurried on with his sales pitch, working through the first case of twenty-four bottles faster than usual. He had about doubled what he had paid the marshal for his license, covered the cost of his materials and now ventured into the arena of pure profit.

He sold another case but saw that, in spite of many remaining in the crowd without shuffling forward to buy, they were anxious not to miss the opportunity to knock back a shot or two of the elixir.

"Money," the doctor said in a low voice.

"Chagrin is a mighty poor town since the railroad bypassed us."

Jerome nodded and began winding up his presentation. He couldn't get blood out of a rock, and the rest of the crowd was stony, indeed.

To his surprise, Dr. Felman stepped up and said, "I heard of Mr. Kincannon's potion, and it's made to cure what ails you. I can't let him go and take away medicine folks in these parts might need. I'll buy what you haven't sold so I can dispense it to my patients as they need it."

Jerome's ebon eyes locked with doctor's muddy brown ones. He understood in a flash what had to be done.

"Your doctor is not only an expert in the medical arts. He is charitable. For you, sir, an entire case of my medicine for only" — Jerome wondered what discount would fly — "for only twenty dollars."

He mouthed, *In coin,* so only Dr. Felman saw. The doctor nodded once, and the deal was struck. Better to sell at half price and let the doctor sell at full price later than not to sell at all. The doctor could prescribe the medicine and possibly get more than two dollars a bottle, but Jerome doubted it since that was the price he had so publicly set.

By Jerome's praising the other man's

medical skills, and going along with Felman's blatant lie about having heard of the elixir and its restorative powers, both of them had come out on top in the deal.

A few of the more timid souls came up after Jerome had transferred the remaining case to the doctor. Felman sold the bottles at the same two dollars Jerome had charged and doubled his money on each bottle, but Jerome didn't care. He had made a handy profit that would keep him searching for the Benjamin gang another couple weeks or until the next town, whatever it might be.

"Come on into the Waterin' Hole," Dr. Felman said, "and I'll buy you a shot of real rotgut." He looked around to be sure they were out of earshot of anyone of the crowd and asked in a low voice, "What's in this witches' brew, anyway?"

"It's a secret," Jerome said, "but a second drink might just loosen my tongue."

"That's my man," Dr. Felman said, slapping Jerome on the shoulder and laughing. "Pack up your wagon and let's get down to serious drinking. The show'll start in another twenty minutes, and you don't want to miss it."

"Show?"

"Ole Jackass — he's the owner — got himself the finest-looking filly what ever trod the boards. Don't ask how he convinced her to stay, but he did. She can sing and dance. Oh, can she dance! It's truly a lesson in anatomy, watching her dance. But her acting is matchless, and I've seen Sarah Bernhardt herself onstage, so I can make a good comparison."

"Indeed," Jerome said.

"I was in Paris and saw her in Victor Hugo's *Hernani* playing Doña Sol. But Molly Davenport's better. I swear it."

Jerome was surprised to find the saloon, deserted only a few hours earlier, was now packed to overflowing. Miss Davenport obviously provided a powerful draw for the Texas town.

"There, over there," Dr. Felman said. "My table's reserved. Hell, it ought to be free, the number of times I've patched up Jackass Morgan after the fights he gets into. But payin' a dollar a performance to get up close is worth it. Believe me."

Jerome figured the doctor was smitten by the female charms or maybe the feminine wiles of the performer. He could understand that after looking out over the crowd of potential customers when he was selling his potion. The women were all plain and weathered with the look of resignation that could not be erased by anything other than moving to a more prosperous town. Even a faint touch of sophistication onstage would have been a welcome sight for the men of Chagrin.

How any such performer had come to Chagrin in the first place, much less remained for more than a single performance, was a mystery. Still, Jerome was willing to share the experience with the doctor. Felman was more educated and likable than many he had encountered. At that thought, he looked around the crowd for the marshal but didn't see him.

The loud calls and claps almost deafened Jerome when the canvas curtains were pulled back. He rubbed his eyes to be sure he wasn't staring out on a grassy meadow at sunrise. The backdrop was cleverly constructed and intricately painted to make the effect almost perfect. Only catcalls and whistles broke the spell.

Then she came onstage. Jerome was hardly aware that he preened a bit when he saw Molly Davenport for the first time. She was everything Dr. Felman had said and much more.

She sang. She acted. The scenery behind added to her performance, taking her away from a stage to somewhere better, somewhere any of customers shared with the lovely woman. The scenery artwork was expert. Molly Davenport was extraordinary.

"She's everything I said, isn't she?"

"She is," Jerome had to admit. He felt a flutter in the pit of his stomach. For almost a year, he had traveled far and wide, hunting for the Benjamin gang, and he had never taken the time to appreciate any beauty he found, much less a beautiful woman. He felt the lack now.

"Don't go thinkin' you can make a play for her," Dr. Felman said.

"She's taken? Yours?"

The doctor snorted and shook his head. "I wish. She made it clear she performs and what we see up there is all we get. Jackass was crazy mad at first, but she put him in his place, and he hasn't even tried to so much as touch her since she arrived a couple weeks back. You have to know what a ladies' man Jackass is for that to mean much, but she's got fire to go along with her other talents."

"Thank you one and all!" the actress called from stage, taking a deep bow that provoked new catcalls and wolf whistles as she revealed considerable cleavage.

The audience stayed back except for one young man, who climbed onto a table, then jumped to the stage. Molly Davenport pushed him back, but he grabbed her and tried to kiss her.

Jerome never consciously thought of what he was doing. He kicked out of his chair and rolled onto the stage, coming to the side of the struggling pair.

"No" was all he said.

As the cowboy turned to him, Jerome unloaded a right cross that staggered him. Jerome stepped forward and drove two quick jabs into the man's belly. The first punch felt as if he had hit an oak plank. The second sank wrist deep. All the starch went out of the man.

"You . . . ?" Molly looked at him, then at the fallen cowboy.

"Sorry about that discourtesy, ma'am," Jerome said.

"You know what you've just done? That's Lark Thompson you just . . . knocked out."

For an instant Jerome thought he had done something to offend the woman. Then she laughed gleefully, grabbed him by the ears, pulled his face down and gave him a quick kiss on the lips.

With that, she dashed from the stage, leaving Jerome alone with the unconscious cowboy in front of a noisy crowd.

CHAPTER TWO

"This stuff actually works," Dr. Felman said, taking a swig of the elixir Jerome had sold him. The doctor wiped his lips, stared longingly at the half remaining, then stuffed the cork back in and dropped the sloshing bottle into his pocket. "You wouldn't be inclined to tell me what you put in it, would you?"

"What? And lose my market if I come back through town?"

"Doubt you'll ever come this way again," the doctor said, shaking his head. "Doubt there'll be much of a town left in another year even if you were so inclined to peddle more in these parts. But that's not why you wouldn't come back. Who is it you're looking for so hard?"

"Does it show?" Jerome finished packing the last of his newly acquired alcohol.

The owner of Waterin' Hole #3 had made him a good deal on five gallons of cheap alcohol, as much to get him out of town as to pocket a few dollars. The brouhaha caused by decking Lark Thompson — Jerome had heard him called Little Larkin more than once afterward — provided some notoriety and had even caused the marshal to issue a stern warning that encouraged all the upright citizens of Chagrin, and that included Jackass Morgan, to see that he was out of town in a hurry.

That suited Jerome just fine. He had mined Chagrin for all the information he could find on the Benjamin gang and had struck nothing but dross. His stay here ended as had so many others: great hope when he rolled into town, only to find nothing useful within a day or two.

" 'Course it shows. You're a driven man. You sell this shit to give yourself an excuse to keep traveling to the next town." The doctor touched the bulge in his pocket where he had stashed the bottle of Jerome's potion. "I've seen enough men with a burr in their soul. You're one."

"So?"

"So it's gonna get you killed, that's what. You don't pack an iron, not that I can see, and you're hot under the collar when it comes to jumping into a fight that's not yours. That's a bad combination for any

34

man, much less one with wanted posters nailed up on the walls in his mind."

Jerome looked at the knuckles on his right hand. They had been skinned from the collision with Little Larkin's stubbled chin. He flexed the fingers and winced. He knew better than to hit a man on the chin, but in the heat of the moment, he hadn't thought about it. He had simply reacted when he saw that Molly Davenport had not wanted the cowboy's advances.

"You're a damned idealist who thinks he can change things. You're wrong. Anybody who thinks they can is likely to be dead wrong."

"How'd you get so cranky?" Jerome asked. "But you're right about me looking for some men."

"The Benjamin gang," Dr. Felman said with some distaste. "And no, I don't know 'em. I just heard you asking after them. How'd you come to think they were lurking in our fair town?"

Jerome shrugged. "Heard rumors farther south. I almost found them in San Antonio, but they'd moved on in this direction."

"You might go north to Fort Davis and ask there. The fort commander's a decent enough fellow, even if he got stuck with the command."

"Stuck? What do you mean?" To Jerome, one frontier post was no worse than another.

"The Tenth, that's what." Felman stared at Jerome, then added, "They're buffalo soldiers. You might not want to spend too much time there."

"I've found soldiers aren't as interested in my potion, probably because there's always an unauthorized still working behind the mess hall to supply them their liquor."

"That's a quartermaster's prerogative, cooking up moonshine for the troopers. There's another reason, at Fort Davis and Quitman and Concho, too. Colonel Grierson isn't inclined to allow booze on any of his posts. He's a God-fearing man with a teetotaler wife, from what I've heard."

"I'm heading northeast, toward Clear Springs," Jerome said. "Might be outlaw activity there and a lawman who can tell me if it's the Benjamin gang creating the ruckus."

"What's your interest in this here Benjamin gang? No! Never mind. I don't want to know. You look after yourself, hear?"

Dr. Felman thrust out his hand. Jerome shook, appreciating the man's compassion for a stranger and even more impressed the doctor saw no reason to dig into another man's motives.

"Boil some mesquite roots along with a few of the green bean pods and add a fair amount of alcohol to create a tincture," Jerome said. "If you want a real witches' brew, use locoweed instead of mesquite."

"What's that? Oh, your potion." Felman grinned. "I might just keep the alcohol and forget the mesquite, and I certainly will avoid anything with datura in it. Those seeds play hob with a man's mind. I even heard tell of a cowboy who chewed on some and went blind."

He hesitated, then said more somberly, "My advice to you is to clear out of Chagrin as fast as your horse can pull that medicine wagon of yours. Larkin Thompson's got a fierce temper and a reputation for being a crack shot. Don't know about the last, but the first is for certain sure the truth."

"I'm on my way," Jerome assured the doctor.

He had run into problems with hotheads in other towns, but this was the first time he had gotten into a knock-down, drag-out fight. Not caring about where he was let him drift on since the search was more important than the location. But from what the doctor had said, Thompson was likely to throw some lead if their paths crossed again. Since the choleric wrangler had nothing to do with the Benjamin gang, Jerome had no quarrel with him.

If only Little Lark had been more of a gentleman toward the lovely singer, none of the unpleasantness would have occurred.

He finished securing the drop-down stage on the back of the wagon, climbed into the driver's box and waved to the doctor. Felman took the bottle from his pocket, stared at it for a moment, took a sip in salute, then walked away, mumbling to himself about mesquite beans.

Jerome snapped the reins and got the horse moving the heavy wagon on its way. He pulled out of the alley where he had parked for the night and turned toward Waterin' Hole #3 on his way to the next town.

"Sir, a moment. Wait!"

Jerome tugged hard on the reins, and the horse obligingly stopped its exertion. He swung about in the seat and saw Molly Davenport in front of the saloon. His eyes went wide when he saw the ugly purplish yellow bruise on her lovely face.

"Sir, I have a request to make of you," she said, hurrying to the side of the wagon and looking up at him. Her bright blue eyes were imploring. "I must leave Chagrin right now and find myself without transportation.

Could you give me a ride to wherever you're going?"

"I'm going to Clear Springs," Jerome said.

She recoiled as if he had hit her. "Th-that'll be fine, sir."

"J. Frederick Kincannon, at your service," he said, touching the brim of his derby. "But that's only what my customers call me. My friends know me as Jerome."

"Jeff," she said, smiling. "I like that. J. F. Your initials." He didn't bother correcting her. "I will need help with my equipment, but I am afraid I cannot pay you. I find myself without funds of any sort."

"Did Morgan do that?" Jerome pointed to the bruise.

Molly touched the spot on her cheek and winced. "No, he's a different kind of bastard," she said bitterly. "He only refused to pay me."

"Would you like me to intervene on your behalf?"

"No! You did enough for me last night with . . . with *him*. I just want out of town."

"Even if it is to Clear Springs?" He watched her reaction closely.

"Yes," she said with some resignation. "I have my scenery. The trunks with my costumes are rather bulky but otherwise there is nothing that cannot be loaded into your wagon easily."

"We can head for some other town," Jerome said, not wanting to.

He had a gut feeling that information about Hank Benjamin and his murderous clan would turn up in Clear Springs. He always chased that mirage, he knew, but this time he was sure. There hadn't been any mistaking who had been responsible for the robberies and killings down in San Antonio. He doubted the gang would light out across the middle of West Texas when they could plunder and kill along the Butterfield Stage Company route.

Chagrin had turned out to be a poor choice for any outlaw band to rob. Clear Springs had to be more prosperous.

"No, no, you are most kind, sir."

"Jerome," he insisted. He coaxed a small smile to her bow-shaped lips. "Glad to be of service, Miss Davenport."

"Molly," she said. "And the scenery is all rolled and ready to be carried out. The two of us might possibly wrestle it onto the roof of your wagon."

"I'm sure I can bring it out myself."

"How noble," she said with a hint of caustic lye in her words. "The canvas weighs more than two hundred pounds."

Together, they dragged the scenery out so

40

Jerome could lift the end to the wagon's roof. From there, he looped a rope around the end and let the horse pull it up. The roof sagged woefully but held. The rest of Molly's gear fit within his crowded wagon — barely. After checking the axles to be certain they weren't in danger of cracking or breaking outright, he hitched his horse back to the wagon and again started from town. This time a lovely dark-haired, blue-eyed actress traveled in the driver's seat next to him.

Jerome was aware of the warmth from the woman's body as they pressed close together, her thigh against his on the narrow seat. It bothered him a mite, but Molly appeared oblivious to the intimacy.

"How'd you end up on the road, Jeff? You sound well educated, unlike most of the peddlers I've come across."

"I never went to a university," he said, "but I read a great deal. Work on our farm was difficult for me but learning chemistry and the art of the apothecary came easily. I apprenticed after my family died and learned even more when I had access to both a good teacher and his entire library imported from England and Germany."

He involuntarily looked over his shoulder into the rear of the wagon. Mr. Poulin's reference books were securely placed on a shelf up high where any chemical spills would not damage them.

"You have learned well. I knew right away you were a gentleman, other than from the way you deported yourself on my behalf, of course." Molly's hand touched the bruise on her cheek.

"How did that happen?"

"It's nothing." When only stony silence followed her obvious lie, she finally heaved a deep sigh. "It was Little Lark. He gets powerful mean when he's drunk, and after you knocked him out and humiliated him in front of all his hands — his pa's cowhands, at least — he had to get back some of his wounded pride."

"So he hit you?"

Cold anger built within him. Jerome felt the same sort of need to pay back Larkin Thompson that he did Hank Benjamin and his clan.

"You don't want to cross that snake," Molly said, putting her hand on his arm. "Please, we need to go. To Clear Springs. He won't bother me anymore if I've moved on. He'll brag and lie about him and me and everything will be fine."

"He shouldn't have hit you. Why didn't you have him arrested?"

"I know better. In towns like Chagrin, the richest men run things. Everything. There's nothing they don't own or think they do. The marshal is in Big Lark's hip pocket. You ought to know how it works, Jeff. You've been around. I can tell that there are considerable miles on both you and this decrepit wagon."

They rode for another mile before Molly asked, "What are you running from? Or is it something you're looking for?"

Jerome almost made a joke and passed it off, but he had been brooding about the injustice of a cowboy like Larkin Thompson hitting a genteel woman like Molly and getting away with it. Worse, Little Lark would brag on it and puff up his own self-importance at her expense.

"You might have heard me asking after the Benjamin gang," he said. "They killed my wife and boy."

"Oh," Molly said softly. She laid her hand on his arm again. "I'm so sorry. But you can't be hunting them down, are you?"

His arm tensed and gave her the answer.

"Oh, Jeff, that is *so* foolish. Not all lawmen are like the marshal back in Chagrin. Tell the Texas Rangers. They don't cotton to killers and are experts at tracking men. If this Benjamin gang is as dangerous as it

43

sounds, you can't handle them by yourself."

"The murders took place outside Fort Smith," he said. "The Rangers have no interest in crimes committed anywhere other than Texas."

"But the gang must have done all manner of illegal things in Texas."

"Probably," Jerome said, his mind beginning to wander along other, older paths. Without meaning to say it, he let his most dearly kept emotions flow out. "I want them to suffer. Seeing them hang isn't good enough."

"It'll eat you up alive," she said softly. "I've seen it too many times."

"She was so pretty. Not as pretty as you, but my Marcie was special. There was a sparkle in her eye and a quick laugh that would brighten the rainiest day. We met at a barn dance at Park Hill. I saw her dancing and couldn't take my eyes off her. I wasn't the only man who felt that way," he said somewhat shyly. "But she was giving me the eye as much as I was her. She was actually interested in how I made a living."

"Apothecary," said Molly.

"Nobody else gave two hoots and a holler. She was so interested in everything I did, we left the dance and I showed her where I worked. Mr. Poulin would have been angry if he'd known, but he never found out."

"He never knew you showed her the store, so to speak?"

Jerome looked away.

"Why, Jeff, you are blushing. You, a grown man blushing. I do declare. What did happen that night?" Molly craned her head about to look squarely at him, then laughed delightedly. "That's nothing to be ashamed about. I think it's wonderful!"

"What do you know?" Jerome said, suddenly angry at himself for revealing such an important moment in his life. "You only need to bat your eyelashes and you can have any man."

"Don't be insulting," Molly said sharply. "You know nothing about me."

"I don't want to, either," he said. "You can find another job in Clear Springs, and I can keep hunting for the Benjamin clan."

"Very well," Molly said, sitting back and crossing her arms.

She glared at him every time he cast a sidelong glance at her. More than once he started to apologize, then knew there was nothing to say. He wasn't sorry.

What he was sorry about was that Molly had brought out such a deliciously wonderful memory — now he remembered all over again how it all had been stolen from him.

45

The image of the fire burning his house to the ground in the bright light of a full moon was so vivid, he almost smelled the charred wood and the stomach-turning odor of burning flesh.

Jerome looked down at his hands, expecting to see soot on them. He had rushed into the house, flames all around as he hunted for Marcie and Arthur. He had found his son, held him, clutched him hard, but it was too late. The young boy had burned to death and was hardly identifiable, other than by the rag doll he still clung to. Two men from the volunteer fire department had reached him and dragged him from the still burning building. It had taken another twenty minutes to put out the last of the fire. He had clutched Arthur the whole while as if his strong arms could somehow squeeze life back into the small body.

No amount of clinging worked to revive Arthur. And Marcie had been burned beyond recognition. The next day was a blur, but he remembered snippets of the preacher's graveside sermon, the two simple pine coffins being lowered, the sound of dirt falling onto their lids.

Hank Benjamin. Leland Benjamin. Curtis Benjamin. He owed them for their mindless killing and arson.

"You hear that, Mr. Kincannon?" Molly half rose from the bench, gripped the top of the wagon roof and swung about to scan over the barren terrain.

"It's only the wind," Jerome said. "That's all that ever happens out here."

He looked ahead along the sunbaked road and saw the endless sand dunes, the mesquite, greasewood, creosote bushes and prickly pear cacti breaking the flow of brown with their own peculiar hues of green. Some patches of buffalo grass sprouted here and there, but along this stretch of desert, it was sparse. But those patches of knee-high grass were not swaying. The wind was calm, allowing the full weight of the sun to bear down on him without a trace of cooling.

"It is not. Sounded like a man. I heard it. And so did you, Mr. Kincannon."

Jerome tugged back to stop the horse, put his foot on the brake and looped the reins about the wood handle. He lithely swung about, skinned up and stood beside the rolled canvas atop the wagon. Shielding his eyes from the sun, he slowly scanned the desert to the right of the road. He was still cranky and refused to admit he had also heard what might have been a man's wordless cry for help. Molly had heard it because it came from her side of the wagon.

"There," he said, seeing what might be an arm flopped over the crest of a sand dune.

Jerome shrugged his shoulders and settled the sheaths holding the knives secreted about his body. He brushed over his right forearm and ran his fingers over the leather sheath there, then decided this was a poor ambush, if that was what it was.

He dropped to the ground with a hard thump and motioned for Molly to stay with the wagon.

"I want to see. Are they in trouble, Jeff? Are they hurt?"

He hardly noticed she again called him Jeff instead of the more formal Mr. Kincannon when she wanted to vent her displeasure. She totally ignored him saying he preferred being called Jerome. He discounted it as just being her way.

A louder moan sounded as the arm slipped from sight. He hesitated, then silently repeated his rationale that this was hardly the stuff of a road agent's trap. He hurried along, his high-topped shoes breaking through the hard-crusted sand. Reaching the crest of the dune, he looked down and caught his breath.

"Who is it, Jeff?" Molly came up behind, gripped his arm and moved closer when she saw the half-naked man sprawled facedown in the sand.

"An Indian," he said. "There are Apaches all over the area. I heard that the Mescalero are off their reservation up in New Mexico, as are several bands of Warm Springs Apaches from over in Arizona. Down in San Antonio, they were all talking about Nana raising hell before sneaking back across the Rio Grande to rejoin Victorio."

"Is he one of them?"

She leaned forward to examine the prone man. She jerked back when he stirred and moaned again.

"I don't know," Jerome said, "but he's not done anything to me. He might belong to an entirely different tribe. I don't know enough about their clothing or weapons to tell."

Jerome kicked a knife away from the outstretched fingers groping for the horn handle. He knelt and rolled the man over. The Indian had been alive only a few seconds earlier, but somehow Jerome expected him to be dead.

Eyelids fluttered and bloodshot eyes as dark as his own fixed on him. Chapped, cracked lips formed a word, but no sound came out. Jerome doubted he would have understood even if he had made out the man's plea.

"Come on," Jerome said as much to himself as to the Indian. "We're going to get you back to my wagon and fix you up."

Growing up in Indian Territory had given him a halting command of Cherokee, but that language was nothing like Apache. Being misunderstood right now was the last thing he wanted, so he decided to stick with English. He got his arm around the Indian's shoulder and heaved him up. Jerome almost took a spill, losing his balance in the soft sand. If Molly hadn't helped, he might have taken a tumble. Together the two of them got the Indian to the wagon, where Molly opened the rear doors so Jerome could swing the Indian around and lay him flat inside, out of the sun.

"Get the desert bag," Jerome said. "He wouldn't survive a sip of my elixir."

"Potent, is it?" Molly flashed him a grin. "Might be I should try a snort. This chaos is all bringing on a faint."

She put the back of her hand on her forehead and let out a low sound, as if swooning. This brought the Indian to a half-sitting position, but he was too weak to remain upright and sank back.

"The water," Jerome insisted.

He knelt by the Indian and examined him

carefully. Molly returned quickly with the burlap bag with the pig bladder inside. Jerome drizzled drops onto the Indian's lips but kept him from drinking.

"Why not give him a good drink instead of torturing the poor man?"

"He'd only puke it back up. Feel his forehead. He's burning up."

"He's been in the sun." Molly hesitated, then reached to lay her slender-fingered hand on the man's forehead. "Why, he's burning up with fever!"

"I don't know enough to help him. It might be nothing but sunstroke, but I've heard of men dying from too much exposure. Or he might have something more . . . contagious."

Jerome looked at her, giving her the chance to back away.

"You're not getting rid of me that easily," she said primly.

"We've got to get back to Chagrin. Dr. Felman struck me as a competent physician. He'll be able to do more than we can out in the middle of nowhere."

"We can't!" Molly looked stricken at the idea of returning to the town.

"I won't let Thompson harm you, I promise."

"You're biting off more than you can

51

chew, Jeff," she said, looking hard at him. "This is only an Indian. What does he matter?" Then she heaved a sigh of resignation. "Very well. You are an honorable man, even if it means both of us will be murdered."

"Quiet," Jerome said. "You're scaring him."

The Indian had taken in their words. In spite of his condition, he understood what they said. Jerome read it in the brave's feverish eyes.

"There, there," Molly said, patting the supine man's arm. "We'll do right by you. Don't worry. I didn't mean it when I suggested we ought to leave you out here."

The Indian tried to speak again, but his thirst-constricted throat still betrayed him.

"Keep dripping water onto his lips and down his throat, but don't let him drink or else he'll bloat like a horse. That might kill him outright."

"Stop your prattling, Jeff, and get us back to that doctor. The sooner we get back to Chagrin, the sooner we can leave again."

Jerome kept the horse moving along at a faster clip than it had gone leaving Chagrin. They pulled up in front of the doctor's surgery just as the sun dipped low over the mountains along the distant Rio Grande. Jerome climbed down as the doctor emerged from his surgery.

"Didn't expect to see you anytime soon. Hell, didn't expect to see you again ever. What brings you back?"

"In the wagon. We found a man out in the desert, and he's in a bad way. There wasn't anything we could do for him, so we brought him back."

"That's a powerful lot of 'we' you're speaking," Dr. Felman said.

His eyebrows rose in furry twin arches when he saw Molly Davenport nursing the Indian. It was hard to tell which surprised the doctor more.

"I can't take him into my office," Felman said uneasily.

"He's hurt. He's got sunstroke, maybe something worse, and may have other injuries. You have to help him. You're a doctor. You've taken an oath."

"You'd know about that, being an apothecary, wouldn't you?" Felman glared at the Indian. "Folks in these parts don't take to Lipan Apaches too much. Can't say I blame them."

"He's Lipan!" Molly exclaimed. "Did you see the way he tensed up when you said that?"

"Oh, he's Lipan, all right," Dr. Felman said. "I've patched up enough folks in these parts after his kind have filled them full of arrows."

"He's hurt. He'll die unless you help him," Jerome said.

"If he dies, ranchers and their kin live," Felman said.

"How far do I have to drive to find a real doctor?" Jerome's voice took on a steel edge that cut deeply. His words seemed to strike a chord with the doctor.

"Oh, hell, what else do I have to do other than get drunk over at Jackass' place? They can lynch me and string me up alongside this red son of a bitch. Help me get him inside."

Dr. Felman grunted as he hoisted the Indian's deadweight. Jerome helped and felt a change in how the Apache moved. He thought the Indian had regained more strength than he wanted them to know.

"Put him on the cot in the back room," Felman said. "I can examine him there. From the feel, you were right about sunstroke."

"I didn't see a horse. How far he had wandered on foot without water, I can't say."

"Do you need any help?" Molly asked.

"No, my dear," Felman said, "I can do what needs doing. You stay out here. And

54

don't raise too much of a ruckus. He's back in town with blood in his eye."

"Little Larkin?"

"Who else?"

Dr. Felman looked as if he had bitten into a bitter persimmon. He gathered his equipment and disappeared through the door into the back room.

"We won't stay in town a minute longer than necessary," Jerome promised when he saw her uneasiness.

"I've been through worse. We saved a man, you and I, Jeff, even if he is an Indian. That has to count for something."

They sat in straight-backed chairs and chattered without really saying anything, their thoughts elsewhere. Jerome jumped to his feet when Dr. Felman emerged from the back room.

"Is he going to be all right?"

"Of course he is," Felman said with ill grace. "That ingrate. I tried to clean him up so I could examine him properly, but he fought me. I finally tied him down, as much to keep him from hurting himself as doing me in. Oh, he's going to be up and about in a day or two. He's a strong one, but they all are."

"We owe you, Doctor," Jerome said.

"Like hell you'll owe me. You're going to

pay for my services. I don't take charity cases. Give me a couple more bottles of that tarantula juice you brewed up. That ought to cover my expenses."

Jerome let a small smile curl his lip, went to the wagon and fetched the bottles. He froze when he saw a dozen men heading toward the doctor's office, marching down the middle of the dusty street. They were all drunk, from the way they wobbled as they walked, but they were determined. Jerome saw that right away.

He hurried back inside and put the bottles on the doctor's desk.

"What's wrong, Jeff?" Molly looked anxious.

"There's a crowd coming this way. I think they saw us bringing the Apache in here."

"Damn," the doctor said. "This could get ugly fast. Too many folks in Chagrin have lost friends and family to those red savages."

"You can't hand over your patient to them!" protested Molly.

"I ought to. He's nothing to me." Felman got an even more sour look on his face and stalked to his office door. "But I won't let them touch him. He's my patient, and I'm responsible for his well-being."

All three of them spun when a loud crash came from the back room. Jerome reached the door first and pulled it open.

"I'll be switched," Dr. Felman said, looking past Jerome into the room. The cot had been overturned, and strips of cloth were scattered about the room. "He got free and hightailed it. With all that was wrong with him, I didn't think anyone'd have it in him to create such mayhem."

"He did," Jerome said, looking around.

The window at the side of the room stood open. He mentally pictured the Lipan Apache brave throwing open the window, crawling over the sill and dropping out into the alley behind the doctor's office. Jerome looked out but didn't see the Indian anywhere.

"He's a sight faster wounded than I am with two strong legs under me."

Jerome saw Molly edging back into the room, her hand over her mouth. The doctor shouted at the men who had pushed their way into his office. In a few minutes, they had gone, but the fear remained on Molly's face. When the doctor joined them, the reason became apparent.

Dr. Felman looked squarely at Molly and said, "You'd better get out of town as fast as that Apache. One of the men in that crowd was Skinny Burke, and he saw you."

"Who's Burke?" demanded Jerome.

"Foreman on the Circle T. Skinny saw Molly, and Little Lark'll know she's in town as fast as his spindly legs can carry him. You two had better climb into that medicine wagon of yours and light a shuck before Thompson comes back with every cowpoke he can round up."

Jerome silently shook the doctor's hand, then followed Molly outside. She already sat on the hard bench seat, arms wrapped around herself, shaking as if she had caught the ague.

He felt the same way; only his shakes were confined to butterflies in his belly.

CHAPTER THREE

"I'm going to be killed if I stay in town any longer," Molly Davenport said anxiously.

Jerome thought she was being overly dramatic until he saw her face. She had turned whiter than bleached muslin.

"Please. Drive, Jeff. Drive us out of here before Little Larkin hears."

"The marshal can't let him do whatever he wants. There has to be *some* law here."

"You don't know the Thompsons' hold on the entire area. Chagrin is theirs, lock, stock and barrel. There's nobody here that's not beholden to them in some fashion. That includes Dr. Felman, though he has more backbone than most."

A chill passed through him. In a prosperous town, gaining such power was harder than in one about ready to dry up and blow away. Chagrin's life hung by a thin thread, and holding the other end of that thread seemed to be Big Lark Thompson. Worse,

Little Lark drunkenly slashed at it with a knife. Who in town didn't owe their livelihood to the Thompsons and their ranch hands?

Jerome snapped the reins and got his tired horse pulling again. They wouldn't be able to get too far before the horse balked from simple exhaustion, but getting out of Chagrin was the most prudent route at the moment. He could deal with Larkin Thompson, elder or younger, but this wasn't his fight. Anything that kept him from finding the Benjamin gang was more of an annoyance than a crusade.

"No, not back toward Clear Springs," Molly said, seeing him retracing their route.

"The Indians won't be prowling along the road anymore," he said. "The Apache — the Lipan — probably scouted for a war party. Or a hunting party," he said hastily. He studied Molly closely to see if she caught his slip of the lip. "They'll have moved on. What reason do they have to hang around?"

"That's not my concern, Jeff. There's no telling what happened to the brave out there, but it had to be pretty serious. The Lipans are tough customers. Whatever trouble that left him on foot long enough to get him into such a condition might still be out there."

"Nothing is permanent in the desert," Jerome said, looking over the barren landscape faintly lit by a silver moon.

The wind restlessly slithered along the sand dunes and brought grit to the sun-baked roadway that crunched under the hooves and wagon wheels. The more Jerome stared over the desert, the eerier it seemed. Ghosts floated at the corners of his vision, and the feel of the soft, increasingly cool breeze might have been the touch of a will-o'-the-wisp. He shivered but kept on the road.

Increasingly, he shared Molly's fear that danger edged closer to them by the second.

"They'll come after us," Molly persisted. "We ought to confuse them and head in some other direction. South. To San Antonio."

Jerome didn't even consider the change in destination. "No," he said.

He had been in San Antonio and had already gleaned as much information about the Benjamin gang as he could. The rumors had brought him north and west into this part of Texas. To return would let Hank Benjamin and the others put that much more distance between themselves and vengeance.

"But, please, Little Lark will bring a

bunch of cowboys with him. They — they'll take turns raping me. You wouldn't want that. I know you're a good man. You didn't once try to . . . you know." Molly faced forward, hands folded primly in her lap.

Jerome glanced sidelong at the woman. The moonlight turned her into something angelic, although he knew better. She worked in saloons and dealt with rowdy, drunken cowboys and soldiers and riffraff for a living. As pure as she appeared, shining like an angel in the silvery light, she was a soiled dove.

"I won't let them," he said simply.

"You won't be able to stop them!" Molly cried. "They're killers."

"So am I."

"Like those outlaws? The ones who killed your family? Do you really believe you're the same as they are?"

"The Benjamin gang *murdered* Marcie and Arthur," he said hotly.

"But you haven't found them. You don't know if you can kill them, do you? You don't even pack an iron. Look around you! Even in a nothing town like Chagrin, most of the men wore six-shooters."

"I refuse to use the weapons they do. I'm better than that."

"So how are you going to bring them to

justice? Talk them to death? That's rich."

She wrapped her arms around herself and seemed to fold inward. Her jaw trembled as she clenched her teeth.

Jerome said nothing, but Molly hadn't run down yet. She heaved a deep breath and plowed ahead.

"You have to face somebody, eye to eye, and then find it inside your very soul to kill. Or do you intend to shoot those Benjamin outlaws in the back? You have that kind of nerve? To face the man you're killing or to shoot from ambush?"

He kept the horse moving, though the mare was visibly weakening. Jerome had spent long hours alone, going from town to town, thinking about this very thing. Did he have the nerve to kill another man? He knew, given the proper circumstances, everyone did. Kill for self-defense, to defend a loved one, simply in reaction. Those were the easy ones. What Molly was getting at and what he had considered was something more difficult. If he had the upper hand on Hank Benjamin and the outlaw was unarmed, could he kill?

"I can do it," he said.

"You are a strange man, Jeff," she said, her arms wrapped even tighter now around her body and squeezing down hard to comfort herself. The woman silently re-treated into her own thoughts and memo-ries.

"Have you ever killed a man?" he asked, prodding her as much to ease his own conscience as to find out more about his passenger.

"That's none of your business," Molly said in a low voice. "I'm tired, and the poor horse is going to keel over if you keep push-ing it much longer. Let's get off the road, hide somewhere and pray to Heaven that Little Lark misses us in the night."

"You're mighty sure he'll come after you."

"Skinny saw you, too. As much as Little Lark wants to have his way with me before letting his cowboys use me, he wants you dead. You made a fool out of him in front of the entire town. That's about the worst thing you could do to man like him."

"His pa wears the pants in the family and Little Lark lives in his shadow. Is that it?"

Molly looked at him sharply. "You get right to the heart of matters, don't you? That's it. Little Lark has turned into a ne'er-do-well and a stone killer. What he wants, he takes. He wanted me, and I fended him off for a day or two, but you decking him the way you did will light a fire in his belly that can't be put out 'til he kills you."

"You make him sound like a mad-dog killer."

"He has the potential. This might be what it takes to push him into a killing spree, because he won't stop with the pair of us. Little Lark might ride back into Chagrin and shoot it up. There're plenty of folks who have riled him."

"You don't know that'll happen," Jerome said, urging the horse off the road toward a sheltered area behind some low dunes.

They weren't tall enough to completely hide the wagon, but in the night, with the moon only a quarter full, a rider might miss them entirely. Jerome wasn't sure Molly knew what she was talking about when it came to Larkin Thompson, but he wasn't going to take too many unnecessary chances. Dying in the desert, even with such a lovely companion at his side, wasn't something he wanted.

The mare let out a whinny of relief when Jerome drew back on the reins and halted the animal's progress. He climbed down, unhitched the horse, found some dried grass for it to crop at and then put on the hobbles. After putting a half barrel of water out for the thirsty horse, he tended to his own needs and ended by splashing some of the precious water on his face. In the chilly desert night, it felt as if his flesh froze when the water evaporated.

Jerome stopped dead in his tracks when he saw that Molly had rummaged through his supplies to cobble together a cold dinner. He had been on the trail so long, he was used to fending for himself. It felt good having someone else to share the chores.

Good and not a little disturbing. She was pretty. Some men might have even said beautiful, but this only distracted him from what he had to do. Jerome wasn't much of a churchgoer, never had been, but finding and killing the Benjamin clan had taken on a religious meaning to him. They had ruined his life. He would end theirs. Such intense belief transcended mere revenge and took on mystical qualities.

"Help yourself. I didn't think it wise to build a fire." Molly looked around. The moonlight glinted off her dark hair and sent argent ripples along its length as she moved. "I don't see much to build a fire from, anyhow. There might be some dried horse shit along the road, but that's too hard to find in the dark."

Jerome shuddered a little at her earthy language. One instant she was the epitome of sophistication and the next she spoke in such vulgar terms that it shocked him. Molly was filled with contradictions that intrigued him even as they repulsed him.

"Thanks," he said, taking the plate of cold beans.

She had found some bread he hadn't known was in the wagon and put it on the plate, too. He used a dipper to fetch water from the horse's barrel and poured some for her into the only tin cup he had.

"We could fix a low fire and boil some coffee, if you like."

"This'll do. Water's just the thing to swill after a day's long, dry ride. This country," she said, gesturing to the landscape all around, "is controlled by the Apaches because they know where the watering holes are. The cavalry chases them endlessly and eventually dies because they can't carry enough water with them."

"Sounds as if the soldiers ought to make it a priority to find those watering holes and take control of them."

"That's easier said than done," Molly replied. She perched on the edge of the dropdown stage at the back of the wagon, swinging her dangling legs to and fro. "The Apaches are sneaky bastards."

"Should I stand watch to keep them from

attacking?"

She laughed. "If I didn't know better, I'd think you were a complete greenhorn. The Apaches never attack at night. They're terrified of rattlesnakes."

"I thought that was just a tall tale," he said, perching on the edge of the stage and letting his long legs swing down under him in syncopation with hers.

"Not so tall," she said, laughing at his naivete. "The truth is always a mite peculiar."

"So what's your truth?" he asked.

She turned toward him with her face hidden in shadow so he couldn't read her expression easily.

"Why are you out here on the frontier with your acting and singing and not in Denver or San Francisco?"

"Fate," she said simply.

"There's more involved than that. How'd you come to tread the boards? That's what you call it, isn't it? You troupers?"

"Well," she said, scooting closer beside him. Her thigh once more pressed warmly into his, making him uncomfortable at such casual contact. Molly didn't seem to notice or be much affected by rubbing up so intimately against a man. "I never got along too well with my mama and papa. They

68

were society people in Austin. My pa is a state senator, and my ma enjoys the social whirl such power brings. That always bored me. I read about Sarah Bernhardt and Lola Montez and Adah Menken. It was what I wanted, everyone looking at you, not because of the political power you had but because you fascinated them. You were so good at singing or dancing or acting out a play that they couldn't take their eyes off you. That was what drew me."

"That's a form of power," Jerome said, scooping in more beans.

They tasted better than he remembered from the first few times he had eaten them. He wondered if Molly had added something from his stash of chemicals and herbs. If so, he couldn't identify what it might be that spruced up the flavor.

"It's not the same," Molly said too quickly, affirming what Jerome thought. She could never compete in a man's world of politics, but she had found another route to acclaim.

"How long have you been on the road with your act?"

"More than two years. I had teamed up — well, sorta teamed up — with somebody else for a spell, but that didn't work out. I decided to strike out on my own and have been doing just well without a partner."

"What was his name?"

"You pry too much, Jeff. I'll paint up the side of your wagon really pretty and that's all you're going to get out of me. *All,*" she said forcefully.

"I'd never try to take advantage of you," he said, startled.

"I know" came the reply.

He tried to figure out if there was a wistfulness to her words or relief.

"I'll sleep inside, if that's all right with you. I've shared my bunk with scorpions and ants too many times lately. I swear, that place where Jackass put me up had more bugs in it than I could smash in a lifetime of stomping and swatting."

"There's a blanket," Jerome said, pointing to a small bedroll. "I'll sleep on top of the wagon. That'll give me a good vantage if any Indians who aren't Apache try to sneak up on us during the night."

"Those'd be Comanches, and you'd never hear them. The Apaches are sneaky bastards. The Comanches are worse," she said solemnly. "Good night, Jeff."

He started to jump down, but Molly grabbed his arm and held him in place long enough to kiss him full on the lips. The taste of her mouth mingled with beans and moldy bread, but it still set his heart pounding.

70

"To the roof," she said, her thumb jerking skyward.

"Good night."

With that, he closed the rear doors to give her privacy, then went for a short walk to find a spot to relieve himself. The desert was alive around him with the staccato sounds of night. The breeze had died down and the nocturnal animals had begun to prowl. Jerome reached for a knife when he saw gleaming eyes peering at him from ten yards off. The shadowy coyote decided there was better, tastier, safer game to be had and slunk away on soundless feet.

Jerome made a circuit of the area, as much to reassure himself the horse was safe as anything else. More than once, though, he turned and stared at the dark wagon, where Molly slept inside. When his legs began to give under him from exhaustion, he realized how long the day had been and how much they had been through. He climbed into the driver's seat, then pulled himself to the roof, hoping he didn't make too much noise. He had been inside once during a heavy hail-storm near Fort Griffin north of Clear Fork on the Brazos River and thought he had been trapped inside a drum. He settled down, lying on his back and staring at the clear, star-filled sky, Molly's rolled-up scenery pressed into his side.

The moon was slipping away at the horizon and the diamond stars burned feverishly. The wisps of clouds looked like spun cotton and then they, too, vanished as he drifted off to sleep, his thoughts on pleasant times now forever past.

Jerome came awake a little before dawn at the sound of horses whinnying. Not his horse. Horses. He rolled onto his side and saw two men with drawn six-guns coming toward the wagon from the direction of the road. The leading man looked familiar; then the man's identity came to him with a crash. Jerome couldn't help it as the name escaped his lips.

"Skinny Burke!"

The sound caused both approaching men to look up. The Circle T foreman lifted his six-shooter and drew back the hammer with a loud metallic click. Jerome rolled over, both hands snaking under his sleeves for the sheaths along his forearms. He threw first one knife and then the other. One knife failed to cartwheel properly and hit the second man sideways in the face. The man staggered back and threw up his hands, causing his six-shooter to veer off target. Jerome's other knife flew true and buried itself in Burke's chest. The rail-thin fore-

72

man fired in reflex, his shot sailing through the dawn air past Jerome's head.

Jerome got to his knees and worked to pull free two more knives, ones sheathed in the tails of his long coat.

"You move one damn muscle and yer a dead man" came the cold command.

Jerome looked behind him and saw Larkin Thompson on a small rise, aiming a rifle at him. At this range the man could hardly miss. What worried Jerome even more than the steady rifle trained on him was Thompson's maniacal expression. He and Molly had discussed killing and killers as they fled Chagrin. This was the face of a man who murdered because he enjoyed the feeling of power it gave.

"There's nothing here for you, Thompson," Jerome called. His fingers turned sweaty on the hilts of the still sheathed knives that he gripped.

"You got to be kiddin', man," Thompson said, laughing. The laugh ripped out of the man's throat and rang crazy. "I want the bitch. Where is she? Inside? How come you ain't in there pleasurin' her? Or you want a pegboy? We got a couple that ride with the herd when we drive 'em up to Abilene. You like a boy better than a woman?"

Jerome knew Thompson was intent on

angering him as much as whipping himself into a killing frenzy.

"Don't go for yer gun, you son of a bitch," Thompson called, seeing Jerome begin to turn. "I ain't alone. I got five more of my men with me. You see 'em? You see 'em?"

Jerome did. Two came from the road, following Burke's tracks. And behind Thompson three others stood with six-shooters drawn. They moved deliberately toward the medicine wagon, causing a sudden wave of desperation to flood over Jerome. He had other knives hidden on his body. Even if he made a kill with each, there remained too many men with guns to fill him full of lead.

And then have their way with Molly Davenport.

Desperation turned to hot fury. Jerome dropped down to his belly as Thompson opened fire. He rolled to the side, crashed against Molly's moving panorama and rebounded. He dodged two more slugs and then pulled free a knife and cast it sidearm. The knife tumbled wrong, so the handle struck Thompson harmlessly.

"You got to do better than that, you pill-peddlin' son of a bitch," Thompson called in glee. "Go on, men, kill him. Kill him dead! I want to dance on his worthless corpse. A hundred-dollar reward to whoever cuts him down!"

Jerome struggled to get another knife out to defend himself when he was deafened by the thunder of a dozen rifles firing simultaneously. He fell facedown over the canvas roll and lay for a moment, wondering if this was what it felt like to be dead. If so, he wanted to see Marcie and Arthur. He craned his neck up and looked around, expecting to see them. Instead, he had to squint because he stared into the rising sun.

He was alive.

And Thompson and the rest of his men were dead.

"What's going on?" called Molly, coming out of the wagon.

"Go back. Take cover," he said, rising to his knees and finally freeing another knife from its hidden sheath at the small of his back.

"My God, that's Little Lark! Dead!"

"Hide," Jerome said when he saw what was going on.

But Molly turned to stone as she looked down the barrel of another rifle, this one held by an Apache brave.

Jerome dropped his knife and raised his empty hands, but the brave with his rifle centered on Jerome's midriff didn't move a muscle. Nor did the dozen others who seemed to grow from the ground like evil weeds. All of them carried rifles, some still smoking from shooting down Larkin Thompson and his men.

Following their leader, the other Apaches took aim on him and Molly. Jerome waited to die.

CHAPTER FOUR

"We're goners," Molly said in a choked voice.

"We're goners unless you do something."

Jerome had no idea what words to say or what actions to take that would save them. He had a couple more knives hidden away. In the face of a half dozen — he corrected himself when a second band of Apaches joined the first — of a score of warriors, he was helpless.

He raised his hands and said in a voice that belied the tremors in his gut, "Thank you for saving us. They were bad men and intended to kill us."

He glanced down at Molly. She had backed against the wagon; whether for support or because her retreat was cut off, he couldn't tell.

"They're not shooting at us," Molly said. "That's a good sign, isn't it?"

Jerome slowly lowered his hands and

stepped to the edge of the wagon's roof. He jumped down and landed hard enough to jar his teeth. He ignored the pain in his knees and stood so he looked up at the nearest Apache. In the new dawn, the Apache looked as if he had been chiseled from rock. Nary a muscle twitched, and his unblinking eyes watched for any sign Jerome was going to put up a fight.

"We surrender," Jerome said, wondering what words would get them out of this predicament.

Offering bottles of his elixir to them might be illegal because it was more potent than most firewater sold in saloons, but he had to think of something fast.

The rifle in the brave's hand never wavered. Nor did he pull the trigger. Jerome wasn't questioning why they had been spared so far.

So far.

"Is there anything I can do to show our appreciation for your . . . bravery?"

The Indians had shot down Thompson and his henchmen from behind. Jerome wasn't going to fault them for that. Given the chance, he would have done the same thing.

From the middle of the tight knot of Apaches came a lightning strike of words, short, sharp and galvanizing. The warrior closest to Jerome lifted his rifle, turned his pony's face and rode away. Others joined him, riding off into the sunrise. Soon only a handful were left.

Jerome caught his breath when the one who had spoken rode closer.

"It's good to see you're able to ride," he said. "We worried about you when you . . . when you disappeared back in town. The doctor wanted to help you some more."

"Are you sure it's the same Indian?" asked Molly. She pressed close to him.

In a whisper, he answered, "It is. Look at how he's wounded."

"Silence!" The Apache roared out the command.

Molly flinched but Jerome never budged.

"I am glad you rejoined your people," he said.

When he got no reply, he started to thank the brave again, then bit his lower lip. Babbling showed weakness. Let the man he had saved before do the talking. All he might do was sign their death warrants by saying the wrong thing or somehow antagonizing their savior.

"You have medicine?" The Apache pointed his rifle at the wagon. When Jerome solemnly nodded, the Indian said, "Give me some. It cures the white man, it cures every-one?"

"It does," Jerome said.

He again forced himself to keep from gushing out a sales pitch. There was no reason other than nerves. The sale had been made.

His and Molly's lives for a few bottles of his magnificent elixir.

He walked to the rear of the wagon, his arm around the woman's waist to keep her from bolting. With gentle pressure he pushed her forward and motioned for her to climb onto the back stage and open the doors. He watched her intently but was all too aware of the four braves fanned out behind him. They all kept their rifles leveled as she worked to swing back the doors.

"That crate," Jerome said, pointing out to Molly one marked ELIXIR. "Push it out onto the stage."

He pried off the lid and held up a bottle. Seeing that his savior was reluctant to take it, Jerome pulled out the cork and took a deep swig before wiping his lips with his sleeve.

Seeing that this didn't convince the Apache, Jerome handed the bottle to Molly. She took it. The way her blue eyes gleamed told him he had no reason to coax her. She upended the bottle and drained half of it. A loud unladylike belch echoed like a gunshot in the still of the morning. Molly held out the bottle, as if considering another long pull. Instead, she took the cork from Jerome and secured it in the top.

Edging outward, she held the bottle far enough from the wagon for the Apache to ride closer. He snatched the potion, thumbed out the cork and drained the remainder of the liquid.

Jerome held his breath. For long seconds the Apache sat completely still. No hint of emotion crossed his face. Then he let out a triumphant war whoop that rolled across the West Texas desert. He threw the bottle high in the air.

With surprising accuracy, he drew a bead on the bottle just as it caught the bright sunlight. The bullet smashed the bottle and sent down a cascade of glass shards damp with Professor of Potions J. Frederick Kincannon's Miracle Elixir.

The brave raised his rifle high and signaled the band waiting behind him. They rode close. One by one, they took the bottle Jerome held out for them. He was about ready to tell Molly to fetch a second crate when the last brave snatched the last bottle and galloped away whooping and hollering as he vanished, riding after the warriors who had already departed.

The leader didn't budge. Jerome started to ask, but Molly nudged him first. She handed two more bottles to him. He held them out. The Apache bent low and grabbed both bottles in one hand. He wheeled about and thundered after his band.

Jerome sank back, elbows on the stage. He held out his hand. Surprisingly, he wasn't shaking.

"You're in big trouble now," Molly said, dropping to sit on the stage. She leaned her head atop his and rubbed his shoulders.

"How's that?"

"Giving firewater to the Injuns is a crime. You'll have Federal marshals and Texas Rangers and even deputies from towns you never heard of after you now."

"I'll have to turn you in as aiding and abetting."

He twisted around and looked up at her. The expression on her face was unreadable. And for the first time he began shaking, just a little, when she bent low and planted a big kiss on his lips.

It was over fast. Molly drew back and hopped into the wagon. She pulled the empty crate behind her, then pushed the door shut and secured it. Jerome wondered about the kiss.

She punched him in the arm and said, "Get the stage pushed up and tied down. We've got to make tracks."

"The law," Jerome mumbled.

"They'll never find out about the massacre. But Big Lark will. When his devil's spawn doesn't show up at the ranch, every last cowboy on the spread will be out hunting for him."

Jerome stepped out and looked over the carnage. The dead bodies stretched a good twenty yards away from the wagon. He knelt and rolled one over. The man's face was mostly gone. The Apache bullet had entered the back of his skull and exited in a bloody eruption where his nose used to be.

The sight of blood and death had little effect on Jerome. He went around the battlefield and retrieved his knives. Most had missed their targets, but here and there, he had scored a hit on his intended target. The first cast to kill had been the foreman. Jerome wiped the blade plucked from the man's throat on the bloodied shirt and moved on. He wasn't able to find one knife, but he had most of his weapons back and secured in their sheaths.

One last look around reassured him that he had been lucky. Without the Apache warriors coming to his rescue, his body would have been drawing the unwanted attention of coyotes instead of Little Lark Thompson and his cowboys.

"Come on," Molly urged. She sat in the driver's box. "Strip them if you have to, but it's better to drive on."

Jerome stepped back from the foreman's body. The six-shooter was missing. A quick check of the other bodies showed their weapons had been taken by the Apaches as spoils of war. He felt mixed emotions about that. The war party deserved something more than the cheap whiskey watered down with a few chemicals, but the settlers and cavalry roaming West Texas became targets using those guns.

If only the Indians turned the captured six-shooters and rifles on the Benjamin gang. That idea made Jerome feel better until he settled beside the woman. Reality crashed back over his head. Whoever died from the looted ammunition wasn't likely to be an outlaw band.

"You're mighty quiet," Molly said after they'd driven for the better part of an hour. When he said nothing, she went on. "There's no telling how much mayhem they'll cause, but we're safe and sound."

"That's not easing my conscience."

"Would getting yourself filled full of arrows take care of your guilt?"

"They all had rifles," Jerome mumbled. "The Indians. They all had rifles. And now they have six-guns, too."

"And ammunition," she said relentlessly. "They'd have them with or without you — us. Little Lark and his bullyboys didn't have a chance against so many warriors. And don't give me any guff about Thompson and his gang staying home if it hadn't been for you." She snorted in contempt. "For us. You saved our hides. I'm mighty grateful."

"You're right about one thing. What I did or didn't do isn't going to matter one whit. Fighting won't come to a halt until the Apaches are rounded up and sent back to their reservations."

"Think of it as them being free just a while longer."

He started to answer, then held his tongue. She was right. They rode for another ten minutes. She took his arm and squeezed gently.

"There's a fork ahead. Let's not go to Clear Springs. Head due west toward the river. We can go to Mexico and —"

"No."

"Please, Jerome. Take me somewhere else, and then go wherever you please."

She sniffed just a little. He looked sharply at her, wondering if she was acting. It was impossible to tell. She had called him by his name, not Jeff as she had been. What had caused this shift was a poser. Surviving the Thompson ambush followed by the Apaches? Or was she only wheedling him into going where she desired?

"It's out of my way. The information I have says Clear Springs was the next town along a trail taken by the Benjamins."

"I didn't hear anything about them when I was there. You've got no call to think they showed up after I left."

"Weeks ago? Is that when you left?"

She sniffed again and said, "Let me off here. Right here. This very spot." She pointed to a weather-beaten signpost marking the fork she had mentioned.

"You figure a stagecoach will be along anytime soon? You could die out here, waiting. I won't do that to you."

"It's not up to you. I'm not your —" She hesitated. "I'm not your slave. Let me down."

He wondered what she had been about to say. It hadn't been "slave."

"Do you want me to dump the scenery in the dirt? And all your wardrobe? It's unlikely a stagecoach would pick up so much cargo.

And a rider coming along?" He shook his head. "There's no way a man on horseback can carry your trunks and the two hundred pounds of canvas."

"I can get more clothes," she said sullenly.

"And your fancy scenery? What about that? It must have cost a pretty penny. You need to find an artist able to paint on such a big canvas. I'm no expert, but I'd hazard a guess that they aren't too common. Not like a housepainter. And whoever painted it was mighty good."

"No, you're not an expert. And what do you know about the quality of the artwork?"

He glanced at the sign, considering for the barest instant driving into Mexico with her. Then Jerome tugged on the reins and the mare obediently took the road to Clear Springs. He jumped when Molly let out a cry of sheer frustration. It sounded as if she was being skinned alive with a dull knife. Then she settled down, eyes ahead, and offered no more argument. She must have thought she was punishing him by remaining silent.

That suited Jerome just fine. He had his own worries. No matter what Molly said, she was better off in town than standing on a desert road, waiting to be rescued. Even the cavalry patrols were few and far between in this remote stretch of Texas.

The day passed slowly, inch by inch, each foot of desert exactly the same as the one they just rolled past. The terrain changed from desert to prairie land that was no less barren for all the gama grass poking up everywhere. The heat broke at twilight. Just as his horse began to wobble from exhaustion, Clear Springs came into view. Jerome topped a rise and stared at the dusty town cradled in a shallow bowl of prairie. Smoke rose from dozens of chimneys only to be caught a hundred feet above by the evening breeze and whipped toward the distant Rio Grande, now hidden by distance and a range of low mountains.

"The town's fixing to go to sleep," Jerome said.

Some folks below were still awake after a long day of commerce but most had finished their work and settled in with family. For his part, he was ready for a long nap.

"You can let me down here. Just dump my stuff. There's no need to — Oh!" Molly made a wild grab for the side of the driver's seat as he lurched forward.

Jerome had no intention of abandoning her even within sight of town. And certainly not at night. At this time of day, the four-legged predators came out to dine. Molly would be a succulent meal for a starving coyote or a pack of wolves come down from the distant hills.

Whatever she ran from here couldn't be half as bad as what they had encountered in Chagrin. The Thompsons were vicious — the ones still alive, Jerome corrected himself.

"The livery stable's over there," she said, pointing down a cross street off the road through town.

The main thoroughfare in Chagrin had meandered about. Whoever had laid out the one in Clear Springs had used a theodolite or, at the very least, hadn't been blind drunk. It stretched straight and true. Jerome brought the wagon to a halt outside the stables.

A youngster of hardly ten came running out. He turned a freshly scrubbed face up to Jerome and asked, "Any special thing I kin do for your horse? She looks mighty tuckered out."

"Nothing special. Just don't feed her too much too soon or let her bloat," Jerome said, jumping down.

He turned to help Molly, but she already stood on the far side of the wagon.

"You a peddler?" The boy peered at the sign on the side of the wagon. From the way his eyes came unfocused, he wasn't able to read.

"Yes, son, I am. And something more. Allow me to introduce myself. Professor J. Frederick Kincannon, dispenser of tonics to cure what ails you. Many call me the Professor of Potions because of my miracle medicines. But you don't have neuritis, neuralgia or the gout, now, do you?"

The boy scratched his head. "I don't rightly know what any of those things are. I had lice a while back." He instinctively scratched his head and tousled his hair even more.

"My special ointment takes care of those nasty little biters." Jerome poked around in the boy's thick thatch. "Looks as if you are free of them."

"Yes, sir, my ma, she used lye soap and a scrub brush 'til I swear I was about ready to —"

"Charles, hush up. This gentleman don't want to hear such things."

A man wearing old denim overalls came from the stalls. He wiped his hands off on his thighs. In spite of that attempt to get clean, Jerome was glad when the man didn't reach out to shake hands. He had been mucking stalls.

Jerome let his spiel slip out. He had sold

too many bottles of his elixir not to tell the stable boy about how a drop or two cured lice. Before he got too carried away with his sales pitch, he added, "But it is not recommended for youngsters to drink. Dab it on the afflicted area and let it work its miracle — on the outside."

"What 'bout us old folks?" the livery owner asked. He cocked his head to one side and looked hard at Jerome.

"Why, sir, you hit upon the very patient most likely to benefit."

He put more alcohol into the concoction than found in most shots of whiskey served in saloons. Jerome knew the alcohol killed lice, but a young man of this size and age would get knee-walking drunk after only a small sip.

"Give me a couple bottles and I'll tend your horse for half price."

Jerome dickered a mite with the man and came to a reasonable fee. Every bottle cost him almost two bits. In some towns, buying empty bottles cost more than the ingredients. About ten minutes into his sales pitch, he got a feel of how prosperous the town was. A bottle selling for two bucks in Chagrin, say, could fetch three dollars in Clear Springs. Or maybe only a dollar.

He unlaced a leather pouch dangling

91

against the side of the wagon. He kept a few bottles within easy reach so he didn't have to break off his sales pitch and root about inside the wagon when he gathered a crowd. The bottles were passed to the stable owner, who sniffed at them like a bloodhound. His nostrils flared and a big grin crossed his face.

"These will do me just fine. I'll see to it my boy gets a drop or two if those lice still bother him, but these will most likely be all mine."

He twisted this way and that. As if by magic, the bottles slid into pockets Jerome hadn't noticed before.

The man pursed his lips, thought a spell, then asked, "You fixing to set up sales here in town?" He watched Charles lead the tired horse into the nearest stall and begin currying it. When he was satisfied his boy was doing his job, he turned to face Jerome. "I got to warn you about the marshal."

Jerome nodded sagely. Most towns were cursed with crooked law dogs. As he had done in Chagrin, he'd come to some understanding here. Right now he was too tired out to think about such bribery.

"What's that you got rolled up on the roof?" The stable owner walked around Jerome's wagon and looked up at the end of the scenery. "You have a tent show like a hellfire-and-brimstone preacher? We had one of them folks come through last summer. He pitched a big tent out at the Underwood place just east of town and spent two solid weeks on a stage he built personally, telling everyone how we was goin' to hell. He thought he was as good a carpenter as Jesus, but he wasn't. The stage collapsed on him just 'fore his last sermon was all done." The man sighed. "There was talk about him and Miz Underwood getting together for a private baptismal out at the stock pond, but ole Will Underwood won't talk 'bout that to this day." He sighed again and grinned. "Best entertainment we've had in years."

"My universal elixir cures what ails you," Jerome said. "But it does not deliver eternal salvation. That claim I leave to others."

"Just as well. The marshal tossed the preacher man into the clink. One day he was locked up. The next he sorta vanished."

Jerome knew better than to ask about the freewill offerings collected during the services. Right now he wanted to crawl into the rear of his wagon and sleep through the night. Then he sagged in resignation. Molly's bedroll was stretched out there. He looked around the stable and started to ask about bedding down on some clean straw in a stall next to his horse.

For the price of a third bottle of his elixir, Jerome was given a clean blanket and room to sleep. He spread the blanket and stretched out. Just as his eyelids drooped, he came awake.

"Molly," he muttered.

Joints aching, he stood and went to the wagon. A couple soft knocks on the rear door didn't bring any response. Gingerly opening the door, he peered inside. Her blanket lay flat on the floor. Wherever she was, it wasn't inside the wagon.

Wherever she had gotten off to was her business. He wasn't her keeper, and she knew Clear Springs and its people better than he ever could. Jerome strained and pulled a bottle of elixir from a crate. Backing off, he closed the door and returned to his own bedroll. A deft flick of the thumb popped the cork. A few quick pulls on the brownish fluid, followed by a warm puddling in his belly that spread throughout his body, erased all his aches and pains.

It was a miracle, and he was truly Professor of Potions.

He lay back and fell into a sleep troubled by nightmares of Molly screaming and the Benjamin gang tormenting her.

Chapter Five

Jerome jumped at every noise. He looked up from the chore of pouring more elixir into a bottle and stared out the back of the wagon. The stable owner had steered him toward a vacant lot on the next block. Situated near the main street, this was a perfect spot for him to begin his sales. First, though, he needed a couple cases more of his potion.

Disturbances only put his nerves on edge. He expected someone to show himself. After a few seconds, when he didn't hear anyone stirring, he sucked in his breath and held it.

Not seeing anyone but increasingly uneasy, Jerome pushed his work aside and made his way to the stage now dropped down. He pointedly stepped over Molly's bedding where she had carelessly left it. He hadn't seen hide nor hair of her since rolling into town, but her wardrobe was untouched and the roll of scenery still weighed down the wagon so that it creaked and groaned as he moved about. Her absence was worrisome but not unduly so. She wasn't likely to go far without her possessions.

At least, he hoped that was true. She had been adamant about not wanting to return to Clear Springs. What there could be in a sleepy town like this that caused her to demand to be abandoned in the desert rather than come back was a mystery he didn't want to explore. He had a mission of his own, and the singer only complicated it.

"So much for being a Good Samaritan," he grumbled.

Jerome stepped out on the stage and stretched his cramped muscles. He had been hard at work for over two hours and hadn't taken a break. Blocking the sun with one hand, he looked around. It was close to noon. By early evening when it cooled off a mite, he'd start his pitch. Clear Springs looked prosperous enough for him to sell at least two cases of his special potion at a decent price.

He pivoted, hand going to a knife sheathed along his left forearm when he heard the telltale metallic click of a six-gun being cocked.

"There's no call for you to point that hog-leg at me," he said.

His fingers worked in a seemingly nervous tattoo as he slipped the knife half from its sheath. A quick spin and powerful toss. The flash of steel in the sunlight. A blade stuck in the man's throat. He worked the scene over and over, rehearsing it mentally. The man kept his gun leveled. The next act of the play seemed more likely to be enacted. Unless one of them backed down, blood would be spilled.

"Now that remains to be seen. Why don't you drop your hands to your side? Without that knife." The gunman turned sideways to present a smaller target.

"You've come to rob me?"

Jerome moved slowly to obey. He slipped his left hand behind his back and touched another knife in the tail of his swallowtail coat. If he had to get shot during a robbery, he'd deliver at least a savage cut to his attacker.

"Nothing like that, mister."

"Professor," Jerome said. "Professor J. Frederick Kincannon."

"Where did you get a college eddy-ca-shun? Or are you claiming to be a teacher kind of professor?"

"A man can call himself what he chooses,"

Jerome said haughtily. "I have studied chemistry and the apothecary arts for years. 'Professor' is an honorific bestowed on me by the most learned scholars in Europe."

"I like that. Apothecary arts." The man edged around to stand in front of Jerome. The gun swiveled to keep him covered. "I've got a bit of eddy-ca-shun myself."

"Fourth grade?" Jerome failed to keep the sarcasm from his words.

"Not that much, but that's not what matters here in Clear Springs. I am an honors grad-you-ate of the school of staying alive long enough to put up with sorry swindlers like you," the man said. He pulled back his coat. The sun caught the marshal's badge pinned to his vest. "I'm the law in this town."

"Marshal," Jerome said softly.

He moved his right hand behind his back and fingered a second knife. After introducing himself, the law dog made no move to holster his six-shooter. That put Jerome on alert there was more coming than a marshal warning a possible lawbreaker to watch his p's and q's.

"It's good to see you twigged to that right away. Common sense always trumps eddy-ca-shun, at least in the real world with guns and knives involved."

The marshal smiled. A gold tooth gleamed in the front of his mouth. He lowered the hammer with his thumb, spun the six-gun around on the trigger guard and pocketed the weapon smoothly.

Jerome forced himself not to cast both knives. He wasn't the target of the marshal's gun now, but deep in his gut, he knew he was still the man's prey.

"We got laws here in Clear Springs about hoodwinking the good folks who might trust a silver-tongued fox like you. Take that bottle of swill you're selling now. There's no proof it does anything."

"I disagree, Marshal."

The lawman ignored him. "Not that I care one teeny bit. How long you intending to stay in my fair town?"

Jerome shrugged. He had no reason to stay any longer than it took to get a lead about the Benjamin gang. If the marshal was any indication of the rest of the townspeople, he understood Molly's reluctance to return.

"I'd say you're only going to be here for one more day before traveling on. Does that sound about right? One more day?"

"I have no objection," Jerome said.

"Then you'll have no objection to a temporary seller's license fee of, oh, twenty dollars." The marshal moved his hand back to the wooden grips on his Colt.

"Definitely twenty dollars. In coin. None of that scrip written on some bank I never heard of." He snorted. "Fact is, I don't trust money issued by the local bank. Leonard Kingman's one step away from getting arrested for thievery."

Jerome scowled.

"He's the bank president," the marshal went on. "But you don't need to know any of this. A double eagle. Or the equivalent. I'll take silver if you ain't got gold coin."

"I don't have that much," Jerome said.

"Then you'd better hitch up your flea-bitten nag and roll on out. No license, no selling. You can be on the other side of the town limits sign by sundown."

"I'd need to sell a case of my medication to get that kind of fee."

Jerome appealed to the man's greed. This dickering wasn't unusual and always went the same way. He almost laughed out loud when the script was read to an end.

"Tomorrow morning," the marshal said. "I'll be by real early for the twenty dollars. If you try to skedaddle, I'll run you down before sundown next, and you'll be slammed into jail for a month of Sundays." The marshal grinned, and it wasn't pretty.

"This wagon and all its trappings will be sold to pay for your stay in my jail."

Jerome considered how fast he'd have to drive to get away if he cut down the lawman. Before he came to a conclusion, the marshal asked something that froze him where he stood.

"That roll of canvas you got draped over your wagon. I've seen one like that before. You traveling alone?"

"I am," Jerome said. "Why do you ask?"

"A real hellion hightailed it from town a few weeks back. I'd like to find her so we can have a little . . . talk. You sure you're all by your lonesome?"

Jerome made a sweeping gesture. The marshal stood on tiptoe and peered inside the wagon. Jerome caught his breath when the man moved from side to side, as if he'd seen some trace Molly left behind. The marshal sank back onto his heels.

"You can believe your own eyes, Marshal. There's no one else here but yours truly." Jerome swept his arm about in another grand gesture.

The lawman grunted and stalked away. Jerome watched until the man rounded a building before sagging in relief. It wasn't that hot, not the way it got out in open desert, but he was sweating like a pig.

He ducked back inside the wagon, scooping up Molly's belongings and stuffing them into a trunk. The marshal wasn't likely to come poking about, but there wasn't any call to run the risk. Jerome had the feeling the law dog had recognized the scenery. How many examples of such extensive artwork ever made it to a stage in West Texas?

He took another look around to be sure the marshal hadn't left a deputy to spy on him, then returned to his work. The specter of having to pay twenty dollars out of his sales goaded him into working faster.

Jerome decanted more of his elixir, chose from a variety of colorful labels he'd had printed up previously and affixed them to the bottles. This time he'd be selling Professor J. F. Kincannon's Liver Remedy and Hair Restorer. He had stumbled on the combination months earlier after a long and hot haranguing. It had been a slip of the tongue and somehow had sparked more interest than anything he'd sold to date.

When he had two cases' worth of his product, he wiped his face, then climbed from the wagon and closed it up. His horse still received good care at the livery. He made a mental note to hold back enough coin from the sales to pay the stable bill.

The crooked marshal wasn't going to deprive that faithful steed of some decent care before moving on.

Jerome stepped out into the main street and looked around. For some reason he felt let down that Molly didn't come running up. Wherever she had gotten off to, she continued to ignore him. He walked slowly past a trio of empty saloons and then saw his destination.

The Butterfield Stage office had seen better days. More than one plank popped loose on the front. The wood and paint were distant companions. Years, Jerome guessed, had passed since the building had looked presentable. All he cared about was the telegraph wire running from a pole down to the roof.

"Stage, telegraph, information," he said softly.

Stride long and anticipation soaring, he went into the cool interior. The fierce smell of the lead-acid batteries made him avert his head. He was used to such fumes in his work as an apothecary, but this small room needed more ventilation.

"Howdy, mister" came a raspy voice. "You looking to get a stagecoach ticket or send a telegram? I can do either for you. Or both. Have your family waiting at the other end of your coach ride with a single message. I even got a special today where both come in a single package, so to speak."

"Nice sales job," Jerome congratulated. "I'm not looking to send information but rather to gather it."

The man stood behind the counter. He topped Jerome by half a head and must have been a hard-rock miner before taking this job. Broad of chest and thick of arm, he showed muscles enough to crush most men with his bare hands. A translucent green eyeshade hid his face and cast an eerie glow to a thick handlebar mustache. A bushy brown beard streaked with gray hinted that he was either older than Jerome thought or had led a hard life so far.

"You ain't one of them bounty hunters, are you? I don't cotton to them. There's one what comes through town too often for my liking. He's a real pest."

"You've got me wrong. I'm not a bounty hunter," Jerome said. He struck a pose, thumbs under his black silk lapels as he tried to look professorial.

The agent sniffed. How he caught the scent of anything over the sulfuric acid fumes was a mystery, but he said, "You got the stink of chemicals about you. What kind of devil's potion do you peddle?"

Jerome decided the man wasn't as dull as he looked.

"You get all the reports about road agents," he said.

"That's true. For all the good it does. The marshal's not likely to do much about such warnings, but I pass it along to the drivers and shotgun messengers. These days that's about every time they leave Clear Springs."

"I'm sure your timely warnings have saved lives and kept valuable freight from being hijacked."

"Spit it out, mister. You're wastin' my time." He looked over his shoulder at the silent telegraph key. "I'm expectin' the evening news anytime now. My partner up in Fort Worth is real good about keepin' me informed of things that are important."

"Any warnings about the Benjamin gang?"

"Benjamin? Not sure I've heard that name, not tied up in a bow around any outlaws in these parts."

"What about your drivers? They'd be the ones who'd need to know such things. The gang has been raiding throughout West Texas these past few weeks. They caused quite a bit of gossip down in San Antonio with their thieving and killing."

The agent shook his head and pushed up

the green eyeshade to get a better look at Jerome.

"What's your interest, if you ain't a bounty hunter?"

"They owe me," Jerome said.

"Stole some of your joy juice, eh?" The agent laughed. "Nothing's worse than stealing a snake oil peddler's wares."

Jerome started to snap back and then knew it wouldn't avail him anything.

"Tell me if you get a click on them, will you?" He gestured toward the silent telegraph key.

"Not much traffic comin' this way the past day or two. Sometimes the Injuns cut the wires, just to bedevil us. Other times it means they're fixin' to swoop down, but the Army claims they've drove most all the Indians back to where they came from." He shook his shaggy head, readjusted his eyeshade and concluded, "Hard to believe everything they say, though."

"So your lines may be down?"

"Didn't say that. Just that traffic's been real slow. That can mean downed lines, but I got a rider out lookin'." He made a sour expression. "If the Indians are responsible, sometimes they cut the wire and tie the ends with rawhide. Looks like a good line but the signal won't go through the leather. But that's not keepin' me from receivin' or sendin'." He fixed a hard look. "You want to send a 'gram? Half the usual rate until six o'clock."

Jerome jumped in surprise when the key began clacking noisily.

The telegrapher turned and went to the desk. He touched the stub of a pencil to the tip of his tongue, then began scribbling down the translation of the incoming message.

Jerome slipped back into the twilight. He had to get back to his wagon and start his evening pitch. There was a rhythm to when to begin his sales pitch. The townspeople needed time to eat dinner and then come out to head for saloons and a night of revelry. First, he had one more well of information to dip a few drops from. He went around back of the stagecoach office and found a large corral filled with a dozen horses. Working to fill water troughs was a youngster hardly into his teens, if that.

The boy looked up as Jerome approached. He called out, "You need to stay back, mister. These horses are all property of the Butterfield Stage Company and not for sale."

"I'm not interested in buying them," Jerome said. He grinned disarmingly. "And

I'm not thinking on stealing them, either."

The boy relaxed.

"Are horse thieves a concern?" Jerome asked.

He climbed to the top rail and swung a leg over as if mounting a horse. He peered down at the boy, who carried two empty buckets. The pails swayed back and forth in quick, nervous arcs.

"It's happened."

"Recently? The Benjamin gang? I've heard tell they're about the worst horse thieves in all of Texas."

He watched the boy's reaction. Then he heaved a deep sigh. As with the agent inside the depot, the name produced no reaction. He might as well have been talking some foreign language for all the recognition he garnered.

"You don't look like a Ranger." The boy stepped closer and gave Jerome more than the once-over. "You're not a lawman of any kind, and I seen bounty hunters. You don't look like one of them, either. One of them what makes Clear Springs his headquarters stinks. He hasn't had a bath since I've known him."

"Everybody in town worries about bounty hunters. Is there a reason for that? Like they're hunting for a notorious gang robbing banks and stages?"

"We're peaceable enough here in Clear Springs. Marshal Bishop's not much of a stickler for keeping the peace, but that might be why —"

The boy cut off his appraisal of the marshal and whirled around, the buckets swinging wide. He ran in the direction of a pump on the far side of the corral.

Jerome didn't have to have eyes in the back of his head to know why the boy had run for the tall and uncut.

"Evening, Marshal," Jerome said aloud without turning. "So is this part of your routine, checking the stage depot before moseying on to keep order in the saloons?"

"You do get around, don't you, Perfesser? Why are you annoyin' the Jenkins boy?"

"I'm just getting the lay of the land, Marshal, nothing more. I enjoy talking to the citizens to find what matters most to them."

"The boy don't have aches 'n' pains. His pa wouldn't like you peddlin' your filthy pizzen to his son."

"Since you hadn't heard of the Benjamin gang, I decided to poke around."

"Ain't nuthin' about criminals in Clear Springs I don't know. Why'd you think to come here? Because the drivers might have

109

gossip? Don't listen to such rumors. The worst of the bunch is Purcell. Because he lives hunched over that telegraph, he thinks he knows everything." The marshal spat, hitched up his gun belt and said, "Don't go annoyin' me anymore."

Jerome swung his leg over the top rail and dropped lightly to the ground. He clanked just a little as his knives banged against one another, but the lawman paid no attention. Marshal Bishop was already walking away. His broad back made a good target. Jerome imagined two quick casts, one knife in each hand. He pushed the fantasy aside. Bringing down men who irked him wasn't his goal.

The Benjamin brothers continued to elude him.

As he rounded the stage depot, the burly agent boiled from inside, looking around frantically. He spied Jerome and rushed to him. With fingers like steel bands, he clamped down on Jerome's upper arms and shook. Jerome's teeth rattled and he cried out. Only that broke the man's obvious panic.

"I found you. I'm surely glad you didn't wander off," the stage agent blurted.

"What's wrong, Mr. Purcell?"

Jerome looked around. He hadn't heard

the stage roll in. Whatever agitated the man came from another source.

"Tell me everything you know about the Benjamin gang."

Memories of Marcie and his son, Arthur, flashed through Jerome's head. Rather than go into that sorry tale, Jerome admitted, "I've never even seen them. I don't know what they look like, other than the poor likenesses off wanted posters I've picked up on their trail. Now tell me what's got you so riled up."

"They . . . it . . . some road agents done up and robbed the San Angelo stage. They killed three passengers and the shotgun messenger. The driver got away by the skin of his teeth. They stole the horses and . . . and . . . and all the mail."

"You sure it was the Benjamin gang?"

"The driver heard one call the leader Hank. Does that mean anything to you?"

Jerome caught his breath. Hank Benjamin. Curtis and Leland. But how many outlaws named Hank plied their trade in this part of Texas? He sagged when he realized there wasn't any way to know. It wasn't an uncommon name.

"How'd he connect the name with the Benjamin gang?"

"The marshal in San Angelo had a wanted

poster with that name on it. Look, you must know about them. Tell me so I can telegraph it to the Butterfield office in San Angelo."

"I can't help out that much," Jerome said, his mind racing. "But you're upset over something else. What is it?"

The man swallowed so hard his Adam's apple bobbed about.

"I shouldn't tell you this."

"Gold?" Jerome saw the Butterfield agent turn pasty white.

"How'd you know?"

"What else could put you into such a state? You need a bottle of my tonic to calm your nerves."

The man looked around as if he had been cornered, although they stood in the street in front of the depot. Then he said, "The ranchers are moving a shipment to a bank in Dallas."

Jerome stared at the man in disbelief.

"You blurt that out to just any stranger?"

"Ain't nobody in town that don't know it. There's a couple of the ranchers who brag on how much they're sending to the big banks."

"In gold?" Jerome pressed.

The ticket agent shook his head. "Some of it might be. Mostly in greenbacks. Their profits for the entire year. A dozen of them.

They're not inclined to trust the local banker."

"Leonard Kingman's not too reputable. Is that it?"

Purcell's bushy eyebrows wiggled about like woolly worms on a griddle. "How do you know about him? Are you sure you ain't a Ranger?"

Jerome waved off the question. He had other inquiries to make and more than one question to get answered.

"It sounds as if they could each have a half dozen cowboys ride along. Such a small army could defend against an entire Indian nation."

"But the outlaws don't know that. If they start holding up every stage because they don't know that, not a one of *my* shipments will get through. They can even kill all the passengers. Who'd ever ride with Butterfield again? We got problems enough what with the railroad takin' so much of our business."

"Especially if they were killed," Jerome said sardonically. "If you're worried about the safety of your passengers, I can ride along as added security."

The agent looked at Jerome's waist and frowned.

"You ain't even packin' iron. But you must know *something* about these robbers that'll help put nooses around their filthy necks."

"Nothing'd suit me more," Jerome said with feeling.

"That's not what I need. Tell me all you can about the gang you're huntin' down, even though you ain't a bounty hunter."

The agent about spat out the words. Whatever cooperation Jerome might have gotten evaporated now that the man's fright was fading.

"Here's all I know about the Benjamin gang," Jerome said.

He named them, then detailed what crimes he knew they had committed since leaving Arkansas a year prior. He neglected putting a name to the woman and boy murdered. The Butterfield agent never noticed the catch in Jerome's voice. Jerome finished with a quick summary of chasing through Texas to find the outlaws.

"That ain't much," the agent said. He spun and started back for the Butterfield office.

"Wait," Jerome called. "What about me riding along?"

The man made a dismissive gesture and disappeared into the depot muttering about "know-nothings." Seconds later the chatter of the telegraph key echoed forth into the still evening. Jerome turned away. He had planted a seed. Whether it grew into anything useful was beyond his grasp now. But he felt more confident of finding the murderers than ever before. The stagecoach company was alerted now and worried about every shipment. News of the Benjamins had to filter to Jerome sooner or later.

He looked around Clear Springs as he returned to his wagon. The streets were deserted, but lights in most of the rooming houses told where the population had gone. The stores were dark, but anywhere people lived bulged with activity. The three-story hotel glowed like a rising sun, interior light shining through cut-glass windows. Even some of the rooms on the upper stories were lit.

At his wagon he lowered the stage and climbed up. Molly's belongings inside were where he had hidden them to keep Marshal Bishop from asking too many questions.

"Where have you gone?"

He shook his head. She wasn't his concern. Yet she was. He had some responsibility toward her because he had rescued her back in Chagrin. The woman hadn't wanted to come to Clear Springs, but he had forced her.

Jerome shrugged it off as he pulled a couple cases of his snake oil to the back of the stage. With the assurance of long months practicing, he arranged his gear around him. Some of it was nothing more than jars filled with a liquid and weird-looking contents. Those were his examples of what untreated — by his potion — organs looked like. Other items were curiosities designed to hold the audience's attention. His stuffed two-headed rattlesnake always caused a ripple of interest. Some claimed to have seen one themselves out in the wild. And they probably had. Most townspeople were intrigued by the display, always edged closer and became more inclined to buy a bottle or two.

"It's coming," Jerome boomed. "Soon. You may not have time to correct this scourge."

It took five minutes of haranguing about the "scourge" to begin drawing a crowd. When he started he had no idea what the scourge might be. He warmed to the subject and convinced a few of the earliest in his crowd they were getting the jump on late-comers.

Jerome spun stories and entertained and showed off his displays to a crowd wanting a diversion. As he did, he spotted her. Molly. She drifted around the edge of the crowd, out near the main street.

He beckoned to her to join him. She was a performer. If he convinced her to render some song — a hymn would be perfect — that would cement the crowd's attention. Molly looked distracted. Distraught.

And then she was gone.

A bear of a man reared up at the far side of the audience, then lit out. Jerome tried to convince himself that the man wasn't chasing Molly. He didn't do a good job and his presentation suffered until he swung back into the rhythm of storytelling.

An hour later he had sold three entire cases of his elixir. Or potion. Or tonic. He had trouble remembering what he'd called it this time, and all the labels were gone. A thick wad of scrip caused a bulge in one coat pocket, but the significant weight of coins in his other mattered more. He had more than covered his nut.

The marshal would be pleased.

Jerome hoped he would be, too, when he had to pull out the next morning even if Molly hadn't returned.

CHAPTER SIX

Jerome sat on the edge of the stage and stared into the darkness. His audience had left, most satisfied that they had bought a bottle of an elixir sure to cure what ailed them. In many cases, that was true. The amount of alcohol in every dose worked miracles at easing aches and pains from everyday living. The other ingredients weren't going to hurt anyone and probably helped some. A few, at any rate.

He felt no remorse at selling his potion because it gave him a reason to travel and a way to make a living while he hunted for the Benjamin brothers. But at the moment a hollowness formed in his gut unlike anything he'd felt since looking down on his wife's burned body.

"Where did you go, Molly?"

Jerome hopped to the ground and closed the drop-down stage. In spite of not being responsible for her, he wasn't going to roll out of town the next morning. He tugged at the scenery dangling down off one side of the wagon.

"I'm not going to dump your clothes and this thing and leave you behind without saying goodbye."

The huge man who had seemed to go after the woman looked as if he had evil intentions toward her. The way she had skedaddled added to that suspicion.

Jerome sucked in his breath and held it until he forcibly gasped. He had been asking around town after the Benjamin gang and now someone who looked like a road agent had pursued Molly. She had come to town with him. The marshal might have guessed — had to have figured it out because of his comment about the canvas roll. And if the law was in cahoots with the gang, kidnapping Molly was a way to get to him.

He wrestled with the question of forgetting about bringing justice to the Benjamins in exchange for Molly's life. Such a deal was still a mirage and might never be offered. But what if it became a reality?

A quick check assured him all his knives were in place. He glanced back at the wagon. He had several firearms there, too, and had practiced long and hard to become adroit with them. Carrying them detracted from his image as a professor helping everyone in town. Never had he known a doctor to carry a gun. So he didn't, either.

But the time had to come when a six-shooter was more useful than a knife.

Mind racing, he decided to hunt for Molly first and worry about strapping on a six-gun later. Although killing a man had caused him a second's hesitation earlier, he was skilled enough so that two quick moves sent deadly steel through the air. A small shift brought other knives to hand. He had enough death riding in sheaths secreted about his body to take care of the shaggy mountain of a man who pursued Molly.

"It must be one of the Benjamins," he said to himself. "Maybe it's Hank himself. He's the oldest one, so he ought to be the biggest."

"Hey, Professor, does your bottled tonic make you talk to yourself? I get mighty lonely a' nights. Should I partake of a swig or two?" A man in shadow sitting in a chair along the boardwalk called out to him.

Jerome whirled about at a bright flash. He settled down when he saw the man held a bottle of the elixir. Half of it was already drained. That much would get the man well along the road to being knee-walking drunk.

"I'm hunting for a friend," Jerome said.

He secured the knife back in the sheath along his right arm and walked to face the man.

Shadows hid the man's face, but Jerome doubted this was one of the Benjamins. The man belched and took another long pull on the potion. If he had meant any harm, he'd had a chance to gun down Jerome from behind. Instead he got a little drunker.

"You live here? In Clear Springs?"

"If you call it livin', I reckon so. More like it's only existin'."

The man thrust out the bottle again so light from the saloon across the street glittered on it. Only a couple swigs remained.

"I'm looking for a woman," Jerome began.

The man laughed uproariously. "Who ain't? 'Cept the ones what got married! To a man they're all lookin' to get rid of a woman."

"Thanks for your views on matrimony," Jerome said dryly. "I'm looking for a dark-haired woman. She's got an oval face, bow lips and the bluest eyes you ever did see."

"Bluer than the Texas sky? Hair down below her shoulders?"

"Yes," Jerome said eagerly.

"Nope. No, sir, never saw her."

The man drained the bottle and stared at it with longing. He shook it and held it upside down in a vain attempt to squeeze just one more drop out.

Jerome reached into his inner coat pocket and drew out another bottle. He held it high enough to catch the light from across the street.

"Might be worth a free bottle if you actually saw her."

The man rocked forward. For the first time, Jerome got a good look at him. The man's eyes were bloodshot, and his face bore the inexorable progress of hot, dry West Texas years. If he tried to smile or laugh or show any emotion, that cured leather face had to crack and break.

"I was thinkin' on a singer what was here in town a couple weeks back. Cain't remember her name, but her lovely face is burned into my memory like a brand on a calf's rump." He reached for the bottle.

Jerome moved it just enough to deny him. "Have you seen her since then? Since she performed here in town?"

The man's eyes darted about. His sun-baked face showed not a whit of emotion. It was too dried out for that. He licked his lips, then wiped them with his sleeve.

"Sometimes it don't pay a man to be too observant."

"But not being observant is thirsty work."

122

Jerome teased him with the elixir.

"Danged bounty hunter," the man spat.

Jerome heaved a sigh of frustration. "Does everybody in Clear Springs worry about bounty hunters?"

"Only one. Him. The cantankerous one."

Jerome said nothing but inched closer. The man's shaky hand touched the slick glass. Rather than pull away, Jerome moved forward until the man's fingers closed around the bottle. Almost.

"Who?" he asked softly.

"Name's Bear. Ain't never heard more 'n that."

Jerome saw he was nearing the end of the line gathering information here. "Why'd he want Molly?"

"That's her name. Molly Davenport. Who wouldn't want her?"

"Where can I find him? I just want to talk, not cause trouble."

"The boy at the Butterfield office. He knows. That little imp knows ever'thing what goes on in this town. Me, I never stir from my chair here in front of the tobacconist."

Jerome pressed the full bottle into the man's outstretched fingers. He clutched it with both hands. There wasn't any way he was going to spill even a precious drop.

Jerome picked up the empty bottle and put it into his pocket. A quick refill and he'd have another sale. Not here in Clear Springs perhaps, but somewhere else on the trail as he hunted down the murderous brothers.

He turned and walked directly to the stage office. It was locked up tight, but a light burned inside. Pressing his nose against a window, he saw movement inside. The hulking telegrapher tapped out a message. Day or night, telegrams had to be sent and received. Jerome started to rap on the window, then stepped away.

The Butterfield agent wasn't whom he sought. He went around back. The horses in the corral stirred restlessly as he approached but didn't put up much of a fuss. Walking the perimeter, he came to a shed. The door stood half open. Light from inside spilled out.

Jerome peered around the door. The boy hunched over a coal-oil lamp. He jumped a foot when Jerome cleared his throat. The boy swung about guiltily.

"What do you want?"

"Reading? A dime novel?"

"What's it to you?"

"It's not something I'd have expected. How old are you?"

"Old enough." The boy picked up the

ragged book with the garish cover and held it close. "It's mine. I paid for it, and you're not taking it."

"I don't want to," Jerome said. "Truth is, I already read that one. You'll like the ending."

His words took the boy by surprise. "You've read it?"

"I wish I had time to read more, but I have technical journals to read and medicinal things to keep up on." He said nothing and the boy stared hard at him, still suspicious of anyone catching him reading. Jerome finally said, "You're the Jenkins boy, right?"

"Yeah. So?"

"Word about town is that there's nothing you don't know. You mentioned a bounty hunter earlier when I was here."

"You wanted to know about an outlaw gang. I hadn't heard a peep about them. Then."

"The telegrapher received a message about robbers that might be them," Jerome said.

"No 'might be' about it. A Texas Ranger's put a name to them. The Benjamin boys. The ones you were asking after."

"You are a veritable fount of information, aren't you?"

"I reckon so, though I'm not real sure

what a fount is."

The boy slid his novel under a thin blanket, then moved to sit on it, as if it might run off — or Jerome might try to snatch it away.

He found himself tossed on the horns of a dilemma. Which road to follow? Molly and whatever predicament she'd gotten herself into or tracking down his family's killers. The decision came easily.

"You know where I can find them?" Jerome cursed under his breath when the boy shook his head.

"But I do know where the woman what rode into town with you is." The boy smirked. "That's the singer woman who lit a shuck a couple weeks back."

"You saw her in my wagon?"

The boy nodded. "As you were coming into town. She's a beauty, that's for sure." He worried the book from under the blanket and held it up. "She's pretty enough to be on the cover of a dime novel."

"I never thought about that," Jerome admitted. "But she's not likely to ever be."

"Not with that bounty hunter stealing her away."

"You know she was kidnapped by . . . Bear?" Jerome tried out the name.

The boy's head bobbed up and down.

"Why didn't you tell the marshal? That sort of thing's illegal."

"Not in Clear Springs," the boy said. "It's nothing Marshal Bishop'd dirty his hands over. Tangling with Bear is real dangerous. More 'n one fool's found that out the hard way."

"He's a big one, but you know what they say about that."

"The bigger they are, the harder they fall," the boy said. "Bear's not gonna fall easy, though. He's tough. Once or twice a month he comes through town to take a gander at the marshal's new wanted posters. He talks to Leon, too, but Leon won't have much to do with him."

"Leon's the telegrapher?"

"Leon Purcell. They look alike. You'd take 'em for brothers if you didn't know better." The boy stared up at Jerome, a cunning gleam coming to his eyes. "The singer 'n' you are more than traveling companions?"

"You're sure Bear kidnapped her?"

The Jenkins boy nodded. "I don't recollect where he took her, though."

"Two dime novels," Jerome said, fishing around in his pocket and pulling out four nickels. "There's no telling what stories you can find."

The boy licked his lips and came to a

127

quick decision. "There's a shack on the outskirts of town, not a half mile from here. Due east along the main road. Bear's not the owner. He's squatting there. The real owner chickened out and just moved on, letting Bear have the place. It's a real dump."

Jerome flipped the four coins to the boy, one at a time. He turned to go.

"Professor Kincannon! You won't tell anybody about me and the book?"

Jerome laughed and said he wouldn't.

"You need a gun if you intend to tangle with Bear. He's a mean son of a buck."

"Thanks for the warning." Jerome touched the knives sheathed all around his body.

"Make it a big gun. The name's well-earned. I read about Hugh Glass shootin' a grizzly bear right betwixt the eyes with a flintlock pistol. The ball bounded right off. Bear's the same way. Shoot him somewhere besides his head if you want to kill him. That skull's too danged hard to penetrate otherwise."

"Reading gives you all kinds of tall tales to think on," Jerome said.

He walked back to the main street. It ran due east toward the shack where the bounty hunter might have been holding Molly captive.

Not for the first time Jerome wondered how involved he should get in this. Bear hadn't seen the woman in the crowd and taken an immediate fancy to her. He had spotted her and known the trail immediately. There was a history between them, which was probably why Molly hadn't wanted to come back to Clear Springs.

Jerome walked with an increasingly sure stride. Molly was his responsibility. Freeing her shouldn't be too hard, in spite of Bear's physique. Jerome lived by his wits and practiced using his knives against the day he found his wife's killers. Talking the bounty hunter into releasing Molly might not be easy, but he felt confident of accomplishing the task before he hit the road at sunrise.

Jerome stopped when he saw a tumbledown shack. A dim glow seeped between the planks in the walls. The door hung from the top hinge, and a tiny curl of white smoke rose from a tin stovepipe. He caught his breath when a shadow passed across the window. Someone moved about inside.

He circled the shack, causing a horse staked out back to neigh and tug on its reins. He quickly moved to the far side to let the horse calm itself, but the damage had been done.

"Who's out there? Show yourselves! If you don't, I'll rip off your arms and beat you to death with them."

That bellicose cry of rage and warning caused Jerome to press his back against the splintery shack wall. His heart hammered away. If Molly was this man's captive, freeing her wasn't going to be as quick and easy as he'd believed.

"You're not taking her back. She's mine!"

Heavy footfalls came in Jerome's direction. He crossed his arms and touched the knives sheathed along his forearms. A quick tug brought the knives into his grip. He turned and readied himself for a quick strike when the man reached the corner of the shack.

For an eternity, he waited. When no one came around, Jerome spun about, ready to fight. He felt his body going numb all over. He had prepared himself to fight, and the man had returned inside. The loud voice echoed as if the entire house was a bass drum.

"Who you got hunting for you now?"

Jerome almost cried out when Molly answered. She *was* here.

"Nobody. There's nobody who'd track me down, Bear. What do you intend to do with me?"

"That's a real silly question. You know what I'm gonna do."

Jerome moved closer to peer past the door. He recoiled when all he saw was a broad back. Bear lived up to his name. If his shoulders weren't a couple ax handles wide, they came so close as not to matter. Jerome twirled a knife about in his left hand, ready to make a powerful stab into the exposed back.

Just as he stepped forward, the bounty hunter took a quick step away. If Jerome launched his attack, he'd miss and reveal himself. In a hand-to-hand fight, Jerome knew he had no chance. Only a lucky strike with a knife would save him.

Dead, he was no use to Molly.

He looked past the mountain of a man to where Molly cowered in the corner of the single room. An iron potbelly stove with an open door cast light into the room and onto the frightened woman's face. Her eyes went wide when she saw Jerome.

He started to enter. His only hope was a quick attack. He had to take Bear by surprise; only Molly gestured to him to stay back. Indecision froze him.

"Bear, you can't go around kidnapping women."

"Didn't," the bounty hunter said petulantly. "You came back to me. Don't deny it. Did that fancy-dressing snake oil salesman spirit you away?"

"It wasn't like that, Bear."

"Yeah, yeah, it was. He took you away from me, but you came back. That's what happened, wasn't it? You came back because you love me."

Molly cried out, "Go! Go away!" The shout was directed at Jerome, not at the hulking man towering above her.

Both men realized it at the same instant. Bear growled like his namesake and half turned, fists the size of hams coming up. Jerome launched himself on what would have been a suicidal attack if he didn't strike exactly right the first time.

He drove the hilt of one knife down hard on Bear's wrist. With his other he made a wide arc, slashing for the man's throat. Bear jerked back in pain from his wrist, causing Jerome's throat cut to miss by a fraction of an inch. Instead, Jerome landed a powerful blow on the man's chin. Bear's head snapped back.

Staggered, he stepped away. Molly threw herself out behind his knees. The huge man tripped over her and fell heavily.

"Come on," Jerome cried. "Get out from under him and run!"

Molly was tangled up with the bounty hunter's legs. He thrashed weakly, adding to the confusion. Jerome leaped over and kicked as hard as he could. The toe of his shoe caught Bear on the chin. His head jerked to one side. Another man would have suffered a broken neck. The bounty hunter only groaned and rubbed the spot where Jerome had hit his chin.

Jerome reached down and pulled Molly free, but Bear, though stunned, still fought. He grabbed Jerome's arm and pulled him to his knees. With a deft twirl, Jerome brought the knife in his left hand around for a swift stroke that would gut the bounty hunter. He lunged forward, all his weight behind the blow.

At the last instant, Molly knocked his arm aside. All he accomplished was to leave a shallow cut on Bear's side. The pain from the inconsequential wound roused him. He bellowed in rage and rolled toward Jerome.

A meaty hand batted away the knife in Jerome's left hand. Bear's grip on Jerome's right wrist tightened like a vise. With an agile twist belying his size, Bear came to his knees and yanked his adversary toward him.

Jerome fought to get his right hand free. The powerful grip turned his hand numb. With his left he reached back to grab

133

another knife. Then he gasped. Bear circled his waist with his arm and drew him close in a bone-crushing hug.

"Let me go. Let me —"

Jerome had all the air squeezed from his lungs. Uttering even a desperate word of surrender was no longer possible. His ribs began to crack, but the lack of air worked against him the worst. He'd black out long before bones snapped under the intense pressure.

Then he fell onto his back. Staring at the roof made him laugh. He saw stars through the holes.

"Come on, Jerome. Come *on*. He's got the hardest head in Texas, except maybe for yours. Why'd you come for me?"

Molly got an arm around his shoulders and helped him to his feet. Jerome took a staggering step, then gained full balance. He looked over his shoulder at the fallen Bear. The iron griddle from the stove top lay on the dirt floor beside him. Molly had used it to clobber the bounty hunter.

"You needed rescuing, that's why," Jerome said.

He herded the woman into the night. The cold night air was like a slap to the face. He regained his senses. When Molly tried to go back into the shack, he shoved her toward town.

"I needed rescuing," she said, "and you need a dose of common sense."

Jerome doggedly kept herding her into town. If they were anywhere within Bear's sight when he came to, there'd be blood spilled — and Jerome knew it was more likely to be his and Molly's.

CHAPTER SEVEN

"I told you not to come to Clear Springs." Molly seethed. "But no, you wouldn't listen, and look at the mess we're in now."

"We'll be on the road before he comes to," Jerome said.

His worry matched the woman's. Bear had a head as thick as the Jenkins boy had claimed. How long before he came to his senses was likely measured in minutes, not hours. Jerome tried to figure out how long before they got into the medicine wagon and lit out.

Only the bounty hunter had a horse and rode faster than Jerome's mare had ever pulled the wagon. The roads out of town were limited. Bear had only to check one by riding a few miles before cutting across country to find another. Chances weren't good that Jerome would avoid the angry man longer than midday.

"The marshal," he said. "Come on.

There's the office."

"Wait, no. What are you doing?" Molly tried to jerk away, but Jerome held her by the elbow. "We can't ask *him* for help."

"Are you wanted for a crime?"

"Well, no, not exactly."

"Then we'll have Marshal Bishop arrest Bear for kidnapping." He caught his breath. "He didn't do anything else to you, did he?"

"Did he violate me? Is that what you're asking?" Molly turned her bright blue eyes on him and fixed him with a hard stare. "What if he did? What would you do about it?"

Jerome's thoughts tumbled and rolled about, then began swirling like a desert dust devil.

She saw the change in his expression. Her eyes went wide, and she clamped a hand over her mouth in surprise. Then she said, "I don't believe it. You'd actually defend my honor?"

"Did he do anything that'd require him to pay?"

"What a quaint notion. Really, Jerome, you are a caution. You keep astonishing me. I'm nothing to you, yet you'd tangle with a man twice your size and ten times as nasty."

"I smell better, though."

"That's because he uses bear grease on

his hair, and you only use a drop of your miracle elixir." She unconsciously rubbed her palms against her dress. "Why risk your neck for me?"

"I gave you a ride," he said, "but it's my fault he kidnapped you. You told me not to bring you here, and I ignored you."

"You would never leave me out on the road, in the desert, on my own." She smiled wickedly. "Even with a case of your powerful tonic to keep me company, you'd never do that."

"You're right," he said. "I'd never leave behind a case of tonic I can sell for almost fifty dollars."

He steered her to the door leading into the town jailhouse. She pulled back, then relented when he refused to let her go.

"This is wrong, Jerome."

"In my opinion, it's the best I can come up with."

"Oh, so now I have to call you Professor because of all that deep thinking? Why'd you get so high and mighty all of a sudden? Because you snatched me away from Bear?"

"My name's Jerome."

"But . . . Oh, all right." She pouted and let him herd her inside the calaboose, where the marshal snored like a crosscut saw going through wood. His head rested on his crossed arms on the desk.

Before Jerome said a word, the law dog jerked erect. Although his eyes were half closed, his hand moved like lightning to the pistol on the desk. Bishop grabbed it, cocked and swung it around with deadly accuracy.

"Whoa, Marshal, wait. Don't shoot." Jerome held his hands out, palms toward the lawman.

"Is it sunup already?" Bishop put his still cocked six-gun on the desk and rubbed his eyes with both fists. He reared back, stretched and yawned. "You're one honest snake oil peddler. I'll give you that."

"I want to report —" Jerome never finished his sentence.

The marshal cut him off. "The money you owe me. For the privilege of selling your pizzen in my town. Now!"

Jerome started to protest, then fished around in his pockets for twenty dollars in specie. Impatiently he waited for the marshal to count the bribe twice and then sweep the coins off the desk into the middle drawer.

"I've got a complaint to make," Jerome started again.

"Ain't givin' you back one thin dime. This money belongs to the town."

"As if the city coffers will ever see any of it. Your fingers are too sticky for that to ever happen."

Bishop craned his head around and looked past Jerome. His face clouded with anger.

"You! You came back to bedevil me. I *knew* that was your canvas-background-scenery thing on top of this thief's medicine wagon."

He reached for his six-shooter again. He stopped when he saw how Jerome tensed.

If Bishop moved, Jerome had two knives ready to skewer him. The marshal wasn't able to figure out what the danger was from a man not packing iron, but he saw the tension and was experienced enough to know he'd be in a world of hurt if he moved a muscle.

"She was kidnapped," Jerome said coldly.

"Kidnapped? Or taken by the hulking bounty hunter you're married to?"

It was Jerome's turn to recoil in surprise. He turned to Molly. She shook her head vehemently.

"I'm not married to Bear. I'm not, Jerome. That's something he made up." She took a deep breath and let it out slowly to compose herself. "It's something he wants, not anything that's happened."

"You and him were real cozy before."

The marshal grinned. It carried more than

a hint of cruelty. He enjoyed watching Molly squirm.

"If she says they're not married, I believe Miss Davenport."

"Thank you, Jerome. That's sweet of you." She crossed her arms defiantly and glared at the marshal.

Jerome felt the undercurrents here flowing beyond anything he knew or maybe guessed. Letting this distract him signed his death warrant and possibly condemned Molly to an even worse fate. The bounty hunter had to be stopped from coming after them. In that instant, he felt a pang of regret that he hadn't slit the man's greasy throat even if that would have been cold-blooded murder.

"Yeah, real sweet of you," the marshal taunted. "We got common law here in Texas 'cuz it's so hard to find a preacher out on the prairie."

"I never lived with him," Molly insisted. "Now, are you going to listen to the professor or not? He's got a complaint to make against Bear."

"He kidnapped Miss Davenport and then tried to kill me."

Jerome started to furnish details, but Bishop cut him off with a chopping motion.

"He may have spirited her off, but he never tried to kill you," the marshal said.

"He's come through town enough times with owlhoots he's caught. If he wanted you dead, you'd be dead. If he intended to rough you up, you'd look a lot more beat up than you do right now."

"I got the better of him."

This caused the marshal to laugh aloud. "You did what? If she wasn't here with you, I'd think we were talking about two different men named Bear." The marshal's laughter died when Jerome tensed again.

A quick toss at this range would drive a knife through the man's throat. Molly laid her hand on Jerome's arm to hold back the deadly cast. Bishop recognized how close he had come to having some righteous wrath brought down on him.

"All right. Bear took her because he considers her his wife and you somehow cold-cocked him. Does that cover the details?"

Jerome realized how quick the marshal's mind worked. He never once suggested that Bear had been killed. If the bounty hunter had died, Jerome and Molly had no reason to ask for protection.

"It does. Arrest him and hold him for trial," Jerome said.

"That's not going to happen," Bishop said, "because you and the chanteuse don't intend to stay in town long enough to testify."

"How long before the circuit judge comes to town?" Jerome asked.

"A week or two, but there's no way I'm holding Bear in my jail until then so Judge Peterson chews me out for not having any reliable witnesses against him."

"Come on, Jerome. We've got to hurry. He's not going to help us." Molly pulled insistently at his arm.

He wanted to argue with the marshal, offer a few more dollars for the lawman to keep a leash on Bear until they had a chance to put a lot of miles between them. Almost a year of pitching to crowds had instilled a sixth sense in him. He had learned when he was wasting his breath and no amount of honeyed words or sharp persuasion would work.

He followed Molly outside. The distant horizon turned pink. From the layer of clouds east of town, a storm worked its way toward them.

"If we hurry, we might get lucky and have our trail hidden by a downpour," he said.

"That's not lucky, not out here. Any storm's capable of filling all the arroyos in a few minutes and washing away a wagon and team."

"We'll stay out of gullies," he said, quickening his pace. Molly struggled to stay even with him.

"We've got to try something else. That worthless lawman's not going to help us," she said. "We have to set an ambush. You have a gun. I saw it in the wagon. You be the bait, and I'll take him down like the animal he is."

Jerome looked at her. The sun poked through the clouds for a moment and made her dark hair looked as if it were on fire — as if a halo formed. What she said was the furthest thing from angelic.

"If you're the bait, the trap'll work better," he said.

"You beat on him and knocked him out. Bear carries a grudge. You don't have it in you to shoot a man down in cold blood." Her jaw set. "With me, it won't be in cold blood." She burst out laughing. "And I am certainly not a man, so I have no qualms about it."

"Have you ever killed anyone before?" He read the answer in her face. "I thought not. Come on. You get things secured in the wagon while I hitch up the horse. We can't outrun him, but our luck's got to change."

"Jerome," she said. She yanked on his arm and spun him around. She reached up with both hands behind his head and pulled him down for a big kiss. She stepped back, looking as startled as he was at the action. "I . . . You . . . go on. Get the horse." Further argument was pointless. He'd lose.

He watched her lift her tattered skirt and rush off. He touched his lips, then hurried to the livery stables. The horse had been well tended and actually bulged at the flanks from eating regularly and well while in Clear Springs. Jerome led the horse to the wagon and hitched it up. Everything he had said to Molly about laying a trap for Bear came flooding back to haunt him.

He wasn't a killer. Not like the Benjamin brothers. Ambushing Bear tore at his gut, but what choice did he have? If the bounty hunter wasn't stopped, Molly would end up his slave — no matter that Bear called her his wife — and the buzzards and ants would have J. Frederick Kincannon's carcass for dinner. He wasn't sure which of those outcomes bothered him more.

"All secure," Molly said, climbing onto the bench seat. "Well, come on. Time's a-wasting."

He stepped up, settled the reins in his hands and gave a loud snap. The horse leaned into the harness and soon Clear Springs lay a mile behind them. Jerome drove westward because the Butterfield agent had hinted that his stagecoaches were in danger from road agents in this direction.

"The Benjamins," he whispered.

He thought he had spoken too low, but Molly's ears were as sharp as her tongue.

"Don't be foolish, Jerome. Get away from Bear before you jump into another pot of boiling water."

"I don't want to lose sight of why I'm out here."

He found himself telling her of Marcie's death and how hard it had been to bury his son beside her. She listened in silence until he finished.

"So this vengeance ride is all because you feel sorry for yourself?"

The response shocked him. "I want justice! They can't get away with murder!"

"Men like that will get their comeuppance sooner or later. Killing your family wasn't their only crime. I'm willing to bet on that."

"So I should forget about them?"

"Get on with your life. If what the Butterfield agent said is right, the Rangers will have rounded up the entire gang in lickety-split time."

"But I want to *know* they've been brought to justice!"

"You want to deal out justice with your own hand. There's a difference. You want revenge." Molly sounded smug in her summation.

He resisted the impulse to shove her out of the wagon, her belongings with her. Then he said, "All right. What you say is true. I want revenge. I want them all to die by my hand. What's wrong with that?"

"You're the one who has to live with it."

"I can. I can if it's one of the Benjamin brothers. Or all of them."

"You don't need my approval. Do as you wish. Be sure to let me off at the next town. I'm not sure what it is, but that's all the farther I want to ride with you, Professor J. Frederick Kincannon." She folded her arms in front of her and stared straight ahead.

Jerome joined her in looking directly ahead. The sun cast a long shadow in front of them. He hoped it wouldn't spook the horse. Then he jumped and craned around. He was only a couple feet away from where Bear rode alongside.

"You pull back on them reins, mister. We got matters to discuss," the bounty hunter said.

Jerome heard Molly gasp. She hadn't seen

or heard Bear ride up alongside the wagon, either.

"All right. Let's have it out."

Jerome halted the horse and wrapped the reins around the wood brake handle. He jumped down and immediately regretted it.

Not only was the bounty hunter half again his weight; astride his horse he was almost twice as tall. If taking the high ground was a sound tactic in warfare, Jerome was already a loser.

In spite of himself, Jerome flinched when Bear jumped to the ground. The bounty hunter caused a minor earthquake. Trying not to be obvious, Jerome reached back and found knives in the tails of his coat. He hesitated to pull them from their hidden sheaths in case he needed to use his hands.

He looked at Bear's fists. If the bounty hunter and he tried to duke it out, the outcome would never be in doubt. He shrugged his shoulders and brought a knife into each hand as he planned his attack. A quick slash at the eyes to distract, then a hard thrust to the heart.

"Don't you go tryin' that," Bear said.

His deep, raspy voice carried no menace. The caution sounded more like advice a father offered to a small child. Such condescension puffed up Jerome and made him mad rather than scared. He'd never fought anyone this size, but Bear'd know he had met a worthy opponent.

"She's not your wife," Jerome said.

"Is too."

"I am *not*!" Molly slid to the side of the bench seat and glared down at the bounty hunter. "We never said vows in front of a preacher."

"Texas law holds that livin' together makes us man and wife."

"You drove me off after a week, Bear. A week!"

"I like you, Molly. You smell good."

Jerome's nose wrinkled. The bear grease slicking back the man's hair had turned rancid. How he smelled anything wearing such an odorous hair cream was a poser.

"We won't set the marshal on you if you ride off and promise never to annoy Miss Davenport again."

"Little man, you ain't got a say in this matter. It's between me and her." Bear half turned.

If Jerome had had a true killer's instinct, a quick thrust of both knives at that instant would have ended the dispute. Bear's flank was exposed. Two knives, both going between ribs and into the man's heart. That'd be all it took.

If Jerome had had a killer's instinct.

He realized he didn't. Not for this man, in spite of the threat he posed to Molly.

"What'll it take to buy you off?" Jerome moved and insinuated himself between Bear and the woman.

"She ain't a slave to be bought and sold. She's my wife!"

"I am not!"

Molly tried to reach over Jerome and strike Bear. Jerome got all tangled up and found himself on the bottom of a pile. The struggling woman and the griping bounty hunter kept him pinned down securely.

"Stop it!" Jerome kicked and finally came to his feet.

Bear saw the knives glinting in the morning sun and sank into a gunfighter's crouch, his hand hovering over the Colt strapped to his right hip.

"You have them toad stickers ready, but I'm quicker. I can draw and fire all six rounds before you so much as twitch. Is this the day you want to die?"

"You stop that right now, Bear."

Molly grabbed his brawny wrist with both hands. If he had tried to draw, breaking such a feeble grip presented no trouble.

"Now, Miss Molly, I don't want to hurt you none."

"Then let's talk this out. And yes, Bear, there *is* something to talk over. I'm not your wife, and I am riding with the professor." She cast a sidelong glance to keep Jerome silent as she argued the point. "I know you pretty well. What do you want? What'll it take for you to ride off and never bother me again?"

Bear sucked on his teeth and looked thoughtful. Jerome worried about the thoughts running through the man's head.

"I can use some help runnin' down a varmint that's been causin' all kinds of devilment," Bear said. "He blowed into the county a week or two back, and he's about the meanest, nastiest son of a gun you ever did see."

"Is his name Benjamin?" Jerome blurted out the question.

Bear looked even more pensive, then shrugged his massive shoulders. "Can't say I've heard a name. What's this Ben fellow look like?"

"Never mind that, Bear," Molly cut in. She knew Jerome had only sketchy descriptions of the gang. "Why do you need anyone to back you up? You work all by your lonesome."

"I do," he admitted, "but you remember that ex-Ranger? Updike?"

"Is he the only one you ever said could whip you in a fair fight?"

Molly shook her head slightly, warning Jerome to butt out. That advice struck him as sound.

"That's him. This outlaw thrashed him good, then outdrew him in what sounded to be a fair fight. I don't want to go against a man who got the best of Ranger Updike."

"Are the Rangers after your quarry, too?" Jerome wasn't able to hold back the question.

"Naw, Updike didn't part company with them on such good terms. Truth is, some'd consider him as gettin' what he deserved. But the telegraph fellow in Clear Springs told me there's a five-hundred-dollar reward on his head."

"How'd we split the money, Bear? After we hog-tie your culprit?" Molly was inclined to dicker.

Jerome wasn't. "We'll help you, and you can keep all the reward," he said, drowning out the woman's protest.

"Why'd you go and do a thing like that?" Bear scratched himself in places where his nails had cut clean through his buckskins. Whatever bugs gnawed on him were persistent and had found a permanent home.

"Because you'll do as Miss Molly suggested and leave her be." Jerome's breathing quickened. "And the man you're after might be one I want brought to justice."

"That Ben you talked about?" Bear looked skeptical. "Ain't never heard nobody call him Ben."

"I'll take the risk," Jerome said. "If Miss Molly wants to stay behind, I can drop her off in Clear Springs while we —"

"No! No way am I spending one second longer than I have to in that town. The marshal has a wandering eye, and then there's the saloonkeeper. He's worse. After a performance, he pinched me on —"

"Molly can ride in the wagon and stay out of sight," Jerome hastily amended. Getting into a verbal free-for-all with the woman was the last thing he wanted.

"Sounds like we got a deal," Bear said. "Let's shake on it."

He spat on his filthy palm and thrust out his hand.

Jerome had to hold both knives in his left hand as he duplicated the bounty hunter's action. They shook. He winced at the pressure and hoped no bones were broken.

More than this, he hoped Bear was on the trail of one of the Benjamin brothers.

Chapter Eight

"You don't know that," Molly Davenport said primly, lecturing him.

Jerome doggedly urged the horse across the prairie, now and then hitting a rock big enough to jolt his teeth. He stared ahead and imagined his dream to be reality. Or was that dream a baseless fantasy?

"Does it matter? We're helping Bear find the road agent. No matter who he is, we get rid of Bear. You'll be free to do whatever you want."

"Jerome," she said in exasperation, "you're sure this is one of the Benjamin gang, aren't you?"

"It's the way to bet."

"It's a good thing you sell snake oil and don't gamble. You'd be broke within an hour of sitting down at a table."

"There's enough evidence to make it a possibility. The outlaw Bear is chasing down just came into the area recently. The Benjamin gang was moving north ahead of me by a week or so."

That alone convinced him he was on the trail. Finally. He had chased this will-'o-the-wisp too long.

"Texas isn't noted for its law-abiding citizens. Have you ever been to Hell's Half Acre up in Fort Worth? No? I didn't think so. You shake hands there and you'd better count your fingers because some slippery character will have stolen one or two of them."

Jerome held his hand in front of him and wiggled the fingers. "I'm doing all right so far."

"Bear said there's only one outlaw he's tracking. You said there were three brothers and another relative. Families don't split up. Why would one go out on his own?"

Jerome had no answer for that. Molly was right about blood being thicker than water. The brothers had fought together for a long time.

"Maybe he's scouting for a special robbery. The Butterfield agent was scared they'd start robbing his stages on a regular basis."

Molly made a dismissive snort and shook her head sadly. The dark locks swayed about her shoulders and caught the sun just right, giving them a luster he had never seen in another woman's hair.

"You're grasping at straws, Jerome. And where'd Bear go? I haven't seen him in an hour."

"He said he was scouting ahead. The road's straight and lonesome. He can make better time alone than if he paced the wagon."

"Your horse does the best it can, but you really need a second one for the team. It's downright cruel making only one old mare do all the work."

She suddenly jumped to her feet and leaned out of the driver's box. As the wagon hit yet another rock, she grabbed for the overhanging roof to keep from being thrown out.

"What is it? Your scenery hasn't slipped, has it?"

For two cents Jerome would have cut the ropes holding the scenery and left it behind in the dust. It added a couple hundred pounds to the load his horse pulled.

"No, nothing like that. I thought I spotted Bear, but it's another rider. There's a fork ahead. The rider's going due south."

Jerome considered what to do. He'd told Bear they'd keep on the westerly road. The bounty hunter needed to locate them and not have to search over endless empty miles if he found his quarry. But what if the rider headed south was the outlaw?

"Where's that road lead?"

"I see a sign." Molly shielded her eyes against the sun and then said, "Yorick's Outpost. That's what the sign says. I never heard of it. Have you?"

"I'm new to this part of the state," he said. "Let's see what's down there. Bear can handle any trouble he finds on his own."

"Can we do the same without him?" Molly swung back and clung to his arm. "We need to be careful."

Jerome was done being careful. He had spent months trying to find the Benjamin brothers with little success. The rider's identity didn't matter too much, but a pilgrim out on the trail had a better chance of seeing or hearing something useful than Jerome tooling about in his slow-moving wagon.

"A mile," Molly said glumly. "The sign claims the outpost is only a mile off."

"You can stay in the wagon. This might be too dangerous for you."

Molly snorted in contempt. "I've put up with more singing in saloons and dance halls than you ever have, grinding up your drugs and selling cheap liquor by calling it a tonic."

"It's not cheap," he said, amused at her protests.

There wasn't any question her life had been rocky, but he'd match his trials and tribulations against hers any day. Even taking Bear into account, he'd match and surpass her life stories.

"There it is. An adobe hut."

Yorick's Outpost existed in its own peculiar world. The road ran straight by it. This wasn't at the crossroads to increase patronage. Jerome had no idea where the nearest town was. If he had to open his wagon and start his pitch, he doubted a half dozen people would stir their bones. From the look of the countryside, there weren't that many within a dozen miles.

"This place defines 'lonesome,' " Jerome said.

"What are your chances of finding any of your family's killers here? Or even the man Bear is hunting?"

Jerome considered rummaging through the wagon and strapping on his shooting iron. Facing one or two strangers in such a desolate frontier settlement posed a bigger danger than if he bulled his way into a crowded saloon, even in a town like Clear Springs. If he was robbed and killed out here where the wind whined out of loneliness, no one would notice or care.

He decided to enter the outpost without a sidearm. Wearing a six-gun was provocation for a lot of men.

"There's the rider's horse. He's been on the road for a long time," Molly said.

"Wait here for a few minutes while I scout out the place," Jerome said. "I'm not joking. This entire outpost screams 'dangerous' to me."

To his surprise, Molly nodded and settled down. She wasn't so much obeying his order as she had decided on her own what was safest.

That bothered him. Driving past the outpost wasn't impossible. He had nothing to find out here, other than asking after the Benjamins.

Before he lost his nerve, Jerome jumped down, settled his coat and checked his knives one last time. He pushed straight through the heavy wood door, ducking under the low lintel, and stepped into a cool, dark room. A bar consisted of a couple planed planks resting on sawhorses. Behind this crude bar were a dirty mirror and a half dozen bottles balanced on a crate. Whether the coppery-colored liquids in each bottle were whiskey or something more vile never entered Jerome's mind.

He went to the sawhorse closest to the door and tried not to feel too uneasy. The barkeep sat on a stool at the far end. Two men huddled together, playing some kind of card game. Neither bothered to look up at Jerome.

"What's your pizzen, mister?"

Jerome jumped at the bartender's question. He blurted, "There was a rider who just came in. Where'd he get off to?"

The barkeep got off his stool, stretched his legs and moved painfully to stand on the other side of the plank from Jerome.

"He's using the outhouse. He your partner?"

"I, uh, no." Jerome took a deep breath to settle his thoughts. Getting flustered was ridiculous. He fielded questions about his potion and often lied with a straight face. "It's just that I ate his dust coming here. I thought I'd buy him a shot of that fine whiskey you've got back there."

The barkeep looked over his shoulder, then back at Jerome. He laughed harshly. "Fine? I got nothing but Gila monster venom and horse piss here."

"So whiskey is out of the question. Tequila? You have the aspect of a man from Arizona. Over in Tombstone? Maybe you

160

have a bottle brought up from Mexico?"

"Rye or beer. Those are your choices. If I had tequila or pulque, I'd've drunk it right down myself."

"Beer," Jerome decided. If he had to die from poisoning, beer probably gave him a few minutes more of life.

"Good choice, mister," one of the card players called out.

Jerome lifted the glass of beer in silent salute. He sipped the brew and almost threw up. The head was less foam and more soap suds.

"Hits the spot, doesn't it?" The barkeep's tone challenged him to disagree.

Before Jerome answered, a door in the rear flew open. Again his nerves betrayed him and he jumped. Filling the small opening and blotting out the sun outside, a giant of a man barreled in. He went to the far end of the plank bar and used his fist to hammer a few times as if he drove nails.

"Whiskey, and not that swill in the bottles. You got good stuff. I want that."

"This is what I drink," the bartender said, bending over painfully and lifting a half bottle from a crate. He lurched back when his customer snatched it from his hand.

The man flicked the cork out with his

thumb, upended the bottle and drank every drop.

Jerome waited for the man to keel over. Even if that was fine Kentucky bourbon, chugging that much alcohol that fast was like a sledgehammer blow to the body.

"More. Gimme more." The man threw the bottle at the barkeep. The bottle missed its target but smashed the mirror. "Don't get me riled."

Jerome carefully set his beer on the plank and rested his right hand over the knife sheathed along his left forearm. The man's tone turned fearsome. With that much tarantula juice in his gut, he'd either go plumb crazy or fall over in a faint. Jerome didn't have to wait but a few seconds to find which it'd be.

The man went crazy.

A huge fist grabbed the barkeep's shirt and pulled him over the bar to crash onto the dirt floor. In a move too agile and quick to follow, he vaulted the bar and landed where the barkeep had once reigned. A full bottle came to hand.

"Glory be," the barkeep muttered, pushing himself away but remaining seated on the floor.

Jerome understood the astonishment. Another half bottle vanished in one long, noisy gulp down the man's gullet.

"I been in the saddle for a week, and it's my time to cut loose," the man said. "It's my misfortune this sorry place is all that's available to me."

He belched and took another long pull on what remained in the bottle. That much would have sent any normal man reeling or even killed him. It only added to the craziness.

"It's hot in here. How'd you do that? You ain't got a fire burnin' back there in the fireplace."

The barkeep pulled himself up to a chair and sat, staring as the rowdy customer took off his gun belt and slammed it onto the bar.

"That's good, sir. Real good. You don't need that hogleg in here. You're among friends." The bartender tried to soothe the anger. If anything, he only fueled it higher.

"I said, it's hot in here. Open the doors. You ain't got windows worth spit." The man threw away his hat, then stripped off his shirt.

Jerome edged toward the door to get back to his wagon.

"You, the pasty-faced fellow. You don't go anywhere. I want to dance and you're going to sing. You can sing, can't you? If not, learn real quick."

"What do you want me to sing?" Jerome drew his knife but held it at his side, hidden from sight.

"Something I like, tha's wh-what."

The man pulled back his long johns and stood bare chested. Then he kicked free of his boots and skinned out of his pants. With sure moves putting the lie to how much liquor he'd downed, he pulled on his boots again and strapped his holster around his waist.

Except for the boots and his gun belt with the big iron dangling at his side, the man was buck naked. He hopped up, sat on the bar and yelped when he got a splinter in his hindquarters. That caused him to climb to his feet, cursing a blue streak.

"Sing. I tole you to sing!"

He whipped out his gun and fired at Jerome. The slug tore past his right ear and blew out a dusty hole in the adobe wall behind him.

"The only songs I know are hymns," Jerome lied. "I don't think 'Rock of Ages' is what you want."

"Warble! Get to warblin' like a saloon wench. Sing!" The gunman pointed the Colt at Jerome with a disturbingly steady hand.

" 'Camptown ladies sing this song, doo-dah, doo-dah,' " Jerome started off-key.

"Louder. I want to dance something fierce."

The man reared back and fired into the ceiling. He had to bend low to keep from banging his head on the vigas. Somehow he avoided bashing himself in the head and started a merry jig that became increasingly uncoordinated.

"That's something you don't see in here every day, Yorick," called one of the card players.

"You sayin' I can't dance?"

The naked man swung around and fired. The bullet hit the man at the rear of the saloon smack in the middle of his chest. He threw up his arms, leaned back in his chair and toppled to the floor, unmoving.

"You kilt him! He was half my regular business!" The barkeep — apparently named Yorick — got to his feet and waved his bony fist at the gunman.

"Wait!" Jerome cried out. Too late.

The naked dancer's bullet hit Yorick in the face.

"Nobody tells me what to do. Not even my brother. I'm sick of ever'body orderin' me about."

He took a shot at the second card player as he ducked out the back door. A sulfurous curse accompanied the dull metallic click as the gunman's hammer fell on an empty chamber.

The man roared and came running down the planks, arms outstretched. Jerome backpedaled and crashed into the wall. He lifted his knife, ready to gut the man if he dived off the plank bar.

The naked man slipped and fell flat on his face. The uneven boards turned under him and spilled him to the floor, where he thrashed about. Being bare-assed exposed parts of the man's anatomy Jerome normally would never have seen. The man's neck and shoulders were a fiery red and splotches across his back looked hot to the touch.

"You laughed at me. Nobody laughs at me!" The man walked on his knees, hands groping for Jerome's body.

With measured care, Jerome waited, judged distances and then kicked out as hard as he could. His boot caught the naked man on the chin. His head snapped back. For an instant his face flushed bright red and his eyes took on a demonic aspect. Then he slipped over onto his side.

"I'm glad I didn't have to save you" came a soft voice from behind.

"I'm glad I didn't have to gut him."

Jerome glanced over at Molly. She held

his six-gun in one hand and braced herself against the doorjamb with the other. Sweat beaded her forehead.

"I warned you to stay in the wagon."

"It's lonely out there, with nobody but the horse to keep me company. And it's hot."

She swiped at her forehead. Jerome wondered how much perspiration came from the heat and how much from fear. She put up a brave front, but he heard a tremor in her voice that betrayed her anxiety.

"Thanks," he said. "You need to have more faith in me, though. I handled this just fine."

She pointed to the two dead men and laughed harshly. "If he hadn't come up empty, you'd be dead. If he hadn't fallen down, you'd never have matched him in a wrestling bout."

"He downed enough rotgut to kill a town drunk. That red flush to his skin's not normal, either."

"So now you're a doctor?"

She stepped over the fallen planks, took one look at the bottles on the back bar and dived into the crate where Yorick had stored his good stuff. She held up a full bottle and let the dim light filter through it.

"This won't kill us outright."

"I hope not."

Jerome found two shot glasses on the floor, wiped them clean and let Molly do the honors. Both sloshed over as she poured. He took this as a measure of how shaken up she still was.

"Cheers," she said, raising her shot glass.

"Salud," Jerome said.

Before he tossed off the liquor, powerful arms circled him, lifted him and threw him halfway across the room. He crashed into a table and turned it into splinters.

Dazed he shook his head to clear it.

"Molly?"

Jerome gasped as powerful arms circled his waist again and lifted him so his toes scraped the dirt. He gritted his teeth and pushed as hard as he could against broad, bare shoulders. His face and the naked man's were only inches apart.

"Stop. Stop it," he got out.

The man had no intention of releasing him. Every time Jerome exhaled, he found it that much harder to inhale as the steel bands of the man's arms tightened even more.

Jerome clapped the flats of his hands onto the man's ears. He knew from experience how painful that was. He barely got a reaction. If anything, the man's face turned redder as he exerted himself even more. Jerome felt ribs cracking. He used his thumbs in the man's eyes to force his head back. If he'd had more time, if his strength wasn't fading fast, this opportunity to slit the man's throat would have ended the fight.

Jerome's fingers felt like bloated sausages. The world turned black, and his lungs filled with fire. He hammered the man's face repeatedly, using his fists. The naked man showed no reaction to the savage punishment in spite of a broken nose and two split lips.

Then the pressure ceased and Jerome fell back. He caught a heel and sat heavily on the floor. He looked up to see that Molly had jumped onto the man's back and raked her fingernails like claws across his face.

"He doesn't feel anything," Jerome gasped out.

He had lost one knife. Another came into his left hand from its sheath. He struggled to get to his knees.

The naked gunman twisted violently and sent Molly flying. Jerome never hesitated. He braced himself and drove his knife straight up into the man's gut. He felt the blade sink deep. Blood spurted around his hand. And the man hardly flinched from what had to be excruciating pain. With a backhand slap, he knocked Jerome to the floor again.

"You stopped singin'." With the knife protruding from his chest, the man lumbered toward Jerome.

Sure that he was a goner but unwilling to give up, Jerome fumbled for another knife. He pulled one out just as the man reared above him. Before he had a chance to stab him again, a shot rang out. The man stumbled away, clutching his side.

"I got here in the nick o' time," Bear said. He lifted his Colt and blew smoke away from the muzzle.

At the same instant, both Jerome and Molly cried, "Look out!"

The gunman pulled Jerome's knife from his chest and lunged toward Bear. The bounty hunter tried to fire again, but a meaty hand knocked his pistol to one side. The other hand clutched the knife and sank it deep into an exposed side. Bear let out a roar of pain and stumbled back. Molly tried to hold him, but the man was too heavy and all strength had left his legs. The pair collapsed in a heap.

"Here, you want me to sing. Let me sing!" Jerome got to his feet and went into a knife fighter's crouch as the naked man turned for him. ". . . racetrack five miles long," he gasped out. He feinted left and struck right.

Again he sank his knife into the man's chest. He felt the blade turn as it slipped across a rib, then he felt nothing.

A fist the size of the Alamo crashed into his head.

CHAPTER NINE

Jerome Kincannon sputtered and fought to keep from drowning. A second tidal wave washed over him. He flinched and wiped away . . . beer. He forced his eyes to open. He stared up at Molly. In any other circumstance, that wouldn't have been hard to do. But not now. Memories flooded through his head, and he fought to get to his feet.

She shoved him back.

"Stay down, Professor," she said sternly. "Do I need to douse you with more beer? Or do you prefer a teeny sip of it? I've got to warn you, though."

"Warn me?" He blinked hard and got his senses back.

"Yeah, it's terrible."

Jerome licked his lips and tasted the flat beer Yorick served — had served. He sat up and looked around the small cantina. The stench of death already infested the single room. Bugs buzzed everywhere, flooding in

172

through the open doors.

"The naked guy. What happened? He —
he —"

"He gave up trying to kill you and ran out,
laughing his fool head off. He left a trail of
blood behind. If he keeps gushing his life's
fluids like that," Molly said clinically, "I
predict he'll be dead within a few minutes.
And out in the noonday sun?" She shook
her head. "He's not got a ghost of a chance."

"Did he ride off?"

"He hopped onto that horse's back like
he was fresh up in the morning and fixing
to lick his weight in wildcats. I've never seen
anything like it." She scowled. "But he's
leaking blood so fast, he can't have a mile
left in him. Less."

"I've seen others act like that," Jerome
said. "If you chew datura seeds, you go all
crazy in the head."

"Locoweed? Why'd anybody do a fool
thing like that? I know how it makes cattle.
The tamest cow turns into a raging bull."
Her eyes opened wide as she understood
what Jerome meant. "So he ate some of the
seeds and he went wild?"

"That's why he was so hot. It causes the
blood to rush to the skin like he had a bad
rash. He probably saw terrible specters

coming for him. Hallucinations are common."

Molly held out her hand. Jerome took it and let her help him stand. He was embarrassed at how puny he felt. Even getting the worst of it in a fight with the crazed gunman, he should have been in better shape. Then he realized that was foolish thinking, and all he wanted was to impress Molly.

"Bear!" he cried. Memories flooded back as he moved around. "He was stabbed."

"With your knife," she said darkly. "I've never seen him in such a bad way. Believe me, I have seen him in terrible condition, too. There was a time he got his hand caught in a sausage grinder." She shivered at the memory.

Jerome pushed past her and went to where the bounty hunter sprawled across a table. Jerome looked away for a moment when he saw his knife sticking out of Bear's torso. Then he tore away the tough buckskin shirt the best he could and ran his fingers around the puncture wound.

"Get a few bottles of my tonic from the back of the wagon."

"Sure, why not celebrate Bear getting himself killed?"

"Now, woman. Go *now.*"

His sharp command made her jump. She

started to argue, then rushed outside while Jerome continued to examine Bear's wound. No blood leaked out around it, but if he pulled the blade free, there was likely to be a deadly gush.

"You? You stabbed me?" Bear's normally husky voice came as a small squeak.

"I'm saving you," Jerome assured him. "The fellow you want to take in did this to you?"

"Curtis," Bear said. He heaved such a deep breath Jerome thought he'd died. Then the bounty hunter's eyes fluttered open, and he fought some more. "That's his name. Found out from a man he and a couple others riding with him robbed."

"Don't talk. This is going to hurt like nothing you ever felt."

Jerome reached back and took a bottle of his potion handed him by a silent Molly.

"Lemme take a swig."

Bear reached out and winced. The movement stretched his muscles around the embedded knife.

Jerome worked fast. He yanked his knife out and poured the entire contents of the bottle into the wound. Bear reacted powerfully. He arched his back and thrashed about. Jerome ducked under the man's log-like arms and poured a second bottle all over Bear's chest.

"He always was a clumsy galoot," Molly said. "I'm surprised he hasn't shot himself before now."

"That's another reason you left him? He's ungainly?"

Jerome had stopped the bleeding, and the alcohol cleansed the wound. Deep inside, though, there might be more bleeding that he couldn't do anything about.

"Here," Molly said.

She tapped him on the shoulder to get his attention, then handed him a cartridge with the bullet removed.

Jerome knew what she meant. He took the cartridge and poured the gunpowder into Bear's open wound. Molly handed him a coal-oil lamp. The wick sputtered. Jerome acted fast before he chickened out. He touched the wick to the gunpowder. With a loud pop, it burned all the way down into Bear's gut.

"That's the best I can do," Jerome said.

"He's not going to make it, is he?"

Jerome stood and stared down at the bounty hunter. He had never seen a man in worse shape. Molly pulled away from him when he tried to comfort her.

"Help me load him into the wagon. There's a doctor in Clear Springs, isn't there? I saw a shingle outside the barber-shop."

"He's a good man," Molly said in a flat voice. Jerome wasn't sure if she meant the doctor or Bear.

Jerome caught one of the bounty hunter's arms and pulled him upright. With a heave, he slung him over his shoulders. He staggered under the weight but got out of the cantina and made his way to the medicine wagon. Molly had lowered the stage. Jerome gratefully dropped Bear onto it. If he'd had to put him down on the ground and then open up the wagon, he wasn't sure he would have enough strength left.

"Let me help."

Molly hopped onto the lowered stage and grabbed a double handful of buckskin. Pulling and pushing, the two of them got Bear into the wagon.

"Make him comfortable. You can ride back here with him."

Molly muttered something as he closed the doors and lashed the stage upright. The horse shifted about nervously after all that had happened. The smell of blood and gun smoke spooked it. This gave it added speed to leave the outpost.

Jerome jumped when the door behind him opened. Molly wiggled through and stepped over the bench seat to sit beside him. She said nothing. He wanted to ask about Bear but held his tongue. When he reached the fork in the road leading back to Clear Springs, she remained silent. It was almost sundown when they rolled into the town.

The saloons already boomed with business. Molly never even glanced toward them. Jerome pulled the wagon to a halt in front of the barbershop. He jumped down and went to the door. He knocked on it several times before a sandy-haired man opened the door. A quick look at Jerome's bloodstained coat answered quite a few questions.

The doctor asked, "You're not the one bleeding enough to cause such a mess. In your wagon?"

"He was stabbed. And shot. I did what I could."

"Right, right. Do you need help getting him inside? My surgery's in the back."

"You might know him. He goes by the name Bear."

The doctor snorted. "I know him. Let's stop wasting time. I need to get some sleep tonight. The sooner I patch him up, the sooner I can get to bed. This won't be the first time I've worked on him." He shook his head. "One time he ran his hand through a sausage grinder. You wouldn't believe what else he's done to himself. It's about time someone else took a turn, I reckon."

Molly lowered the stage and opened the wagon's back door. She and Jerome slid Bear onto the stage. With the doctor's help, Jerome wrestled the deadweight into the barbershop and through to the rear.

He was buoyed by Bear fighting him a little. The weight he lugged wasn't entirely dead. Yet.

"On the examining table," the doctor said. He pulled back the blood-sticky buckskins and peered down at the knife wound. "You probably saved him. This is as good as I could do, under the circumstances."

"Can you get him sewed up?" Molly spoke for the first time since reaching the doctor's office.

"He'll have a huge scar to brag on. And yes, he'll likely survive me poking about. Hand me that bottle on the desk."

"The whiskey?" Molly asked.

The doctor nodded. He took the bottle from her, knocked back a long swig, then put the bottle on the floor near the table.

He looked at Jerome and Molly. "I need it more than he does. Now clear out. Come back in the morning. And get into some clean clothes. The two of you are a sight."

He made shooing motions, then turned to his work. Bear started screaming as the doctor probed for the bullet in his side.

Jerome steered Molly through the barbershop and out onto the street. He vented a huge sigh of resignation. Marshal Bishop leaned against the wagon, thumbs tucked into his gun belt.

"I reckon you two missed Clear Springs so much you had to come back."

"We'll leave as soon as our" — Jerome started to say "friend," but Bear was hardly that to either of them — "colleague gets some much-needed attention from the doctor."

"That 'colleague' wouldn't happen to be a gent called Bear, now, would it?"

"He caught a knife in the gut trying to bring in a killer named Curtis," Molly said. "Have you seen a wanted poster on anyone with that moniker, Marshal?"

"Curtis?" Bishop shook his head. "Don't know any desperado on the run around here by that name. And I just got in a stack of brand-spankin'-new wanted posters." He looked archly at Jerome. "I made special sure to check for your ugly likeness, but you've escaped notice elsewhere, it seems."

"You got any objection to us staying the night?" Jerome was too tired to put up with more of the marshal's snide remarks.

Bishop looked from Jerome to Molly. The leer said it all.

"Now, Mr. Snake Oil Salesman, you can get on the road and I'd never give two hoots. She can stay as long as she likes. I even got a bed for her to sleep in."

Jerome grabbed Molly's arm and held her back. She hissed like a snake and then subsided.

"We're traveling together."

"Do tell?" Bishop stepped closer and fixed his gaze squarely on Jerome. "Does that mean the three of you, or just her and you?"

"We'll be on the road as soon as the doctor says Bear's not going to kick the bucket," Jerome said.

"If you're not sellin' any of that witches' brew, I won't ask for another license fee. You'll spend a good, long time in my jail if I catch you peddling even one teeny drop. You understand?"

Jerome nodded. Answering aloud carried the risk of him telling Marshal Bishop what he thought of him, his jail and his entire town.

Bishop sauntered off, whistling tunelessly through his teeth.

"Oh, that man," seethed Molly. "If I had

one of your knives, I'd make sure he never
—"

"We need to find a place to park the wagon. You'll be safe enough sleeping inside."

"Where are you going to sleep?"

She turned hot eyes on him, as if daring him to give the wrong answer. For his life, Jerome wasn't sure what that was.

He answered the only way to avoid a new argument. "I don't expect to get much sleep. Come on."

He held out his arm for her. Molly pointedly ignored him and stepped up into the wagon without his aid. Jerome convinced the horse to pull the wagon just a bit farther. He circled around back of the Butterfield Stage office and parked near the corral.

"Will they mind?" Molly asked when he unhitched the horse and put it into the corral with the stage company's remuda.

"The Jenkins boy will take care of everything," he said confidently. "You'll know him when he asks. Don't let him rook you out of too much money." Jerome fished around in his pockets and came up with a few coins. "This'll take care of everything."

"Where are you going?"

"Just around to the talk with Leon Purcell

— the agent. Get some sleep."

He pointed to the rear of the wagon. Molly nodded tiredly and crawled over the driver's seat and disappeared into the bowels of the medicine wagon.

Jerome hesitated, wanting to be sure she was settled, but he knew if anyone could take care of herself, she was the one. She still carried the six-gun she'd taken from his cabinet.

He wondered about her attachment to Bear, then pushed it aside when the tall, burly ticket agent stepped from inside the depot to see what the ruckus was all about.

"I thought it was you comin' back," the agent said. "You don't know how pleased I am to see you."

Jerome smiled ruefully. At least someone in Clear Springs was welcoming him.

"Just passing through," he admitted, "but you talked some with Bear."

"The bounty hunter fella? Yeah, I did. The wire's been burnin' up with warnings about a gang of road agents out there."

"One of them named Curtis got Bear hurt really bad."

"I was afeard of that. Every dash and dot says only a posse ought to track down the gang. Or maybe a company of Rangers."

The agent went back into the office and

kicked the door shut behind Jerome. The heavy cloud of sulfuric acid and lead vapor made Jerome woozy. To regain his senses, he leaned against the counter and found a current of air blowing through the open front door that revitalized him.

"Are you after more of my elixir?"

"What? Elixir? No, nothin' like that, Perfesser. Not that you don't have a fine medicinal tonic, mind you. I tried a snort and was mighty taken with its qualities." Purcell looked around as if someone was spying on him. He leaned over the counter and whispered, "You said you'd ride guard on a stage. You still want to do that?"

Something frightened the agent about reports of the outlaws holding up stages — something more than usual.

"What're you shipping that's so special?"

"What? Who told you?" Purcell jumped back, looking frightened at the idea of a spy. Then he grinned weakly. "Reckon I made it purty obvious, didn't I?"

"It's got something to do with Curtis and the gang?"

"Other than the one time, I ain't never heard names mentioned. I tole Bear that. It don't much matter who's robbin' the Butterfields. This shipment's got to get through to Fort Concho."

"A payroll for the soldiers? Why didn't the fort commander send a squad to protect it — or even have the paymaster escort it themselves?"

"The Comanches have been kickin' up quite a fuss of late. The major's got too many patrols out chasin' 'em down. That don't stop the bluecoats from wantin' to get paid." He reared up and struck a pose. "The Butterfield Stage Company contracted to deliver the payroll."

"At a hefty price, I am sure," Jerome said. "Tell me more about the road agents who've been holding up your stages."

"Not just ours. They've robbed a couple banks in nearby towns. The ranchers complained to Marshal Bishop about rustlers takin' their cattle, but he won't budge out of Clear Springs. There's a passel of thievery goin' on out there, and nobody's workin' to stop it."

"You're offering me a job as guard?"

"Well, not exactly like that. Ride along and pretend you're a passenger. Then you can get the drop on them varmints if they try to rob us."

"I'll think about it," Jerome said.

"Time's up. There's the stage now, all rarin' to go. We're drivin' at night to confuse the desperadoes."

"I've got other concerns."

"Get on out there right now, Perfesser. Please. Hop in and keep the cavalry payroll safe. You need a gun? Here." The agent shoved a derringer into his hands.

"Maybe some other trip."

"This is the one they'll most likely rob."

Something in the way the agent said it put Jerome on guard.

"Why do you think I'll just pick up and go?"

"This Curtis fellow. He's one of the gang. A cowboy on the Triple K saw him and said he was all shot up. Your doing?"

"Partly," Jerome said, "but —"

"You wanted to know if I heard of the Benjamin gang. A single message came along the wire this morning. Curtis Benjamin's been identified as one of this gang. Some folks think he's riding with his kinfolk."

Jerome felt as if he had stepped off a cliff. One of the Benjamin brothers had danced at the tip of his knife, and he'd let him get away. Somehow, saving Bear seemed like wasted effort now when sating his own vengeance had been so close at hand.

"They're pullin' out, Perfesser. Better get aboard. Old Frank's up there in the box, him and Squeeze Box Malone ain't gonna wait."

Jerome saw the shotgun messenger with a long-barreled Greener goose gun resting in the crook of his arm. On the other side Old Frank looked intent on getting his team under control and moving out.

"You're not joshing me about this being the Benjamin gang?" He saw the Butterfield agent was deadly serious.

Without a second thought, Jerome dashed for the door and leaped, catching the side of the compartment and pulling himself in as the stage rattled out of town. He swung inside and sat down, wondering what the hell he had gotten himself into.

CHAPTER TEN

"What have I done?" Jerome Kincannon panicked.

He opened the stage door and leaned out. His cries to the driver were choked off with a cloud of dust kicked up by the stagecoach wheels. Old Frank used his long whip to good effect. The snap from the whip's crack just above the lead horse's head drove it on at a full thundering gallop.

"Stop. Let me off!"

His call was drowned out further by the rattle of wheels and the creaking leather springs. In desperation he looked out into the night. Clear Springs wasn't that far behind the stage.

If he jumped, the walk back wouldn't be that long. He had left Molly without a word about his intentions. What would she think? He caught his breath, coughed out a lump of sludge, then realized she would sleep through the night and not discover his absence until morning.

A crazy thought fluttered about in his head. She'd go back to Bear. *Go back?* Jerome coughed again and popped back into the compartment. Such thinking implied she had left Bear and . . . been with him.

Jerome had no reason to make an assumption like that. All he had done was give her a ride when she needed it. Nothing more. Catching the Benjamin brothers and putting them into graves had to be his only goal. Justice. Revenge!

He fingered the two-shot derringer the Butterfield agent had given him.

"Two shots. For an entire gang of outlaws," he mused.

Then panic gripped him again. He patted himself down. Two of his knives had been used back at Yorick's. Those sheaths along his forearms were empty. He had three knives left: two in the coattails and another in a sheath dangling around his neck down his spine, where he could reach it as if scratching the back of his head.

His impulsive behavior had doomed him, if the Benjamins — or any gang of road agents — held up the stage.

Curious sounds drifted back from outside. He poked his head through the narrow window and looked up. The shotgun guard played a concertina with more gusto than skill. How he produced anything approaching a recognizable tune was a small miracle. The stage groaned with strain, the horses' hooves pounded on the sunbaked road and, he had to admit, his pulse hammered frantically in his ears.

He leaned back and got into the rocking motion. For this kind of travel, he preferred a train, but the Benjamins weren't out to rob a train. They wanted the cavalry payroll riding in the boot.

Or some outlaws wanted to steal it. Jerome fought down pessimism that he was waiting to be attacked by some gang and would never find his family's killers.

He closed his eyes, wiped away a layer of dust and calmed himself. If he'd had time to think, not only would he have carried something more deadly than a derringer but he'd have a couple bottles of his special tonic sloshing about in his pockets. A nip of the alcohol used in his elixir would go a long way toward cutting the thirst.

So much for being the Professor of Potions, able to cope with any situation.

Jerome returned to the window and leaned out. The driver and the guard had to have a bottle with them. Just a short snort would do him a world of good. As he craned his neck, he saw eerie movement on the moonlit prairie. He wiped his eyes clear and spotted a second rider. The full moon turned them into silver ghosts flying along, matching the stage's speed and presenting a menace that set his pulse pounding again.

"Frank! Malone!" Jerome shouted, but they didn't hear him.

The guard enthusiastically pumped away at his concertina and bellowed out a song.

Jerome risked his neck by creeping out onto the step and pulling himself up outside the stage. Wobbling about precariously, close to being thrown off by the rocking stagecoach, he grabbed for the shotgun messenger's arm as much to keep from being thrown off as to get the man's attention. His fingers raked Squeeze Box Malone's arm, startling him.

"What're you doin', you danged fool?"

"Riders. Straight out from us riding parallel to the road." Jerome tried to point and almost lost his grip.

The guard dropped his concertina and grabbed the shotgun. He hefted it and triggered a loud blast. Jerome flinched from the debris kicked out of the muzzle. Specks of half-burned powder and fiery cardboard from the shell singed his face.

"Let them get closer," he called.

His advice wasn't heeded. Squeeze Box fired wildly. The long-barreled shotgun had the range to do damage to the riders, but Jerome wanted them to get closer. From this position he had no chance to join the fight. He slipped back into the compartment, out of breath from anticipation and itching to use the derringer.

He wanted to be sure they were brought down and not chased off. Only by examining the corpses did he have a chance of identifying them. Let the Butterfield employees claim any reward. He wanted scalps — the scalps of the Benjamins.

The robbers left their flanking positions and fell back to the road, content for the moment to only follow. They galloped along for a half mile, then made their attack. They closed the gap until they rode with only the length of the stagecoach between them and the guard. Squeeze Box flopped belly down on the top of the stage and kept firing at the riders. When Jerome heard Squeeze Box curse, he swung about and looked out the window on the other side.

Another pair of riders closed in on them.

He clutched the derringer, but the range was too great for the short-barreled weapon. It fired a hefty .45 slug, but accuracy wasn't a consideration. As many men had died from having their clothing set on fire when the derringer was jammed into their belly and fired as from the bullets. Jerome wished he were close enough to use the weapon like that.

Then he changed his mind. Bullets ripped through the compartment, sending splinters flying in all directions. The wood sides were thin enough that any lead drilled through one side and sailed out the other. That wasn't much of a consolation for him. He needed something solid to keep the wild firing from ventilating him.

He chanced a quick look out the window from where he crouched on the floor. He rocked from side to side and that saved his life. He was thrown back an instant before a bullet tore through the air where his head had been.

"Curtis," he cried. The rider closest to the stage firing furiously was the naked gunman back at Yorick's. "Curtis Benjamin!"

His heart caught in his throat when the outlaw reacted. The brilliant light from the full moon showed the surprise on the man's face at being identified.

"Leland! Somebody inside knows me!"

The rider farther away spurred his horse to ride parallel with Curtis.

"You're crazy" came the shouted reply. "You eatin' them seeds again?"

"Benjamin!" screamed Jerome. He braced his elbow on the windowsill and fired at Curtis Benjamin. The derringer spat two feet of orange-and-yellow flame along with its bullet. "Come on. Fight me!"

"He hit me, Leland! He hit me!" Curtis Benjamin slumped and started to veer off when the roar of Squeeze Box's shotgun deafened Jerome.

"No!"

Jerome leaned out the window and grabbed. Curtis was too far away now. He had tumbled from his horse. Jerome got a quick look of pitch-black blood all over the man's shattered face. The shotgun blast had done more than taken him from the saddle. It had killed him.

Squeeze Box Malone fired some more, but the three remaining road agents turned cagey, riding back and forth behind the stage in a scissors action, becoming constantly moving targets to confuse the guard. To Jerome's dismay, the tactic worked. Squeeze Box's pellets no longer found targets but went ripping off harmlessly into the night.

"They're not givin' up. You got more firepower to add, mister?" The shotgun guard shouted at Jerome, who clutched the derringer.

Only one shot remained, and he didn't have any more ammo for it after he expended that round.

"Let them get closer. We need to take them alive."

"Mister, you're plumb loco. Ain't no way we're capturin' any of *them.*" Malone's shotgun blared again, filling the night with spooky tendrils of smoke and blinding flashes from the shotgun's muzzle. "They get close enough, they're ready to be planted six feet under."

Jerome's reply disappeared as all three of the remaining desperadoes cut loose with a storm of bullets. The guard's shotgun belched fire once more and then fell silent.

"Squeeze Box? You there?" Jerome listened for an answer, any answer. Nothing.

He cursed as he opened the door and clambered up the side of the rocking coach. He grabbed a rail atop the compartment and pulled himself up. Malone lay flat on his belly, clutching his shotgun. He didn't stir. Jerome pressed a hand onto the man's back, waiting for a breath to stir the body. He'd have to wait a very long time for that.

"Frank!" He picked up the Greener and rummaged in the dead guard's pocket for more shells. "Frank! He's dead. A bullet caught him smack in the top of his head."

Jerome tried to look away from the wound. Lying prone, Malone had presented the smallest possible target to the robbers. A chance shot had entered the top of his head and killed him instantly.

"Dead? He cain't be! He's my brother!"

"He's a goner, Frank."

Jerome settled onto the roof and fired. His first few shots were tentative. Then he got the feel of the bucking shotgun and learned how to snug it firmly against his shoulder to keep from being knocked all around. The first shot had almost unbalanced him enough so he'd tumble off the stage.

Jerome tried to lure the road agents closer. He was positive now these were the Benjamin brothers. Curtis and Leland and probably Hank. The fourth had been the relative he'd never heard named. A cousin perhaps? The three brothers were his primary targets, but he wanted them all, and now Curtis was gone.

"They killed my brother!" Old Frank wailed like a banshee as he drove.

Jerome started to ask why the driver slowed, then took this to be the perfect ploy to draw the gang in where he had a better shot at them. When the stagecoach rattled to a halt, Frank surged from the driver's box to kneel beside his dead brother. He sobbed noisily.

"He's all the family I got left. Had left. He — he —"

Frank stood, pulled a six-shooter from his waistband and starting shooting. One outlaw was a better shot.

Frank grunted and fell from the stage. Jerome watched him hit the ground. He wasn't dead, but he was close. He moaned softly and kicked feebly.

Then Jerome had his hands full as the Benjamin gang came at him from both sides. Jerome gave up any notion of capturing them to stand trial. He fired until he ran out of shells. Then he slipped down to the driver's box and from there jumped to the ground. He hit hard, rolled and lay still, waiting.

He clutched the derringer with its single remaining shot, waiting for the right instant to fire. He wondered which of the moonlit figures coming in was Hank Benjamin. He was the oldest and the leader, by accounts.

Jerome wasn't able to see their faces. Hat brims cast shadows across their faces, but the moon turned their six-shooters into pure silver.

"In the back. Check there, Luke." One

rider snapped orders and tried to keep his skittish horse under control.

"Luke," Jerome whispered.

Luke had to be the relative who wasn't a brother. Hank and Leland ripped away the canvas. They dragged out a large box. Jerome winced when the one he pegged as Hank fired his pistol to blow off the lock.

The three gathered around. Jerome knew he'd never have a better shot. He steadied his hand to take the single shot when all three wheeled their horses about and galloped off.

"No!" he screamed. "You can't ride off like that!"

They had robbed him of his best chance at killing another of them.

Jerome lay on the ground, sobbing in frustration and fury at being denied. It took a full minute for him to get his feet under him and stagger forward. The fall from the stage had jarred him more than he cared to admit. Step by step he went to the strongbox. The lid was open, and the shot-off lock hung from the hasp.

The box was empty. He held his head as pain shot through his skull. None of the Benjamins had taken anything from the box after they blasted it open.

"Empty? The payroll wasn't in this box?"

He leaned against the stage and poked through the boot, hunting for a second iron box.

Nothing.

He sank to the ground and fought the pain in his head and body. Then he made his way to where Frank lay beside the stage.

"You going to make it?"

"All broke up inside. I hit a rock when I fell. Get me back to Clear Springs. And my brother. He deserves a Christian burial."

"The strongbox was empty. There wasn't anything in it. Nothing."

Jerome got his arm around the driver and heaved him into the compartment.

"Decoy. We was a decoy."

"Where's the payroll?"

"Special courier. On horseback. Saddle-bags stuffed with greenbacks. Stuffed."

Frank passed out, leaving Jerome to fume. He had been duped into riding along. Worse, he hadn't killed any of the gang.

He climbed into the driver's box and turned the team around, heading back to Clear Springs. Getting fooled into risking his life ought to have infuriated him, but he had done some of what he'd spent almost a year attempting.

One of the Benjamin clan was dead. There wasn't any way Curtis Benjamin had survived a shotgun blast to the face. And he had identified the Benjamins' relative.

Luke. He didn't know the man's last name, but this was more than he had learned in the prior nine months.

"I've run you down, Hank Benjamin. You, Leland and Luke. You're all going to pay now."

He pressed his hand into the derringer he had stuffed into his vest pocket. Then he snapped the reins and got the team pulling on the return to Clear Springs.

In spite of everything, his first run-in with the whole gang hadn't been a complete failure. Now he could get down to business and eradicate the survivors like the mad dogs they were.

CHAPTER ELEVEN

"I ought to hire you," the doctor said, shaking his head. "You've brought me more work in a couple days than I've seen in a month. I only wish you'd find some who aren't so badly shot up. If they start dying on me, it'll hurt my reputation." The doctor wiped his hands on a rag. "Not that I care too much. I'm the only sawbones within twenty miles and the only good one within a hundred."

"Is he going to make it?" Jerome tugged on Old Frank's feet to get him out of the stagecoach. "He took a fall."

"Let me examine him," the doctor said. He put his fingers into his mouth and let out a shrill whistle. Like an obedient hunting dog, Bear came from the barbershop. "Don't hurt him too much more getting him into my office."

Jerome watched in surprise as the huge bounty hunter scooped up the driver and carried him inside as easily as toting a bag of grain. Trailing, Jerome tried not to feel too useless. He had done all he could for the driver getting him back to Clear Springs.

"You got a knack for bein' there when others get all shot up," Bear said, wiping his hands on his filthy buckskins. " 'Cept in my case, I got stabbed with one of your knives. So make that shot and all cut up."

"It was the Benjamin gang," Jerome said. "And the shotgun messenger killed the one that stabbed you."

"Curtis? Do tell. You fetch back that body? He's got a few dollars in reward money on his head. And it's mine, no matter that the guard did the actual shootin'. I'm owed."

Bear pressed his hand into his side and made a face. Bandages showed through the rips in his buckskins to provide mute evidence of his claim.

"The body's somewhere out along the road," Jerome said. "Identifying him isn't possible. He took a shotgun blast to the face."

Bear snorted in contempt. "Don't matter to me if I can identify his face. I saw other parts in the cantina when he was dancin' around all naked as a jaybird."

"Go on and hunt for him. The coyotes and buzzards have had a feast by now."

202

"You aren't askin' for any of the reward?" Bear stared at Jerome as if he had lost his mind.

"He was one of the Benjamin boys. Dead is good enough for me." Jerome collapsed into a barber chair and leaned back. His body ached and concentrating became harder by the minute. "You sure healed up fast. The doc must be a miracle worker."

"I got the constitution of a grizzly," Bear said. "That's what I've always been told. Must be true."

Jerome heard the bounty hunter's voice fade away. The chair was better than the softest bed he'd ever stretched out on. He jumped when someone shook him hard. He sat upright and went for the derringer tucked into his vest pocket. Molly glared at him.

"You left me. You hied on out of town and never once told me what you were doing." Her lips were pulled back into a thin line and her eyes flashed.

"Bear's recovered enough to defend you." Jerome lay back and closed his eyes.

She shook him even harder. "Don't you ever do that again."

"I will if you don't let me get some sleep."

She kept shaking him. "What am I supposed to do? Drink all those bottles of tonic you have in the back of your wagon to try and forget you? We can't stay in Clear Springs. We sneaked in and the marshal's fuming mad about it."

Jerome heaved himself out of the comfortable chair. He rubbed his stubbled chin. Not only had he failed to get any sleep; he hadn't even gotten a shave. The chance to leave Clear Springs unnoticed evaporated before his feet touched the floor.

Marshal Bishop stood in the doorway, hand resting on his six-shooter.

"You came back," the lawman snapped. "You shouldn't have done that."

"The Benjamin gang held up the stage and killed the guard."

"I heard. News like that gets around quick-like when somebody like Purcell won't stop runnin' off at the mouth. That doesn't change anything. You can't just waltz into my town anytime you please, not after I ran you out."

"If you get a posse together, you can catch them. There's three of them left. There's Hank Benjamin. He's the leader. And —"

"I'm not spending good money for a posse. You got this bug up your butt about these owlhoots. They aren't any concern of mine."

"Squeeze Box Malone is dead and his

brother's in a bad way. Doesn't that mean anything to you?"

"I heard all that. The robbing took place outside town limits, so it's not my concern. On the other hand, you are my concern since you keep coming back like a bad penny." Bishop turned to Molly and eyed her. "She can stay. I'll make a special exception. Do you like that notion, Miss Davenport? Or should I throw you into a cell next to him? There's not a whole lot of privacy for a lady in any of the cells."

"Give me an hour for everything I need to do. Then I'll be on the road again. If you won't track down those murderers, I will."

Jerome rested his fingers on the derringer hidden away in his vest pocket. One shot. Marshal Bishop. The temptation was great.

"An hour and not one second longer," Bishop said. He spat on the floor in front of Jerome, then took his leave.

"Jerome, wait." Molly grabbed his arm. He pulled away. "Hunting the gang will get you killed."

"You can go or stay, as you see fit. Bear is up and about now. He can look after you."

"Look after me!" Molly's voice rose in anger. "I don't need him — or you — to look after me!"

Jerome stared at her in wonder. Her reac-

205

tion was far out of proportion to his suggestion.

"We're up against some dangerous men. Are you sure you can deal with them?"

"You don't know what I can do. My pa had a stroke and could hardly move. My ma killed herself. My two worthless brothers and sister lit a shuck. I never saw them again. They left me to look after him when I was only fifteen." Her face flushed with fury. "I'd still be there looking after a man who couldn't do more than drool if he hadn't died. He died and I was glad! So don't tell me I can't look after myself." Her eyes welled with unshed tears.

"It's your call, then," Jerome said, knowing how cruel that was.

She might have fled Clear Springs before on account of Bear, but Marshal Bishop had to be part of her reasons for never wanting to return, also. The lawman showed an obvious letch for her.

Jerome climbed up into the stagecoach driver's box and eased the horses down the street and behind the Butterfield office. His medicine wagon remained where he had parked it what seemed a lifetime ago.

For the shotgun messenger, it had been a lifetime. And for the driver, it might have been, as well.

After putting the team into the corral, he went into the office and saw the telegrapher working furiously on the key. The clicks and clacks ceased, and the burly man sank back in his chair, his face haggard. He turned bloodshot eyes to Jerome.

"Thanks for getting Old Frank back to the doc 'fore he croaked," he said.

"Wish I could have done the same for Squeeze Box." He heaved a deep sigh and asked, "What news has come in about the Benjamin gang? Anything I can use to find them?"

"You got a blood feud with them, don't you?" The agent pushed to his feet and came to lean over the counter. Purcell's face was inches from Jerome's. "The marshal's not gonna recruit a posse, is he?"

Jerome had no reason to answer. They both knew the marshal wasn't budging from Clear Springs for any reason.

"I got a plan," Purcell said, whispering as if someone might overhear.

They were alone in the office. Even the telegraph had fallen silent for the moment.

"Is it any better than your last one?" Jerome laid the derringer on the counter.

The agent shoved it back. "Those road agents will be hightailing it to parts unknown since Squeeze Box killed one of them and they looted an empty strongbox."

"Seems that'd make them angry, not scared."

Jerome watched the cunning look show on the agent's face. He agreed, and his plan played on Hank Benjamin wanting revenge for the death of his brother and being made to look like a fool for falling into the trap so easily.

"You're right, Perfesser. What we need to do is use that need for revenge against them."

Jerome felt as if a strong current carried him to the middle of a river to drown. Even worse, he wanted to let it, even if he died. The chances of tracking down the gang were small if he kept going on his own. The Butterfield agent had a plan. It had to be better than the previous one.

"They don't know that the Army payroll's already been delivered. We spread a rumor around town that you're carrying it in that wagon of yours to sneak it past the road agents. Only there'll be armed men inside the wagon to gun down the lot of them."

Jerome hefted the derringer, then tucked it back into his vest pocket. For such a war wagon to work, he needed a better pistol. Keeping this one as a hideout gun struck him as a good idea, though, no matter what iron he slung at his hip.

"Who're you thinking of having join me?"

The agent smiled and launched into his plan.

"He's hunting for you again, Jerome," Molly warned. "You can't stay in town much longer. The marshal is determined to throw you in the hoosegow since you broke your word about leaving." She heaved a deep sigh. "And I'll be in the cell next to you." With a wide grin, she added, "It might not be so bad if we were in the same cell."

"Bishop's searched the wagon several times, but he never found the false floor." He stretched and moaned softly. "If I have to stay pressed down any longer, I am going to have every joint freeze on me."

"Keep warm with your tonic," she advised. "I need to talk to the women at the general store. That'll spread the news about a secret mission as fast as anything."

"A drink sounds good to me," Jerome said. "I'll go to the saloon. Oh, don't worry. Bishop's not going to get back to town for another hour or two. Purcell sent him on a wild-goose chase."

"I don't trust him," Molly said.

"The Butterfield Stage Company does. So does the telegraph company. And this is his plan because he wants Malone's killers brought to justice. Purcell feels responsible for the man's death."

Jerome didn't add that he did, too. Purcell's cockamamie plan had been loco from the start. He was sorry he had gotten rushed into taking part, even if he had gotten to see Curtis Benjamin die.

"Old Frank's still in no shape to come along, but the doctor says he's kicking up quite a fuss, so he's on the road to recovery."

"He'd be a good addition," Jerome said. "Avenging his brother's death is a powerful reason to join in. But Purcell and Bear are about all the wagon can hold."

"Do you have to leave my scenery behind?" She sounded as if she was ready to bawl. "I painted it myself."

"You told me that an Indian painted it using mystical symbols of his tribe."

"He told me which symbols to use," she said lamely. "But I'd feel better if we moved it into the stagecoach office. Leaving it out here by the corral in the rain and weather's not good for it."

"It rode on top of the wagon in the hot sun and survived. A few more days outside isn't going to hurt it none," Jerome said.

The things that worried the woman continued to amaze him. The chances of everyone riding in the wagon getting shot up — killed! — were great. Hank Benjamin and his surviving family weren't likely to surrender.

"I got it" came a loud call from the office. Purcell dragged a heavy canvas bag behind him.

"What do you have inside?" Molly asked. "If it's supposed to be gold coin, that's enough to buy and sell half the ranches in West Texas."

"Do you think I overdid it?" The burly agent stared at the stitched-up canvas bag. "Naw, it's got to look good."

"Bear's on his way," Jerome said. "I'll pull the wagon around to the front of the office so we can load there, but Bear and you'll already be hidden. We can roll out in a few minutes after making sure folks have seen that bag being shoved into the wagon."

He turned to Molly, but she pointedly ignored him. It was just as well. She was safe in town or as safe as possible until the marshal returned from the wild-goose chase Purcell had sent him on.

Jerome and Purcell dragged the heavy bag to the front door. The agent dusted off his hands, picked up a rifle leaning against the counter and said, "Let's go. I'm as ready as I'll ever be."

They went out back. Purcell hopped inside and joined Bear. Jerome closed the doors and fastened the stage in place. He was glad the heavy roll of Molly's scenery had been stashed along the back of the Butterfield office. The wagon moved as if it was dipped in molasses due to the added weight of the two bulky men. The slowness of the wagon made it obvious they'd have to deal with the gang wherever they were stopped. There wasn't going to be any prolonged chase as there had been with the stagecoach.

Jerome set the brake and jumped down when he reached the street in front of the depot. Loading the sack so it rode at his feet in the driver's box was quite a chore. He wished Purcell hadn't been so eager to make it look as if they hauled a ton of gold, but he drew some attention. If the word hadn't reached the road agents before, it would now. Everyone would gossip about watching the medicine wagon leave town with its heavy load.

His poor horse strained to get the wagon moving. Barely had he reached the outskirts of Clear Springs than Marshal Bishop came trotting up from the opposite direction.

"There you are. I told you to clear out. I even gave you an extra hour, and it's been most of the day. I ought to lock you up."

"Marshal, you're getting your wish. I'm leaving."

"Where's the singer woman?"

"She —" Jerome was cut off as Molly pushed past him as she emerged from the rear. She settled down beside him.

"I'm going, too, Marshal. You're rid of both of us."

"Where were you?" Jerome whispered.

She smiled and said, "You're right. That hidey-hole under the floor is quite small. A tight fit." She ran her hands down her sides to get wrinkles out of her dress.

"I don't want to see you in my town again," the marshal said with ill grace.

"Good day, Marshal," Molly said.

Jerome touched the brim of his derby hat, then snapped the reins. In a few minutes they'd gone far enough so that the marshal couldn't possibly overhear them.

"You get down right now," Jerome said angrily. "This is going to be dangerous."

"Not as dangerous for me as staying in Clear Springs without you or Bear to defend my honor. That so-called lawman is a vile man filled with evil intentions."

Before Jerome could argue, Bear poked his head out and handed a bottle of Jerome's elixir to Molly. "This is real good rotgut, Perfesser. It goes down smooth. Try it."

"Don't mind if I do," she said, grinning wickedly. She knocked back a full inch of the potent tonic, then offered it to Jerome.

He grumbled and kept the horse moving. They had outlaws to bring to justice. There'd be time for celebration later. He hoped.

Chapter Twelve

"This feels like walking to the gallows to be hanged," Molly said. She stirred uncomfortably next to him and looked around the countryside anxiously.

"Do you know that from firsthand experience?"

Jerome tried to keep the conversation light, but the weight of their mission bore down on him as heavily as it did on the woman. At any second one of the Benjamin brothers might pop up from hiding along the road and open fire. Molly and Jerome were sitting ducks for such an attack.

"There!" Molly half stood and pointed west. "Do you see them?"

"Him," Jerome corrected, squinting into the setting sun. "There's only one rider and he's galloping so hard, he'll run his horse into the ground within another mile."

"What's his big hurry?"

Jerome had no idea and remained silent.

They drove at a glacial pace, hardly moving. The prairie around them showed enough bumps and gullies for an entire army to lie in wait. Molly was so nervous, it made him nervous. As much as he hated to do it, he took the bottle Bear had passed forward when leaving town, and took a nip. He smacked his lips in appreciation.

"Do you always sample your own medicine?"

Molly sounded bitter about it. She snatched the bottle from him and downed another slug. The way she looked at what remained worried Jerome.

"Don't drink too much or you'll be seeing double."

"Wonderful. Your tonic cures single vision."

She took another drink in defiance, but not as much. She made no move to hand the bottle back. Instead, she clutched it as fiercely as she would a lifeline saving her from drowning.

He shouted back over his shoulder, "Purcell, where are we? There're more riders, all going in the same direction as we are."

"San Angelo's only a dozen miles off," the agent answered. "There's a railroad depot there. And a telegraph office. That's where most all of my news comes from. From there and Fort Worth."

"If they don't attack soon, we're going to be in town. I can't imagine them trying anything there. How many people live in San Angelo?"

"Twice what's in Clear Springs. Maybe more and it's growing by leaps and bounds. They've got a train. We don't." Purcell sounded aggrieved about that.

Jerome remembered Chagrin and how that town had close to dried up and blown away. The train ran too far from it. The surrounding ranches were all that kept it struggling to survive. And if a spur was ever run down to Clear Springs, there'd be no reason for the smaller town to exist.

If no spur dropped down to Clear Springs, it'd become the next Chagrin. The iron horse gave and took in equal portions. Eventually even the stagecoach route would disappear, guaranteeing the town's death.

"More riders," Molly said. She gripped his arm. Then she sagged. "They're escorting a couple of freight wagons."

"And there's the train," Jerome said.

Billows of black smoke curled into the bright blue sky. As the wagon topped a rise, Jerome and Molly had a good look at the tracks running into San Angelo.

"Why not just drive onto the tracks and

let the train hit us?"

If Purcell sounded upset about the train not coming to Clear Springs, Molly was even more bitter about their attempt to lure the Benjamin gang into attacking them.

"Like them fools?" Bear poked his head out from the back and forced Jerome to slide over in the seat. While Jerome didn't mind pressing closer to Molly, his attention went to what the bounty hunter saw.

"They're robbing the train," Jerome said. "That's a pile of rocks and brush on the tracks!"

"Why pile the bushes?" Molly ended with a small "Oh" when the brush barrier exploded into ten-foot-high flames.

"That's got to be the Benjamin brothers," Jerome said.

He veered off the road and cut across the rugged prairie, heading directly for the spot where the robbers intended to stop the train. Metal-on-metal screeching as the engineer applied the brakes filled the quiet evening.

"Whoa, slow down," cautioned Purcell. "You're throwin' me all around back here."

Jerome ignored the Butterfield agent. Ignoring Bear was harder, as the bounty hunter kept pushing him to one side to clamber into the driver's box. Bear waved his Colt around and whooped like a Comanche.

"You want off?" Jerome asked Molly. She clung to the side of the wagon for dear life. "This isn't your fight."

"I'd kill myself jumping off. And you're going to kill the lot of us tearing along like this."

The mare began to tire from the breakneck speed, but they were within a few hundred yards of the bandits. The rattle and clank of the wagon drew the train robbers' attention. One shoved another in their direction, urging him to stop the wagon before they interrupted the robbery.

"They're coming for us," Jerome said.

"Only one of them," Bear said, squinting. "I know that varmint. That's Marshal Bishop."

Jerome's eyes widened in surprise. He wanted to tell Bear he was full of beans, but he couldn't. If this wasn't Bishop riding toward them, rifle pulled up to his shoulder, it had to be his twin brother.

"Shoot, Bear!" Molly reached in front of Jerome and shook the huge man's arm. "Shoot him!"

The marshal's first rounds sang high and missed. He continued to pump the lever on his rifle and got off three more rounds before Bear fired his six-shooter.

Jerome stared in amazement. Marshal Bishop threw up his hands and toppled backward off his horse and lay still on the ground. The lawman had missed with five shots. The bounty hunter took out his target with a single shot from a handgun fired from a bouncing, rolling wagon. Somehow, Jerome doubted Bear had been lucky.

The bounty hunter looked at Jerome, noted his surprise, then laughed. "I practice a lot. Nobody's a better shot 'n me. Nobody."

"Yeah," grumbled Molly. "You hit your foot practicing that fast draw. I know. I patched you up."

"It wasn't like that," Bear said. "You distracted me. You walked past wigglin' your —"

Jerome yanked back hard on the reins and brought the wagon to an abrupt halt. Too much happened all at once. The fiery barrier across the tracks crumpled into embers so that sparks leaping from the locomotive's wheels flashed brighter and fiercer than the fire. The robbers all yelled amid the screeching of steel against steel and ran forward brandishing rifles.

"What're you stopping for?" demanded Bear. "Them's the owlhoots you want. That

I want. There's got to be a huge reward on all their heads by now."

Jerome stepped past Molly, ignoring her complaints, and jumped to the ground. The setting sun glinted off Marshal Bishop's fallen rifle. Scooping it up, Jerome ran toward the tracks. He levered in a round, dropped to one knee and fired. In the chaos he wasn't sure if he hit any of them. A second round whined off the locomotive's cowcatcher. There wasn't a third. Bishop's rifle came up empty.

With the rifle clutched in his hands, he ran toward the robbers, screaming at the top of his lungs. One masked man spun on him. Jerome crashed into him. The rifle butt knocked the outlaw's pistol from his hand, and they went down in a struggling pile.

"Shoot him. Get him off me!" the writhing outlaw called to his partners for help.

Jerome looked up, sure he was a goner. He had forgotten he had allies in this fight. Both Bear and Purcell shot at the gang. Added to the mix, the engineer and his stoker had unlimbered weapons and shot at the robbers. Unfortunately, they didn't choose their targets well — or maybe they considered anyone on the ground to be their enemy.

Purcell screeched as a round nicked his

neck. He slapped his hand over the shallow wound and danced around, the fight forgotten. Jerome tried to stop a robber from drawing a bead on the Butterfield agent, but the one he wrestled with had other ideas. They rolled over and over fighting for any advantage.

Jerome ended up pinned to the ground. The outlaw's hands closed around his throat. Feeling the life creeping from his body, Jerome gasped out, "I killed Curtis. I mowed him down with a shotgun."

The surprise in the man's eyes rippled down. For an instant his grip on Jerome's throat eased. A heave to the right let Jerome reach up and around, find the knife sheathed just under his neck in back. One quick slash across the outlaw's forearm completely loosened his hold.

A thrust upward drove through an exposed throat and up into his brain. With a single convulsive twitch, the man died. Jerome kicked out from under the deadweight and grabbed for a fallen six-shooter.

He looked around frantically for a target. The deathly silence, save for the hissing steam engine, mocked him. Slowly getting to his feet he went to where Purcell sat cross-legged on the ground, moaning like a banshee.

"They kilt me. They shot and kilt me! I'm bleedin' to death! I'll die of lead poisoning. Oh, oh!"

Molly stood behind the Butterfield agent. She yanked away his collar and laughed derisively.

"If that's all it takes to kill you, they wasted a bullet. They could have just called out 'Boo!' "

Nervous release made Jerome laugh, too. Purcell grumbled, but the wound was trivial. The only blood on his shirt came from Bear, who bled like a stuck pig. The bounty hunter stomped around, then let out a whoop that must have been heard miles off in San Angelo.

"You folks fought like a pack of rabid dogs. The railroad thanks you kindly."

The engineer took off his tall striped cloth hat and wiped his forehead. He tossed his rifle to the side. His young stoker caught it clumsily, trying not to drop his own shotgun.

"Did you see what direction they rode when they hightailed it?" Jerome turned in a complete circle.

The moon had set, depriving him of any chance to see the escaping riders.

"Two of them sidewinders went that way," the engineer said, pointing toward the southwest. "If they got a lick of sense, they're heading for Mexico. Won't see them in these parts again. No, siree. And we got y'all to thank." He took a deep breath, pursed his lips when his set eyes on Purcell and amended, "Most all of you."

"Do you recognize the one you killed, Perfesser?" Bear nudged the dead outlaw with his toe.

Jerome shook his head. He had never seen any of the Benjamins, and the wanted posters had been poor representations. If he had to be honest, he looked as much like the pictures as the gang did.

Bear rifled through the dead man's pockets. Jerome said nothing when he watched the bounty hunter slip all the coins from a vest pocket into his own waist pouch. This was going to be all the reward Bear was likely to see. Then he fumbled out a sheet of paper and held it up.

"Can't read it in the dark. What's it say, Perfesser?" Bear held it while Jerome struck a lucifer.

By the flare, Jerome read, "This one's carrying his own wanted poster. He's got a hundred-dollar reward on his head."

"But which one is he?" Molly crowded close to read over his shoulder.

"Hank Benjamin's cousin, it says," he

replied, fighting the depression that washed over him like a black tide. "Luke Keyes."

"A hunnerd dollars is a fair price," Bear said.

"It's not yours to claim," snapped Molly. "Jerome deserves it. He was the one that almost got killed."

"Do you think there's a reward out on Bishop?" The bounty hunter stepped back as they all stared at him.

"We're better off not mentioning him," Jerome said uneasily.

"That the first one you shot out of the saddle? That was mighty fine marksmanship, yes, sir," the engineer said.

"Bear's a good shot," Molly said. "But we won't bother ourselves over that one. Will we, Bear? Will we?"

"He —" Bear fell silent.

Jerome knew the explanations needed if another lawman found Bishop's body would slow them down. The two Benjamin brothers — the survivors of the gang — had to be tracked down before they got into Mexico. That country swallowed up men on the run, sometimes for good.

"So Hank and Leland are still on the loose. What are you going to do?" Molly took Jerome's sleeve and tugged. "Isn't it good enough you've got two of them?"

Even in the dark she saw his expression.

"Take Purcell on back to Clear Springs," Jerome said. "You can handle the mare. She's tuckered out and won't give you any trouble."

"Wait a minute. I'm coming with you!" Molly stamped her foot in defiance.

"He needs tending." Jerome pointed at the Butterfield agent, who still grumbled and moaned as if he had one foot in the grave. "You get my wagon back safely and stay in town. There's not going to be anything there to give you any worry now with Marshal Bishop dead."

"Not the marshal and not Bear," she said in a disgusted voice.

"I need to know how to find you," Jerome said.

"Me or your damned medicine wagon?"

She whirled around, skirts flaring. Reaching down, she caught Purcell by the ear and lifted. With him protesting, she led him back to the wagon like a schoolmarm taking a misbehaving student to the woodshed.

Jerome watched as she became cloaked in the inky night. He knew she was able to look after herself once she returned to town. Jerome shook his head. Molly was able to look after herself no matter where she was.

"This snake's worth a hundred, eh?" The

engineer walked around Luke Keyes' body. "What do you say we load him onto the train — in the coal tender so we don't spook the passengers more 'n they already are — and turn him over to the sheriff? You can ride along and pick up the reward. I'm more 'n happy to let you claim a seat in first class."

"Go on, Bear," Jerome said. "I've got a trail to follow."

He grabbed the reins of Marshal Bishop's horse as it came back to poke about curiously, nudging its former owner with its nose.

"I found where they staked their horses. I'm taking this one," Bear said. "It must have belonged to the one you skewered."

"I'll pick up the reward soon," Jerome said to the engineer, doubting he'd ever do such a thing. "If I don't and Miss Davenport comes by asking, give it to her for her trouble."

"She's a real purty lady from what I can see," the engineer said. "So you two are chasing after the pair that escaped?"

"The reward's bigger on their heads," Bear said. "For the kind of money galloping away, I can live like a king for a month or two."

"Well, sir, I wish you luck. Tracking

anybody in the dark's no easy chore. Them two lit a shuck, and I don't blame them. Not with you fellows on their trail."

The engineer and the stoker hefted the corpse and carried it to the engine.

"They can push aside the rocks on the track without us," Jerome said.

All around the once quiet night filled with sounds. The engine built up a head of steam and used the cowcatcher to crunch through the rocks Henry Benjamin had piled up to stop the train. Molly snapped the reins and turned the wagon about, heading for Clear Springs. And the most disturbing noise was a pack of coyotes ripping away the marshal's flesh as they dined on a fresh kill.

"Are you gonna set and ponder the whichness of the whys or are you coming along?" Bear pointed toward the southwest, where the engineer had said the Benjamin brothers had fled.

Even with the bounty hunter trotting at his side, J. Frederick Kincannon felt strangely alone in the Texas night.

CHAPTER THIRTEEN

The morning sun warmed Jerome's back. He shifted uncomfortably in the saddle, touched the six-gun thrust into his waistband and stared at the empty land ahead.

"Ride faster. I found the trail," Bear bellowed from a dozen yards to Jerome's right. "They tried to get sneaky by doubling back, but I'm too good for them."

Jerome obediently turned the horse's face and walked to where Bear peered at the ground. The bounty hunter had dropped to all fours and sniffed around like he was a hound dog. Laughing at him got Jerome nowhere, but the sight was silly.

"What's there?"

Jerome didn't point out that Bear had "found" the trail four times during the night. It had led them here, but nothing proved to Jerome that the hulk of a man had seen or heard or sniffed out anything. The night had been almost pitch-black, even after the clouds cleared and the stars shone down. Now that the sun was up, heavy clouds rolled down from the north, promising a frog strangler of a storm later in the day.

"Hoofprints. What do you think? I can taste it now. A fine steak, a bottle of the best whiskey, a side of taters and apple pie with a dab of fresh churned cream for dessert. That's what I'm going to splurge on with the reward money. After all the trouble they're puttin' me through, I deserve every bite of that meal."

Jerome's belly growled. All either of them had eaten was a tough strip of jerky chased down with tepid water. The Benjamins hadn't planned far ahead for their getaway. The saddlebags were bereft of food. Expecting anything more in the marshal's gear was a fool's errand, too. The man had rushed from Clear Springs to tell his cronies to ignore the medicine wagon because there wasn't any payroll aboard.

How the train robbery had come about was another matter. Hank Benjamin might have planned it all along, and the marshal had dealt himself in. But food? Their saddlebags were empty except for the pieces of jerky tough enough to loosen their teeth.

"Do you think the marshal saw wanted

posters on the gang?" Jerome asked.

"I wouldn't have put it past Bishop to join up with them, if they were nasty enough to make a few dollars with their thievery." Bear stood, stretched and began leading his horse almost due west.

As Jerome followed, he saw the deep hoof-prints. He wasn't much of a frontiersman, certainly not as good as Bear, but the prints looked wrong. As he rode along, it finally occurred to him what was wrong.

"There're too many horses. Only Hank and Leland got away from the robbery." He made a quick count of spoor on either side of the trail. "At least six horses made those prints."

"It's a busy section of prairie," Bear said. "You tellin' me I'm wrong? You climb down, Mr. High-and-Mighty Perfesser, and you find the trail."

"I'm an apothecary, not a tracker. But we started after two men. Count the sets of tracks. There might be more than a half dozen, and all of them came riding through at the same time."

"How do you know that?"

"Some of the tracks are on top of others that are equally fresh. The wind hasn't rounded the edges of each print."

"They got friends who joined up," Bear

231

said. "See?"

Jerome reached for the six-gun tucked in his waistband. Not a half mile ahead rode six men, fanned out but all heading in the same direction.

"They're riding abreast so they won't miss a trail. They're tracking someone." He caught his breath. "That's a posse hunting down the Benjamin brothers!"

"Now that's a load of bull flop. How'd they know to come this way, Perfesser? What town sent them out? And how'd they get ahead of us if they came from San Angelo?"

"The engineer said it'd take close to a half hour for him to steam on into town. If the sheriff went around knocking on doors in the middle of the night, it'd take a goodly spell before this many men were deputized," Jerome said. "It doesn't explain how they got ahead of us."

Jerome worried that Bear had led them in circles all night long, giving a posse plenty of time to get on the trail. He wasn't about to point this out. The bounty hunter was in a good mood, thinking he was close to claiming the reward. There wasn't any call to upset him by pointing out they weren't any closer to finding the outlaws than they had been back at the site of the train robbery.

A trailing rider spotted them and passed the word. All six riders drew rein and reversed course, coming back. Shooting it out with this many men was a one-way ticket to the graveyard. And Jerome didn't hold out much hope galloping off would cause the half dozen to give up chasing them down. They looked determined.

"There's an arroyo," Bear said. "We can make our stand there."

It pleased Jerome that the bounty hunter thought along the same lines he did, but Jerome was more observant.

"Stand your ground. There's nothing to be afraid of."

Bear growled something and started to pull a rifle from the saddle scabbard.

"They're lawmen." Seeing that Bear ignored him, he added, "The morning sun's reflecting off their badges."

"Ain't no way the sheriff in San Angelo put all them boys out here so fast," Bear said.

He didn't point his rifle in their direction, though. For that, Jerome was thankful. It kept them alive just a little bit longer.

"Where are you gents heading?" The man leading the others pulled his brim down to shield his eyes to get a better look at Jerome and Bear.

"We're on the trail of two train robbers," Jerome said. "They've been on a killing spree from all the way back in Arkansas."

The posse fanned out. Any chance Jerome had of running for it disappeared. They expertly hemmed him in. If shooting started, he and Bear were in a deadly cross fire.

"What about you, mister?"

"He's —" Jerome began.

"Not asking you. I want to hear him answer. What's your reason for being out here?" The lawman rested his hand on his six-shooter, waiting for Bear's answer.

"I'm after the money on their heads. My friend here, the perfesser, he says I can have it all. Ain't that right, Perfesser?"

"Who might you be?" Jerome asked, curious now.

His and Bear's answers had sent a ripple through the posse. All six of the men relaxed and took their hands away from their weapons. Whatever brought them to this part of Texas, it wasn't pursuit of the Benjamin brothers. Nothing either he or Bear had said proved their identity — or disproved they were ruthless killers from Indian Territory.

"I'm Deputy Federal Marshal Sutton from over in Arizona. Me and my men are hunting four Mexican bandidos that did some mighty terrible things in Prescott."

Jerome heard another of the posse mutter something about raping the governor's wife. That made him sit straighter in the saddle. It explained why a posse had ventured so far from their stomping grounds. They had probably been ordered not to return until the men responsible were brought to justice, even if the posse had to ride to the ends of the earth. Being in Texas south of San Angelo, they about had reached that point.

"I assure you, we're not Mexican bandidos," Jerome said.

"The vaqueros we're after don't speak English. Mostly, they don't want to," the deputy said. "Listening to your accents tells me you weren't lying about being from Arkansas. Now your partner, he's harder to pinpoint. I'd say he hails from someplace up north. Montana?"

"Idaho," Bear said.

The deputy nodded knowingly. "I haven't lost my ear. That's plenty close enough, and it's not Jalisco."

"We haven't seen any Mexicans," Jerome said, "but then we're hunting for an outlaw band. The leader goes by the name of Henry Benjamin and the others riding with him were all kith and kin. We whittled their number down to two — Henry and Leland

Benjamin."

The deputy looked at the posse. No one spoke up. He turned back to Jerome and said, "Sorry to disappoint you. If we come across anyone answering to those names, well" — he shrugged — "we'd let them ride on by, just like you two."

"No riders at all?" Bear growled deep in his throat.

"None."

"How much of a reward on the heads of these desperadoes you're hunting?" Bear asked.

The deputy cleared his throat and said, "That's a matter of some dispute, but the governor all by himself's offering a thousand a head. The territory's chipped in another five hundred for each one."

"That's a princely sum," Bear said. "How do you intend to divvy it up?"

"Me and the others are collecting a daily fee of a hundred dollars in exchange for the reward."

"How much?" Jerome blinked. If it took a month to find the four rapists, somebody was out a huge sum.

"The governor's no pauper. Both he and his wife come from considerable fortunes, so the governor's willing to spend money."

"If I joined your posse but didn't ask for

236

that hunnerd a day, I could collect the rewards on their heads?" Bear leaned forward.

"You any good at tracking?" The deputy studied Bear more closely.

"The best there is in the state of Texas. I'd claim to be the best there is west of the Big Muddy but that's harder to prove."

"The six thousand's yours if you help us find and catch them," the deputy said. "We're already tallying a decent reward being deputized and riding for the governor of Arizona."

"Bear, the Benjamins . . ."

Jerome saw his words fall on deaf ears. The lure of so much money for the Mexicans proved overwhelming. If he hadn't been so focused on the men who had committed such atrocities against his own family, Jerome had to admit he'd have been tempted to throw in with the posse. A man could live a very long time on even a sliver of that much money.

"I might be able to lend some help right away," Bear said. "I know the terrain around here a little. You think those Mexican varmints are hankering to return to Mexico?"

The deputy nodded.

"That's the way you want to go, then,"

Bear said, pointing due south. "The land between here and the Rio Grande's drier than an old lady's teat. But that way there's water."

This set off an argument about how well the fugitives knew the land. Jerome listened in stunned silence. He had no real skill as a trailsman. Without Bear's aid, he might wander in circles until he died.

"You convinced us, Bear," the deputy said. He turned to Jerome. "You coming along? How you and the bounty hunter split the reward's your concern, but an extra gun's always appreciated in this land."

"Clear Springs is back that way," Jerome said, looking over his shoulder. "I don't think I could miss the road if I rode north ten miles or so."

"Call it fifteen," Bear said. "Or you can backtrack our trail and get to San Angelo in a day or two. You'll probably cross the railroad tracks before that, so you'll know where you are without gettin' lost too much."

Jerome made his decision. He thrust out his hand and said, "You've been a help, Bear. I hope riding with the deputy here works out for you."

They shook.

"I'll make sure it comes out in my favor,"

the bounty hunter said. "You look after Molly, you hear?"

"You'd better catch up. The deputy's already on the trail."

Bear let out a whoop and galloped after the posse, catching up with them as they reached the top of a low rise. In seconds they vanished. Jerome sat on the horse alone.

He turned north and walked slowly, thinking hard what to do next. He had spent the better part of a year finding the Benjamins. He considered how he'd feel in a week or a month or even another year if he quit hunting for Hank and Leland. Curtis was dead, as was Luke, the Benjamin cousin who'd taken to the outlaw trail with them.

"Guilty," he said aloud. The word caught on the wind and whistled over the prairie.

He found the double-rutted road and started back toward Clear Springs. Once, he saw a cluster of hoofprints in the earth heading toward the northwest. It took some willpower not to follow them farther than a hill a quarter mile off the road.

Atop the hill he tried to make out any riders ahead of him. He saw nothing and realized the better way of hunting for the killers was how he had worked for so long. Sell his magical tonic laced with alcohol, drive his medicine wagon to a new town and ask after the bandits. It was slower that way, but more likely to give him the killers. Not now, maybe not immediately, but eventually.

Jerome wondered at why he felt as if a weight had been lifted as he rode back to Clear Springs and Molly Davenport.

CHAPTER FOURTEEN

He felt as if he rode into a ghost town. Clear Springs was hidden in shadow, and no one moved about in the evening streets. He touched the six-shooter resting in his waistband, but where was the danger to evacuate the town? When he came to the Red Ruby Saloon in the dead center of Clear Springs, the answer to his questions flooded out into the street.

If it had been possible, the saloon walls would have bulged outward from packing so many customers inside. Men hopped about just outside the open doors, trying to get a good look inside. The waves of smoke and loud talk from inside boiled out and swept past Jerome like a summer thunderstorm. He closed his eyes and rode on. Even if he had been curious about what packed the house like that, getting inside amounted to an impossibility.

He stabled his horse. As in the rest of the

town, nobody showed himself when he dismounted. Jerome reckoned the horse was his now. If he had a chance to break it to harness, his other horse wouldn't have as big a load to haul any longer. In spite of being dusty and aching from the trail, he curried the horse, made sure it had water and a fair amount of hay, then walked to the Butterfield office. He expected to find Leon Purcell inside, hunched over the telegraph key as dits and dahs flooded in from all over the state.

The office door stood open. Purcell had vanished, leaving his precious telegraph untended. If Jerome had been smarter, he could have interpreted the chatter of the key. All he did was cough at the sulfuric acid fumes from the ranks of batteries. Purcell had left the door open to air out the office, but the accumulation of noxious vapors was still overpowering.

Jerome walked through the narrow office to the rear door and went out to the corral, expecting the Jenkins boy to show up. Like Purcell, he was absent.

"At least you're still here," he said, addressing his medicine wagon.

"Where else would you expect me to be?"

Jerome jumped. For a moment he thought the wagon had answered him. He walked around to where Molly Davenport worked furiously with a paintbrush, dipping it into the nearest of three cans open on the ground. Quick, sure strokes up and down against the side of the wagon pleased her.

She stood back, hands on her hips and said, "Better. Much better. But I can make it impossible to ignore, given more paint and time."

Jerome looked from the paint-spatted woman to the artwork she had left on the side of his wagon. He wasn't a prude, but he blushed.

"That's mighty . . . bold," he got out.

"You don't like it? I can paint a strip here and another there." She demonstrated.

"She's not as naughty," Jerome allowed. "Could you add even more covering?"

He eyed the cans of paint, estimating how much it took to completely paint out the racy filly Molly had so accurately drawn for God and everyone to see.

"I know your show's not like that, but you need to get their attention. This'll do it."

She dabbed a bit more paint over a strategic area and scowled. She obviously liked it with the naughtier cleavage.

"In spades," he agreed, "but about half my sales go to women. If they see something like that, they'll avoid me like the plague."

He held back his appraisal that they'd keep their husbands from buying even a drop of his miracle tonic, too.

"You don't like it," Molly said. She stamped her foot. "This is some of my best work. Look at the proportions and the colors. You can't see them too well in the dark, but take my word for it. They're vivid and eye-catching."

"Garish," he said to himself.

"What time is it?" she asked abruptly. "I've got a show at nine o'clock over at the saloon."

"The Red Ruby?" Jerome guessed.

"Does that joy juice you peddle make you a mind reader? That's potent stuff." She pressed close to him and looked up into his eyes. "I doubted you'd be back."

"But you still worked on my wagon?"

She pushed away as she said, "I can work on it some more come tomorrow. I need your help now." She mumbled to herself. He heard, "Should have done it earlier but there wasn't anyone to help me."

"What do you need?"

Jerome ached from the trail, and as happy as he was to see her, he wanted nothing more than to curl up and sleep for a week. It became obvious Molly wasn't going to allow that.

"The scenery. We need to get it to the Red Ruby and nail it into place on the wall at the back of the stage."

"Carry it?" Jerome wasn't up for that, but her solution was even crazier.

"Drag it," she corrected. "Oh, not by yourself. Get a horse from the corral. That annoying little boy's not there to act all high and mighty. He's probably at the saloon waiting for my show. The urchin has that look. I can always tell, no matter how old they are."

"That look?"

She turned and pressed against him again. Her hands circled his head and drew his face down until their lips almost touched. Before a kiss developed, she released him and once more stepped back.

"*That* look. Now get a horse so we can hitch the canvas to it and drag it to the saloon's back door."

To Jerome's surprise, it took only a few minutes to hitch up the canvas roll and pull it to the saloon. Even wrestling the heavy canvas inside wasn't too difficult, but once they positioned the roll where they wanted to nail it up, Jerome ran out of steam.

"No more," he said. "No matter what you promise, no matter how much I get *that* look, I'm at the end of my rope."

"Pulleys," Molly said. "Block and tackle. Wait a minute." She slipped off the side of the stage.

Jerome sank down and watched the curtain ripple and bugle, surge and flow back as the restless crowd on the other side grew impatient for the show to begin. He came awake when Molly returned with the barkeep and another man all decked out in a gambler's finery. It took only an instant for Jerome to figure out this was the Red Ruby's owner.

He stepped away and let them do the work. They fastened ropes onto the edges of the canvas, then pulled it up from the roll. As it revealed itself, Jerome wasn't sure whether to laugh or stare in utter bemusement. No Indian shaman had ever painted this, not unless they led more colorful lives on the reservation than anyone ever thought.

"Go, go," Molly said, shooing him into the wings. "Stay there or go out and watch the show with the rest."

Jerome stayed put. He wanted to see the show but had already seen how packed the saloon was. After so many hours on the trail, jostling about in a sea of lustful cowboys was the last thing he wanted.

Molly came to stand by him. "You can open and close the curtains. I'll cue you."

She ran her hands over her painted-spattered dress and looked forlorn. "No time to change into a decent outfit, not that they'll care. But I should look presentable for every performance. I have standards, after all."

The piano player began hammering out a raucous song that whipped the crowd into a frenzy of anticipation. She took a deep breath, composed herself, kissed Jerome on the cheek, then hurried to the middle of the stage, found her mark and struck a pose. She looked back at Jerome and winked to signal him. He opened the curtains to an avalanche of noise louder than any cattle stampede.

He watched a few minutes as she danced and teased the audience; then he had to sate his thirst. He longed for a shot of whiskey more than he'd expected with such a fine performance unfolding.

"Undressing," he muttered.

How Molly managed to expose a little bit more skin as the dancing and singing progressed bothered him, but she did it tastefully enough. She knew exactly how to egg on the audience so they always wanted more.

And somehow, even when she didn't give them what they wanted most, they kept jeering and cheering, sure she would relent . . . soon.

Jerome went around the curtain and hopped down to the saloon floor. The easiest way to get to the bar was to hug the wall since the crowd pressed ever closer to the stage. If they pushed any more, they'd crush one another. Worse, they'd climb onstage with Molly.

At the far end of the bar nearest the door into the street, he caught the barkeep's eye and signaled for a drink. Jerome wondered what he'd be served, not that it mattered. Anything to quench his thirst and ease the aches and pains from riding all day across the arid prairie was the prescription he needed.

A shot of something pretending to be rye dropped in front of him. He knocked it back and held it out for a refill. The barkeep leaned forward and shouted in his ear to be heard.

"You was out at Yorick's Outpost, weren't you?"

Jerome nodded. He sampled the second shot rather than downing it in a gulp. The first already tore at his belly and made him a trifle woozy.

"You know him? The big galoot holding forth back there?"

Jerome glanced over his shoulder. The booze burning a hole in his stomach turned to ice. He put the shot glass down and reached for his six-gun.

"So you do know him? He claims he was there when Curtis Benjamin danced nekkid on the bar."

"He wasn't there," Jerome said, "but he should have been. It was quite a show."

He recognized the man's clothing, having seen the outfit recently. During a train robbery. This might be Henry Benjamin or his brother. Whichever it was, Jerome didn't care. He was too burned out, and why would either of them come to Clear Springs? Their protection here was dead along with Marshal Bishop.

"He's mighty boastful, but nothing of what he says makes any sense. He'll say something and a minute later contradict it. Most gents don't get that way until a few drinks. He came in all mixed up, and if I read him aright, he was sober."

Jerome doubted the man seated at the table, ignoring Molly's show in favor of buying drinks for a couple men with him, was confused about anything. He was a Benjamin and casting about for information. Just as Jerome hunted the gang for killing his family, Hank and his brother hunted him for killing Curtis and Luke.

Hunters hunting hunters.

Jerome took a deep breath and regretted even sampling the second shot of rye. He needed a clear head and deadly aim for what was going to happen.

Killers killing killers.

Amid the blaring music and catcalls, the press of scores of men and the pungent odors of spilled beer and sour sawdust, Jerome carefully drew his six-gun. He cocked it and aimed at the man across the room. Before he drew back on the trigger, a blow to his forearm ruined his aim.

"I don't care who you are, professor or pimp for the gal onstage. You're not starting a gunfight in my saloon."

The man dressed as a gambler who had helped nail up Molly's scenery had jumped halfway over the bar to keep Jerome from shooting one of the men responsible for murder and thieving and who knew what else.

Jerome jerked his hand free and stepped away from the bar. The saloon owner swarmed across, hands grabbing to stop him.

"You're not murdering anybody on these premises!"

He flopped onto Jerome, and they went

down in a heap on the floor.

Sawdust flew all over as they fought. From a distance it had to look like a gopher digging a hole. Jerome wrenched free and sat up, the six-shooter still clutched in his hand. His target had jumped to his feet and slapped leather. They both fired at the same instant — and both results were identical.

Benjamin shot the saloon owner in the back, and Jerome's errant slug found a berth in the arm of the man listening to Benjamin's stories about Yorick. Both shots went unnoticed by most of the men in the saloon. Such was the stage power and attraction of Molly Davenport.

Jerome got off another shot at Benjamin as he disappeared through the door. He struggled to his feet and staggered outside, heedless of walking straight into an ambush. The cold night air hit him like a slap in the face and brought him to his senses. Twisting hard, he threw himself behind a water trough before chancing a longer look around.

The only signs of life in town came from inside the Red Ruby. And the thunderous applause told him Molly was close to finishing her act. Catcalls and demands for an encore rang in his ears as he edged around the saloon and looked down an alley.

Jerome jerked away at movement high up, then relaxed his finger on the trigger.

"You coulda shot me," the Jenkins boy said in disgust. "Not even a pint of that poison you sell heals bullet wounds."

"Did you see him?"

Before Jerome described whichever Benjamin he pursued, the boy held up his hand.

"Of course I saw him. There's nothing in Clear Springs I don't see." The boy turned cagey. "For the right price I can even remember where he went."

"How much?" Jerome patted his pockets for coins.

"Not money." The boy looked up. Jerome followed his eyes and saw a platform nailed to the wall above head level. "If the show's interesting enough, I watch from up there. I drilled a couple peepholes in the wall so I look down right onto the stage."

Jerome was frantic to find Benjamin. By now the murderer had had time to mount and hightail it out of town. Jerome might have identified the man as one of the brothers, but he knew that he was now known to the gang. Before, neither had had a chance of recognizing the other. It was easier now for the other Benjamin to sneak up on him unobserved.

"I want to see her. Miss Davenport. From

up there I only got a glimpse of her. I want to see . . . more."

"That's not up to me," Jerome said.

He started to push past the boy when Molly called to him from out in the street.

"What happened? Who shot Mr. Galen?"

"I spotted one of the Benjamin boys and shot at him. He returned fire and missed me. The saloon owner got in the way."

"He *killed* the saloon owner," protested Molly. "This town is cursed. I thought with Bishop gone and Bear riding with the posse, I'd find some peace. But no, you get me mixed up in a shoot-out and —"

"Just an ankle," the Jenkins boy said in a husky voice.

Molly came over and stood beside Jerome. She saw the expression on the boy's face. It was what Molly had described earlier as *that* look.

"What's going on between you two?"

"Nothing," snapped Jerome.

"He promised me a look at your ankles. Both of 'em."

"Professor!" Molly pushed Jerome away in outrage.

Jerome had no time for such a discussion.

"He's lying. I said no such thing."

He spun to continue his hunt, but Molly grabbed him hard enough to swing him about. Using the momentum, she slammed him into the saloon wall hard enough to jar him.

"He saw where Benjamin went and won't tell you unless —"

She read the answer on Jerome's face. She made a disgusted noise, then lifted her skirts and showed more than ankle. She flashed bare skin all the way to the knee.

"I . . . I —" the Jenkins boy stuttered. His legs turned to rubber and he sat heavily when Molly went to him, bent over and planted a kiss on his forehead.

"Tell him what you know, you little imp."

"I saw him shoot Mr. Galen," the boy said, touching his forehead reverently. "He burst out of the saloon and headed down yonder alley. He got over to Rock Island Street and turned left. That's what I saw. That's all I saw, damn it." He obviously wished he had more to impart if Molly was feeling generous about dispensing her rewards.

Jerome sprinted in that direction. He heard Molly's skirts swishing about as she matched him step for step.

"Stay back. I want him alive to find where his brother is," he gasped out.

"I'm not letting you blunder into an ambush," she said. "You're as bad as Bear when it comes to getting yourself into trouble. At least you haven't shot yourself yet. Have you?"

"You should never have given in to that little extortionist. He'll think that's the way to getting whatever he wants now."

Molly laughed. "Who'll believe him? If he tells his old man, he'll get a tanning. And friends? Not a one will believe him. Never." She grabbed Jerome's arm with both hands and yanked hard.

The bullet tore through the air between their heads. The fight was on to the death.

CHAPTER FIFTEEN

"He's trying to kill us!"

Molly Davenport sounded startled at the very idea. It was as if she hadn't heard a word about the saloon owner being cut down or remembered anything else Jerome had told her about the Benjamin brothers.

"Get back to the saloon," Jerome ordered. "The marshal's dead, but you might recruit some of the crowd there to form a posse. This is our best chance at catching or killing him."

"Mr. Galen's dead. I'm not sure anyone in there cares one way or the other. Soapy Jones, the barkeep, will see that as his chance to take over the Red Ruby, so he's not willing to budge. And it's a good thing Marshal Bishop is dead. He'd thrown in with *them.*"

A bullet tore into the wall beside her head. She ducked and clung to Jerome. He swung her around behind him, as much to protect her as to give himself a better shot at whichever Benjamin had ambushed them. He chanced a quick look around the corner of the building and was rewarded with another bullet. This one tore off a piece of wood. The splinter almost blinded him. Ducking back, he picked at the wood and pulled it from his cheek. It hardly bled but hurt like hellfire.

"Go on. Vamoose."

He tried to shoo her away. She resisted. Telling Molly to do anything was like pushing a rope.

"You can't tangle with a murderer like that and hope to come out alive. Get help." She tugged at his arm.

"Good idea. Go get help. In the saloon. Somewhere else?"

Jerome crouched, spun and fired. Without a distinct target, he was firing blind. Two more rounds sailed off into the night to no avail. He had hoped to draw fire so he could home in on the outlaw's muzzle flash.

Benjamin was too cagey for that trick. He intended to draw Jerome out where he had a good target. A single bullet was all it'd take and muzzle flashes after that killing shot meant nothing.

"He's hiding across the street," Jerome said. "I'm going to circle and catch him from the side."

He gripped Molly's arm and pulled her along behind. He had no idea where Benjamin hid, but this proved the best way of getting the woman out of the line of fire. They stopped across the street from the Red Ruby. Judging by the boisterous noise inside, no one had noticed that the owner had been shot or that a deadly gunfight had raged inside just minutes earlier.

"Jerome, I know what you're doing. I don't need to be hidden away where it's safe." Molly snorted in disgust. "Where in this godforsaken town *is* safe? Get someone to back you up. Please."

She sounded so forlorn in her pleading that he hesitated. Who was there in town who could help him? Bear was off on the trail of Mexican desperadoes because the money was better. The marshal would never have dropped his boots off his desk, much less drawn his six-gun and joined the fight.

"I can get Purcell. This is his fight, too, since the gang held up one of his stages. More than one," he amended, "and they've killed his drivers and guards."

She looked skeptical but realized this was as good as she was going to get. Molly gave him a quick peck on the cheek and said, "Don't get yourself killed. I'll need help taking down my scenery."

Jerome waited for her to enter the Red Ruby before running down the street toward the Butterfield office. Purcell hadn't been there before, but since Molly's performance in the saloon was over, the telegrapher might have returned to his work. Wary of getting shot from ambush, Jerome edged along in front of the office, then ducked inside. As before, the heavy sulfuric acid fumes almost overwhelmed him. Purcell sat behind his desk, staring at the silent telegraph key.

"I need your help," Jerome blurted.

Purcell looked up with dull eyes. It took a few seconds for him to respond, as if he'd had to translate what Jerome said into Morse code to understand.

"No way, Perfesser. I got shot up helping you before." He put his hand on the bandage at the back of his neck. "I coulda been killed. Those are dangerous outlaws you're hunting down."

"It's one of the Benjamin gang. He's here in town and killed the Red Ruby's owner. You helped drive them off so they weren't able to rob the train. You're keeping them on the run so they'll leave the Butterfield stages alone. Help me again. Please!"

"Even the marshal was in cahoots with

them. No, sir, I'm not budging from my chair, where I'm all safe and sound." Purcell gripped the edges of his desk with such intensity, his knuckles turned white.

"Your bosses will give you a medal. A bonus! A promotion!"

Jerome felt a mixture of frustration and anger. He was the perfect salesman. He sold snake oil, but his words failed to sell the agent on lending a gun hand when he needed it most.

"Get the bounty hunter. Bear's fool enough to do what you want." Purcell hunched over even more and muttered into the desktop, "For that Miss Davenport, he'll do anything, no matter how crazy it is."

"They weren't married," Jerome said in exasperation. "And Bear's gone. He's chasing other road agents with bigger rewards on their heads."

"If she's in town, he'll be back, mark my words." Purcell jumped when the key began clicking.

Jerome saw he had no chance of persuading Purcell to help capture — kill! — the gang member roaming around Clear Springs. He reloaded, then cautiously looked out the door for any sign.

"I'm coming for you, Benjamin!" he shouted at the top of his lungs.

Playing cat and mouse led one way — to his death. Flushing the killer into the open gave him a better chance. He gripped the Colt tightly and made his way along the wall. As alert as he was, he still didn't see or hear his attacker. A bullet broke the window behind him and showered him with glass shards.

Jerome dived forward onto his belly. He braced his elbows on the boardwalk and held the six-shooter in both hands. Jerome fired at a hint of movement in shadows across the street. Whether he was lucky or good didn't matter. His shot caused a loud groan.

"Give up, Benjamin. You're not going to get out of town alive."

"Why are you dogging us so? You're the one what kilt Curtis. I know it! I read it in your eyes back in the saloon."

"Which one of you am I talking to? Are you Leland? I'd wager that's who you are. Leland Benjamin."

"Who are you that you know my name?"

Jerome felt a surge of confidence. He had guessed which of the brothers he faced. With more patience than good sense as he lay exposed on the boardwalk, Jerome waited. And waited. When he was sure Benjamin had slunk off into the night, he saw movement.

He began firing as fast as he could in the hope of hitting Leland Benjamin. His pistol came up empty before he drilled even one hunk of lead into the killer.

"I'm going to kill you!" Leland Benjamin launched a full-out assault, running from across the street, his six-gun leading the way. He had turned into a force of nature. His face was masked in shadows and his feet hardly touched the ground as he ran.

Jerome was helpless to stop him. His hammer fell repeatedly on empty chambers, and there wasn't time to reload. He flinched as a shot rang out. He waited for the pain of death to flood through him, but it never came.

One eye opened tentatively. The outlaw was nowhere to be seen. Jerome hastily reloaded and came to his knees, looking around like a prairie dog popping from its burrow. Another deafening shot echoed down the street, but it was farther away. When a fusillade came, the reports were already fading into the distance.

Jerome propped himself up against the stagecoach office and wiped sweat from his eyes. He spun, pistol coming around when a huge shadow detached itself from the building across the street and moved in his direction.

"I'll kill you, Benjamin!"

"Don't go gettin' an itchy trigger finger. I just saved your worthless hide from gettin' filled with holes."

"Bear? What are you doing back here?"

The mountain of a man stopped a few paces away. He cradled a Sharps in the crook of his arm and laughed.

"I reckoned you needed my help."

Jerome cursed nonstop for several seconds, then finished with "Thanks for saving me. Benjamin had me dead to rights."

"You sure it was one of the gang with a reward on their head?"

Something in the way the bounty hunter said that told Jerome what had happened.

"Did the Federal marshal chase you off?" Jerome slid his six-gun back into his waistband. "They worked out a way to cheat you out of your reward for the Mexican bandidos?"

"Something like that. We were closin' in on them, thanks to my expert trackin', of course, when a dozen others swooped in. There wasn't much of anything left of those bandidos. And those claim jumpers demanded all the reward money. That Arizona marshal agreed."

"So you hurried back because the reward

is still riding on the Benjamin gang."

"That's part of it. My wife's likely to be here in town somewhere. I was fixin' to hunt her up when I heard a ruckus and came to pull your fat out of the fire. Arrived in the nick of time from the look of it. It gave me a chance to try out my new rifle. I took it off one of them cheatin' lawmen as my due for helpin' out." Bear swung his buffalo gun about, then lowered it as Purcell poked his head out of the Butterfield office.

"Leland Benjamin," said Jerome. The bounty hunter looked at him quizzically. "That's the one you ran off. Now we have to find him before he tells his brother what happened."

"They'll run," Bear said thoughtfully. "That'll be better. Out on the prairie, I can track a snowflake in a blizzard. In town's harder. Too many places to hole up. Then there's all the folks gettin' in the way. Be a waste of good ammo if I have to shoot them to get to that Benjamin varmint." Bear shifted from one foot to the other in his eagerness to get down to the fight.

"We've got to be sure he lit a shuck," Jerome said. "He might be hiding out in town, waiting to ambush us."

"I don't read him that way. He's a coward. He'll turn tail and run."

"If he does, trailing him in the dark's more than even you can do."

Jerome remembered the last time Bear had tried such a stunt. They had ended up riding in circles.

"Naw. If we carry a couple torches —"

Both men stared at the other and said at the same instant, "Molly!"

Bear followed Jerome for a few paces, then caught up when their destination became obvious.

"How's that varmint know about her?" Bear loped along, reloading his rifle as he ran.

"He might have spotted her in the medicine wagon at the train robbery. Or if he asked anybody in Clear Springs, they'd have spilled the beans about her and me," Jerome said.

"What about you and her? She's my woman." Bear growled like his namesake.

"Later. We can argue later, once she's safe."

Jerome pounded through the wide-open doors and burst into the saloon. The owner's body had been removed to make room for more customers. They had climbed onto the bar to get a better look at the stage.

Jerome wasn't able to see Molly but heard her belting out "The Old Whorehouse Bells

Were Ringing."

"She must be doing a second show," he said. "That's crazy with Benjamin hunting me — and her."

There wasn't any trace of Leland Benjamin, but the outlaw was a slippery snake. A lump formed in Jerome's gut when he realized he had no idea what Henry Benjamin looked like. There had better be a close family resemblance or he'd miss him entirely. Leland could be gone and his brother left behind. Henry could identify him and Jerome would never know.

"Anyone paying us more attention than to Molly is a suspect," he shouted in Bear's ear.

"I'm gonna get her off that there stage. The way she's dancin' is downright dirty. No wife of mine's showin' off her legs in front of a rowdy bunch like them. Listen to what they're catcallin'! How dare they say that about her?"

Jerome was too frantic to argue. Let the bounty hunter cause all the commotion he wanted. Identifying the Benjamin brothers was more important. They had figured out his connection with Molly and how he'd return here eventually. Pushing his way through the edge of the crowd, he worked to the stage. Jerome swallowed hard when he saw how Molly hoisted her skirts and kicked high in a cancan as the piano player blasted out "Hell's Gallop." For a second, he agreed with Bear about this being too lewd for a respectable lady.

Men behind him jostled him around. He let them push him toward the back of the hollering crowd. When he reached the wall, he swiveled about. He heaved a sigh of relief that the Benjamins hadn't come in to kidnap her — or worse.

Jerome let out a cry that disappeared in the tumult Molly created with her dancing. He slipped along the wall and back to the door where Bear stood looking glum.

"Cain't get within ten feet of the stage. I'm thinkin' on burnin' down the whole danged saloon if that's the only way to make her stop showin' off like that."

"Bear," Jerome said, shaking the man. He might as well have tried to move a mountain. "They want to kill all of us. That's the way they operate."

"Purcell," Bear said, shaking his head. "He was along for the ride. He got himself all shot up, though."

Jerome took off at a dead run for the Butterfield office. Bear lumbered along behind, more reluctant to follow because of Molly remaining in the saloon. As he turned a corner, Jerome saw a flash from inside the office. His gun filled his fist by the time he reached the door.

He didn't bother shouting a warning. He fired. Leland Benjamin leaned over the counter waving his six-shooter around. From somewhere under the counter came pitiful cries for help. Purcell had been shot again. If his pleas were to be believed, this wound was far more serious than the tiny nick from back at the train robbery.

Benjamin jerked away and fired at Jerome, forcing him to retreat outside.

"Got you now, you miserable cayuse," Benjamin shouted. "Why are you so determined to get in the way?"

"You killed my family!"

Jerome fired several more times. By now Bear had arrived. The bounty hunter hefted his heavy rifle and loosed a round that missed Benjamin but tore a fist-sized hole in the back wall. This put the fear into the outlaw.

"Who are you? We ain't killed any women-folk in months."

"And you'll never get the chance to again," Jerome cried.

He reloaded and burst inside. Benjamin had disappeared like a puff of smoke. Then he heard Purcell calling from under the counter.

Blood hammered in Jerome's temples, and he lost all sense of fear. He walked in, judged where someone might be behind the counter and fired. Bullet after bullet ripped away the wood. His wild assault brought two different cries. Purcell shouted for him to stop firing. Leland Benjamin grated out a curse that warned Jerome that Purcell had bitten the man's hand as he tried to grab him.

He vaulted the counter and hunted for the man who had murdered his family. Benjamin fired at him pointblank. For once Jerome's luck held. The outlaw's pistol blew up in his hand, knocking him flat onto the floor. Bits of six-gun tore at Jerome's face, momentarily causing him to flinch in reaction.

"You're going to die now." He took careful aim at the fallen outlaw.

"No, wait. Turn me over to the law. You'd rather see me swing than die with a bullet in my gut." Benjamin scooted away like a crab.

"Bishop's dead, so he's not going to let you get off scot-free."

Jerome's trigger finger tightened. A hammer blow knocked him back into the banks of lead-acid batteries.

"Get out of there, Leland."

"Kill him, Henry. Kill him dead!" Leland Benjamin got to his feet, hobbling from a wound in his leg.

"My pleasure." Henry Benjamin pushed through the rear door and rounded the counter, his six-gun cocked and ready.

Jerome got off a shot that missed. Henry Benjamin fired — but Jerome wasn't hit. Purcell had jumped to his feet at the wrong instant. The slug drilled into his back and exploded out his chest. Blood spewed everywhere, landing on the lead-acid batteries and hissing like fat spilled into a campfire. The telegrapher moaned and pressed his hand to the wound in his back. He tried to also stanch the exit wound in the front, but he only flopped about. From the way he cursed a blue streak, he wasn't in danger of kicking the bucket anytime soon.

Jerome dodged to the side to get another shot at Henry. Both brothers were heading out the door. He screamed in defeat. Then the roar of Bear's Sharps rifle filled the room.

"Dang, missed. You gonna stand around or are you comin' with me?"

The bounty hunter ran for the rear door. He poked his head around, then ducked back as a hail of bullets greeted such carelessness.

"Stand back," Jerome called.

He knelt for a moment and pressed his fingers into Purcell's neck. The Butterfield agent's pulse throbbed. He opened his eyes and tried to bat Jerome's hand away.

"Go get him. I want you to give him what for!" Purcell propped himself up under the counter, where a box of rags gave him rude bandages for his wounds.

Jerome reared up to give the agent room and a curious calm came over him. He held the six-shooter behind his back as if hiding it, lowered his shoulder and ran full tilt into the back wall. The flimsy wood splintered, and he crashed into the alley. Jerome tried to keep his feet but got tangled up in the debris from his precipitous assault on the wall. He landed hard on the dirt.

"No!" he cried out when Henry Benjamin smashed one bottle after another of his potion against the medicine wagon. Behind him Leland Benjamin fumbled to light a match.

Jerome emptied his six-shooter at the younger outlaw and forced him to drop the match.

"He's outta ammo, Henry. Get him, get him!"

The leader of the gang came around the

271

wagon and leveled his pistol at a helpless Jerome.

"I don't remember doing a danged thing to you or your family, but right now I wish I had. It'd give me real pleasure all over again." Henry Benjamin made sure Jerome saw the gun pointed at him.

Again came the ferocious roar of Bear's Sharps. He hit Henry in the arm. The huge slug lifted the outlaw off his feet and caused him to skid backward in the dirt. The bounty hunter came from the stagecoach office, swearing as he tried to reload his rifle.

"They're getting away. Bear, stop them!"

Jerome came to his knees and dropped his empty six-gun. A year of practice guided his hand to a knife sheathed in the tail of his coat. He found the hidden blade, pulled it free and cast it with practiced ease.

"You got him. Dang me if you didn't!" Bear threw down his rifle and charged forward to where Henry Benjamin thrashed about on the ground.

The outlaw had not only been hit by the Sharps round but had taken Jerome's blade in his arm. The bounty hunter stretched out his powerful hands, intending to wrap them around the fallen outlaw's throat.

Jerome cried out a warning too late. Leland Benjamin had retrieved his brother's fallen gun and used it, firing three times into the approaching bounty hunter. Then he turned and fired at Jerome.

Jerome's head snapped back, and he fell to the ground. He stared up at the night sky — the sky where dawn threatened to drive away darkness once more. Then the world turned blurry, and Jerome lost track of where he was and what he did.

CHAPTER SIXTEEN

Jerome choked as liquid dribbled over his lips and down his throat. He tried to turn aside and avoid the downpour. Someone held his head in a viselike grip. He blinked open his eyes and saw the sun turning the top of the Butterfield office a warm yellow. The day was beginning.

"St-stop pouring that down my gullet," he gasped out. He looked up at Bear, who held an almost empty bottle of elixir taken from the medicine wagon. "That's a dollar a bottle. More if I can get it."

"I had to bring you around. I thought you was a goner."

Bear held up the bottle, judged what remained, then upended it. A single long swallow left the bottom drier than the West Texas desert. He smacked his lips and tossed the empty bottle over his shoulder.

"If I had more than two nickels to rub together, I'd be first in line to buy this. It goes down real smooth. I can feel the power flowin' through my veins and rejuvenatin' me."

He reared back and stretched his arms out to either side of his body and let loose a rebel yell that made Jerome's head ache.

"I saw Leland Benjamin shoot you. Three times," Jerome said, the memory of the gunfight still vivid in his mind. He reached out and pressed his fingers into Bear's torso. He looked up in surprise.

Bear laughed and used his knuckles to rap on his chest. The metallic ring told why the bullets hadn't killed him outright. The bounty hunter pulled back his buckskins. Dangling on a rawhide strip around his neck, an iron plate gleamed where bullets had left silvery streaks as they bounced off.

"I come prepared ever since that train robbery. It's how I keep on breathin'. You should do the same, but it'd ruin the line of that fancy coat."

Jerome tugged on the coat lapels. Bits of cloth came free. His "fancy coat" was the worse for wear and tear. After sitting up, he patted himself down. All his knives were gone. Then another memory hit him.

"Henry Benjamin! He caught one of those slugs you fire from that howitzer. And I skewered him with a knife. Where is he?"

"We both blacked out for a few seconds. That's all it took for them lily livers to turn rabbit and hop off. I'm never gonna collect the reward on their miserable heads."

On hands and knees, Jerome searched the ground. He avoided the mud patches caused by Henry Benjamin dousing the wagon with bottles of his elixir. The impressions in the soft dirt gave him enough of what had happened after he passed out to feel he knew as much as if he'd witnessed it.

"Henry fell back here. There's plenty of blood, but not so much it's going to kill him. His brother stood over there and shot at you, then me. The tracks are all scuffed up, but Leland dragged Henry off toward the corral."

"Once a thief, always a thief. They done took all the horses. Put that on their list of hangin' offenses. The stage company had at least a dozen horses penned there."

"And my horse," Jerome said, anger rising.

He still had a horse taken from the outlaws after their failed train robbery over in the livery stables, but this was *his* horse. A year of work had taught the steady, sturdy mare how to pull his wagon without bolting or balking.

"I'm headin' over to the saloon. Molly's

got to be done by now. It's dawn! I need to reassure her I've been doin' everything I can to protect her." Bear puffed up his chest, then lit out with a long stride and complete determination.

"Wait. Wait for me."

Jerome forced himself to match Bear's pace, in spite of every muscle and joint in his body screaming in pain. He found the dizziness assailing him even more debilitating. There wasn't much of anything in his body that worked. He wondered if he wasn't in serious need of his own medicine.

"Professor Potion, heal thyself," he grated out.

"You're not that bad off. Purcell's all shot up," Bear said, "but he'll live." He hefted his rifle and tugged and banged at the receiver. "That's more 'n I can say for this ole buffalo gun. It's shot its last desperado."

Bear tried to work the lever but the falling block on the carbine refused to budge. He swung it around his head and let it sail away. "I need to get me a Winchester. No more of them single-shot rifles for me."

"We can send the doctor by to patch Purcell's wounds," Jerome said. "They looked pretty nasty."

"Pour some of your magic juice into the holes. That'll patch him up faster. Maybe it'll even get him a tad drunk."

Bear laughed. He slowed and stopped outside the Red Ruby.

"What's wrong?"

"You sure they left town? I don't want them goin' after Molly the way they did Purcell, just 'cuz he helped us run them off before they robbed the train."

"Killing the marshal probably irked them more than anything else," Jerome said. "Other than not getting the payroll from the train. And having their kin gunned down. And —"

"It's real nice for an outlaw to have a friend in the marshal," Bear rambled on, not hearing Jerome. Or not caring what he said. "You think they're holed up some-where around Clear Springs? Someplace Bishop let them use as a hideout?"

"They stole all those horses rather than hiding out in town. They're out of town by now, but you're right about one thing. They probably have a camp not too far off. Something's holding them around here, something more than wanting to stop me — us."

Jerome hurried up the steps and pushed into the now deserted saloon. What Bear had said about Purcell applied double for Molly. She'd be a target.

"There you are," the singer called from the stage. "It's about time you showed up."

She sat on the edge, her legs dangling down. With a quick hop, she landed lightly and went to them.

Jerome caught his breath wondering which of them she meant.

"You should be ashamed of yourselves. Both of you, shooting up the place like you did. It sounds as if the entire town is moving on to greener pastures," she said.

"What do you mean?"

"It turns out the bank owns this place. Mr. Galen was mortgaged up to his earlobes. That means the barkeep's not staying around since there's no way he can ever own the place, even if the Red Ruby goes into bankruptcy."

"From what the marshal said, the banker's crooked," Jerome said. "I'm not sure what that means, coming from a man like Bishop."

"Soapy Jones said the bank's moved all its money up to San Angelo," Molly said.

"The train went right on by the town," Bear said sadly. "A place like Clear Springs can't survive without a train."

Jerome wasn't interested in listening to how Clear Springs was dying. He had another mission to complete.

"The barkeep's leaving, too?" He needed to know everything Soapy Jones did before letting the man go on his way.

"He's talking about leaving town first thing." She stood on tiptoe and looked past Bear. "He's leaving at sunup, which it already is."

"He's got a real good idea," Bear said. "We oughta clear out, too."

"That's just like you," she said sourly. "You're clumsy and shoot yourself in the foot and even fell off your horse. You weren't even drunk then."

"I never —"

"You did!" she raged. "I was there. I saw it." Molly turned her wrath toward Jerome. "And you're no better." She grabbed his pistol and yanked it from his waistband before he could stop her. "Dance, Professor, dance." She fanned the hammer. It clicked on spent rounds. She started to lift the muzzle and stare down the barrel.

Jerome grabbed it from her. "I need more cartridges. I went through a powerful lot of them. And a holster."

"And you should stock up on more of them fancy throwing knives you're so fond of," Bear said.

"No ammo? What happened to all the knives?" As if for the first time, she saw their disheveled condition. She sniffed and then sneezed from the gunpowder lingering on their clothing. "What happened?"

"Nothing important," Jerome said. "Why'd you come back here?"

"I . . . The show had to go on," she said. "And I figured if anybody knew anything, it'd be the barkeep. That's when I found out about him abandoning the town."

"What about the man with Leland Benjamin? The one he was talking to before the gunfire started?" He held Molly at arm's length when she started to turn away "Did you get a good look at him?"

Molly frowned. "Not too good a look, I suppose. I was doing so many things on-stage, and they were out here by the doorway."

"Do you have any idea where to find him?" Jerome took her by the upper arms to keep her from turning away. She protested and Bear growled. "Do you remember seeing him from the time you were in town earlier?"

"Where's this goin'?" Bear demanded.

He tried to interpose himself between Jerome and Molly, but the woman lithely sidestepped him.

"I'm beginning to think the Benjamin gang came here weeks back, bought off

Marshal Bishop and were fixing to stay a spell. The fellow with Leland could be someone they recruited."

"There's enough money here to interest them," Bear said thoughtfully. "Leastways, there was at one time. The whole place is packin' up and leavin'."

"If they have been around since you were here," Jerome said to Molly, "it's not out of the question they recruited a few locals to scout for them and maybe even ride with them on some of the robberies."

"Soapy will know," Molly said. She hoisted herself onto the bar and peered behind it toward the back room. "He's not there. We'd better hurry to catch him before he leaves town for good."

Jerome was already making a beeline for the stage. He hesitated when he reached where Molly had performed. For a fleeting instant, he looked out over the now empty saloon and felt a pang. He missed being the center of attention as he peddled his snake oil. And he felt a pang of jealousy at how easily she had captivated a crowd many times the size of any he had ever harangued. He pushed it aside. They put on different shows and aimed to entertain in different ways. He spun and ran for the back door.

"Stop!" Jerome called out to the barkeep

as he loaded a case of whiskey into the back of a buckboard.

"You're not stopping me from taking the rotgut. It's my due. Galen never got around to paying me."

Soapy Jones pulled back his coat. He had two Colts thrust into his belt cross-draw style.

"Take all you want," Jerome said. "That's not my business."

"Good, since you're the one who got the boss gunned down. It shoulda been you taking the slug, not him." Jones stepped back and reached up to pull himself into the driver's box.

When his hands were well away from his six-shooters, Jerome moved. He shoved the man hard against the side of the wagon and held him until he stopped trying to get away.

"You fixing to rob me? There wasn't much in the till."

"Liar," Jerome snapped. "Molly brought in the biggest crowd this place has ever seen. But that's not what I want, either. Who was the man talking with Leland Benjamin, the man who shot your boss?"

"I don't know. Let me go!"

Soapy Jones wiggled, but Jerome tightened his grip on the barkeep's collar. He lifted him onto his toes so he lacked leverage to escape.

"Wait," the barkeep said. "All right, I know him. He lives here in town. His name's Franklin. Don't know his first name. Never heard it, but I heard folks call him Bronco, like he broke horses." Jones snorted in contempt. "I never saw a bronc buster with weaker hands. I shook hands with him once, and it was as limp as a wet bar rag."

"Bronco Franklin," Jerome repeated, fixing the name in his head. "Where do I find him?"

"Danged if I know. Maybe a boardinghouse. There're only a couple around the edge of town. To the south."

Jerome released him and motioned for him to clear out. The barkeep made tracks, leaving the Red Ruby and J. Frederick Kincannon behind in a cloud of dust.

He looked back through the door into the saloon and saw Bear and Molly standing nose to nose and shouting at each other. This decided him. Trying to keep Molly out of the line of fire and worrying that Bear would shoot him in the back for a few dollars' reward looked too much like his future. Without them noticing, he left.

It took less than ten minutes to get to the south section of Clear Springs. He spotted two boardinghouses side by side. All hesitation was gone now. He was a man on a mission. Two quick raps on the first house's door brought a harried-looking gray-haired woman. She wiped flour from her hands.

"We don't serve breakfast 'cept to residents. And we're all full up. Go find some other place to stay."

She gave him a look of disdain. He was filthy, covered in dried blood, and his tattered clothing hung on him like he was a scarecrow. He didn't blame her for her reaction.

"Ma'am," he said, politely touching the brim of his derby, "I'm looking for Mr. Franklin. I think he goes by the name Bronco."

She glared at him when he mentioned the name. Not answering, she tried to slam the door. Jerome got his foot in the jamb. She was irritated. In dark intensity, her face rivaled any summer thunderstorm blowing across the prairie.

"Next door. If you're looking to give him a sound thrashing, punch him a couple more times for me. He shot my dog. Claimed it attacked him. Old Smoke'd know better. Biting that son of a bitch would poison him. He was smart enough a dog to know that."

Jerome took his foot from the door. The landlady slammed it in his face, but Jerome didn't care. He vaulted over a low picket fence to go to the next boardinghouse when a man rushed around the side of the building. For a moment he and Jerome stared at each other.

Jerome went for his six-gun at the same instant Bronco Franklin went for his. A cold chill passed through Jerome when he remembered he was out of ammunition and that his pistol was empty.

"Drop it," he barked, holding the empty weapon in front of him. "I won't shoot if you lower your gun."

Franklin looked around like a trapped rat. "You're the one Leland shot."

"He missed me and killed the saloon owner by mistake. Galen's dead, not me. And if you're smart, you'll keep on breathing because you dropped your iron."

"You're not a lawman. You with that bounty hunter? The one calling himself Bear?"

"Let's do this in a different way. I'm putting my gun down. You do the same. We can talk this out."

Jerome carefully shoved his six-shooter into his waistband, aware of the danger. Franklin kept his weapon pointed at Jerome's breadbasket.

"Leland had a reason for shooting at you. Who are you?"

Franklin's aim wavered a mite. Jerome knew he had been right about the outlaws recruiting locals. Franklin wasn't a killer, not like Henry or Leland Benjamin. That didn't mean he wasn't as dangerous as a stepped-on prairie rattler.

"We had a dispute back in Arkansas. I wanted to smooth his ruffled feathers so we can get on better terms."

"You're the magic healer man, the snake oil peddler. How'd Leland come to know you?"

"He liked my tonic, but he got a bad bottle and ended up with a pain in his gut that almost didn't go away." Jerome edged closer. "I wanted to make it up to him with some good liquor."

"Yeah, that's what I figgered. The snake oil's got a healthy dollop of whiskey in it." Franklin nodded, assuring himself he had been right about his suspicions.

"You riding with him and Henry?"

"How'd you know that?"

"They came to Clear Springs a few weeks back and told you all about the easy pickings here: the stage with only one guard if that; the train; how the cavalry was all tied up hunting down Indians. It's a sweet setup and not one you're likely to find in many places." Jerome saw that Franklin worked over what he'd heard, deciding if he trusted anyone who wasn't already in the Benjamin gang. "With Marshal Bishop looking out for you, it was even better."

"Warn't no risk of gettin' throwed in jail," Franklin said with a touch of admiration for such a clever scheme. "So why'd you and Leland swap lead back in the Red Ruby?"

"A mistake. We each thought the other was shooting at us. You weren't hurt too bad, were you? That was a foolish accident on my part, but you stepped right in front of Leland when I returned fire."

"That's what I thought. You shot me." Franklin's finger drew back on the trigger.

In that instant the air filled with billowing white gun smoke and deadly lead. Jerome reacted by throwing himself to the side, but from the corner of his eye, he saw Franklin recoil as a slug tore into his shoulder. The choking fog hung all around, giving Jerome the chance to scuttle away and hide behind a low hedge. Daring a quick look, he popped up to see who had saved him.

"Bear, don't kill him!" Jerome called out. "We need him."

"I need the bounty on his head. There's

got to be one, and it's all mine!"

Jerome retreated, but Franklin scattered bullets all around, making it too dangerous. He sank back behind the hedge, flat on his belly. Even though Jerome was hidden and presenting such a small target, Franklin's bullets ripped through the vegetation close enough to make him cringe.

"Dead or alive," Bear bellowed. "It don't matter a whit to me."

He started walking, firing a Colt with a rhythm that matched his every step. When he came up empty, he swapped that pistol for another tucked into his belt.

When Bear got close enough, Jerome lurched up and tackled him. His arms circled the bounty hunter's legs at the knees and toppled him. They wrestled about, Bear kicking and hammering away. He landed the pistol butt on Jerome's shoulder. Waves of pain shot through him as fierce as if he'd been shot.

"Stay down, will you? We need him alive."

"You want the reward. I'm not lettin' you steal it from me."

"Keep the reward. I want him to lead us to the Benjamins' camp so we can nab the entire gang."

For a horrifying second, Jerome thought the bounty hunter had died. All fight went out of him, and he stretched out limp and unmoving. Then he rolled away.

"That's a good plan — if I get the rewards."

"Take it all," Jerome said in exasperation. "All I want is for the Benjamin brothers to pay for what they've done."

"Why didn't you say so?"

Bear sat up, dragged his pouch around and reloaded his pistols. Jerome made a grab and took a handful of cartridges, too. He not only reloaded but also gained enough spares to fill his coat pockets.

"How good are you at tracking? Really?" Jerome asked, sneaking a look over the hedge.

"You know I'm the best. Why?"

"Franklin's lit out like his hair's on fire. He's not smart enough to head for the tall and uncut."

"He's goin' to the gang's camp," the bounty hunter said. A huge grin split his face. "Let's go get some reward — and vengeance."

Jerome couldn't have put it better.

CHAPTER SEVENTEEN

"He must be hidin' his trail," Bear complained. "That's the only explanation."

"You can't find anything?"

Jerome stared at the dry ground. A confusion of hoofprints was etched in the ground, evidence that riders had come this way after the last heavy rain. Their horses left prints in mud that dried into perfect castings. But more recent riders? Jerome saw no hint that Franklin had come this way.

"I'm not Kit Carson or St. Vrain," the bounty hunter said. "I'm good, but I got limitations."

Jerome fumed. They had delayed almost an hour getting on Franklin's trail after he left Clear Springs. It had been necessary to get ready, find food and pick up a couple boxes of ammunition. But Bear's insistence on testing one rifle after another until he found one that "set right" against his shoulder had been the real problem. As much as firepower was likely going to be necessary taking on the entire gang, any rifle would have been a decent replacement for the Sharps.

For his part Jerome had strapped on a gun belt and filled the loops with spare ammo. He felt ready to whip his weight in wildcats or at least gun down what remained of the Benjamin gang.

"Which way do we go?"

Jerome stared into the midmorning sun, then slowly studied the ground all around. The road gave no evidence of any rider's passing this morning.

The bounty hunter closed his eyes, tipped his head back and let out a howl rivaling that of any lovesick coyote.

"What's that all about?" Jerome went for his six-shooter, then stopped when Bear cut off his cry as suddenly as it began.

"Gettin' the feel of the air." He sniffed, then leveled his arm and slowly moved it around until he pointed south. "That way. He went that way."

Without waiting to see if Jerome agreed, Bear tapped his heels to his horse's flanks and rocketed away.

Jerome watched for a few seconds, took one last look around and figured this was as good as any other direction. He galloped after Bear. When the bounty hunter topped a low hill and stopped, Jerome almost ran over him.

"You see him? Where?"

Jerome used his hand to shield his eyes as he stared out across a barren prairie. No trace of travelers kicking up dust or otherwise showed the bounty hunter had found their quarry.

"Farther," Bear said. "I feel it in my gut."

He thumped his belly and winced. Too many bullets had torn chunks of his flesh out for him to be completely healthy. Even so, even shot up and beat up, Bear was a formidable foe and one Jerome wanted fighting at his side.

Only now it felt as if he valued his sense of tracking too much. As far as Jerome could see, the lonesome land stretched to the south devoid of any human life.

"There aren't even buzzards circling up there," Jerome said, pointing to the cloud-flecked sky. "This place is so desolate, nothing's coming here to die."

"I smell the reward money. This way." Bear urged his horse down the far side of the hill.

Jerome watched the bounty hunter go. If Bear felt this was the trail to follow, Jerome's gut told him the opposite. Franklin hadn't had enough time, even with an hour's start and a fast horse, to get out of sight this way. More than that, the man was wounded and scared. Making the effort to drag brush behind him to hide his tracks or doing anything but making a beeline straight for the Benjamins' camp would have never occurred to him.

"The road," Jerome muttered. "He's not leaving the road."

He made his way back and retraced his route. When he reached the road, he again looked eastward. They had found a couple people back in town who claimed Franklin had gone east. Jerome wasn't much of a gambler, but he rolled the dice now and put his bet on finding the fugitive before Bear.

A half hour trotting along the road brought Jerome to a stand of scrub oak. A stream meandered along through the small forest and provided a cool, refreshing spot for travelers to pause. Or outlaws to camp. Clear Springs was only a couple hours' ride away. San Angelo lay to the north, with its railroad terminal and riches shipped along tracks connecting the rest of the state.

Jerome sat a little straighter when he heard chains clanking and leather harnesses creaking. Hoofbeats hammered the ground and a whip cracked like thunder. He moved off the road as a stagecoach lumbered past. The driver bent over, using his whip to keep the team pulling hard. A sharp-eyed shotgun guard half rose in the box and gave Jerome the once-over. Jerome waved. The guard nodded in his direction and then the stage rumbled past.

The dust cloud choked him for a moment; then Jerome blinked until tears caused muddy tracks down his cheeks. If anyone intended to rob the stage, this was a good place. The vigilance of both driver and guard warned that holdups were expected along this stretch of road. Were Henry and Leland Benjamin so stupid they'd camp where they robbed stagecoaches?

"Or are they that crazy?"

Jerome decided they were neither. If the Clear Springs marshal had been one of their gang, why not bribe other law dogs in the region to look the other way? This was an isolated section of Texas and one filled with huge acres of cattle ranches and farms. The few marshals and sheriffs made this a safer area for road agents than in bigger cities like Fort Worth or San Antonio.

Jerome sneezed to get the clot of dust from his nose. As he inhaled, he perked up. Woodsmoke. A hint of meat cooking. A nearby camp!

With greater deliberation now, he rode along the road, eyes peeled for a hint of smoke rising above the treetops. He quickly found it. Jerome was tossed on the horns of a dilemma. Tackling the entire gang alone was more than foolish; it was suicidal. He ought to track down Bear. Enticing the bounty hunter back with the lure of reward money was child's play.

He ought to do that. *What if they broke camp and rode on?* A dozen other reasons for not fetching Bean rattled around in his head. As he thought, he trotted a quarter mile farther along the road. When he came to a decision, he slipped from the saddle, made sure his six-shooter was ready for action, then hiked through the woods. The trees were sparse and not much undergrowth sprouted up here. That made visibility in the forest a hundred feet or better.

"No guard," he whispered over and over to himself. "Don't let them post a guard."

On cat's feet he approached the camp. The scrub oaks were thick enough to provide some cover, but he kept pressing into the trunk of the largest tree around to be sure he wasn't seen. Within ten yards of the camp, he flopped on his belly and peered over a fallen log. Two men crowded close to the fire, although the day was warm.

One man screamed, threw up his hands and fell onto his back. The other half stood. In his hand he held a small branch that he used as a torch. Jerome tried to piece together what was going on. When Franklin sat up, he clutched his side and the smell of burned flesh wafted toward Jerome, who understood. Franklin's wound had been severe enough for his partner to cauterize it with the branch after taking it from the campfire.

"I thought I was gonna die," Franklin rasped out.

"You would have if the bleeding had gone on much longer. You're lucky you got back here when you did."

"I'm lucky," Franklin said, "neither Henry nor Leland saw me like this. They don't like anyone to slow them down."

His partner used the branch to stir the fire a mite. "They don't like much of anybody who's not family."

"They're sore," Franklin said, "that Curtis got killed, him and their cousin. We haven't scored that much, either."

"The marshal musta double-crossed us. That's all Leland talks about, but Henry thinks all the blame lies with the medicine show potions peddler. The one what shot you."

"I go along with Henry on that. I was lucky to get away."

Jerome listened to the pair accusing everyone for their misfortunes. He was happy to accept blame all by himself, though some of what they griped about could have been laid at Bear's doorstep.

"What're we gonna do?" Franklin's partner spat into the fire. "We can't rob the stage with just four of us. We need at least one more. A couple would be better."

Jerome wondered at the concern. Given careful planning, two men were more than capable of sticking up a stage. If the robber cared nothing for taking a life or two, one man was plenty. Snipe the driver and guard, then rob the passengers, who'd be cowed by the first two deaths. He listened more intently. Some detail was missing.

"When are they coming?" asked Franklin. He looked around.

Jerome froze when the outlaw stared in his direction. When Franklin gave no sign he'd spotted the spy, Jerome sank down farther behind his meager cover.

"They're not due back here for a while. Both of them are in San Angelo trying to recruit a few more guns to help us. Time's getting short, real short. If they can't do it, we'll have to make do. With you all shot up, that's an added burden for the three of us."

"I can pull my own weight," Franklin declared. "Let me rest up. I'll get my strength back real quick, I promise."

"Ain't me you need to convince." The man pulled out a pocket watch and squinted at it. "I'm due back in town to do some scouting." He shot to his feet and stepped over the fire on his way to his and Franklin's tethered horses.

Jerome turned over all the things possible to do without getting filled with lead. If he believed Franklin's partner, the man was heading to Clear Springs. What he intended doing there was a mystery. Figure it out and capturing the Benjamins would be easy as pie. But the brothers were returning to this camp eventually. Jerome didn't have to catch the outlaw going to Clear Springs if he stayed put and got the drop on the men he hated most in the world.

The steady clop-clop of hooves disappeared as the outlaw wound through the trees, heading for the road back to Clear Springs. Jerome settled down behind the log to wait. He had to prepare himself to act in a flash because the Benjamin brothers were likely to return with several gunmen recruited up north.

He worked through his plan to get the

drop on them when he heard unsteady footsteps approaching. He froze. Franklin hummed to himself. The sound of falling water made Jerome edge away. Then urine splattered all over him. Franklin was relieving himself on the other side of the log.

He reared up, going to his six-shooter. He wasn't sure who was more startled, him or the outlaw. He went for his gun. Franklin stepped away and sprayed him in the face with a flood of urine.

Jerome fired wildly as the liquid blinded him. He got off another round and knew he had missed with it, too. Franklin ran like a frightened deer back to his camp. With a wild swipe, Jerome got most of the fluid from his eyes. Franklin reached for the rifle in his saddle sheath and swung it around.

Both Jerome and the outlaw fired at the same time. Neither came close to hitting the other.

"You," cried Franklin. "How'd you get here? I'm gonna end you right now!"

Jerome twisted to the side and landed hard. A bullet tore into the other side of the rotted log and burrowed through. It kicked up dead leaves beside him. He swung around, poked his pistol over the top of the log and fired until he came up empty.

"You're the snake oil salesman, the one

that shot me up good," Franklin called out. "You're never gonna let me be, are you? I ain't done nothing to you."

Jerome sneaked a look around the end of the log, saw Franklin's hat poking up over a stump and squeezed off a round. The hat went flying. The instant he fired, he knew this had been a trick to get him to reveal himself. Franklin was a dozen feet away behind a thick-boled tree, waiting. He opened fire a fraction of a second after Jerome shot a hole in his hat.

The bullet tore through Jerome's sleeve and pinked his right wrist. He dropped the gun and pulled back behind the log and the dubious safety it offered.

"You give up right now, and I won't cut you down."

"You'll save me for Henry and Leland?"

Jerome reached for the gun and yanked his hand back when another bullet tore off a bigger hunk of skin. Whatever he did had to be done fast. Franklin would figure out he'd pulled his enemy's fangs and walk right on over, big as you please, and empty the rifle's magazine.

"Why bother doing that? I don't know what feud you have with them or them with you, but all I want's for you to leave me be. Get on your horse and ride away. That's all

I want."

Silence descended on the forest. The crackle of the dying fire and occasional drops of sap exploding were the only sounds. All the animals were quiet, waiting for more gunfire. Jerome picked up a rock and settled it in his hand. It wasn't much of a weapon, but he had forgotten to replenish the sheaths with his spare knives. He cursed Bear for distracting him back in Clear Springs. He was a skillful knife thrower, but the distance was too great, even if he had a couple blades.

Jerome started to retort. A different tactic came to him. Like the birds and small animals all around, he hunkered down and made no sound. He wished there was a burrow big enough for him to crawl into.

"What do you say? Come out and I'll tie you up, set you on your horse and let it take you back to town. By the time anyone finds you, me and the rest of the gang'll be done with what we're planning."

Jerome bit his lip to keep quiet. He longed to pop up and see what Franklin did. The hammering of his heart had to be loud enough for the other man to hear. But Jerome bit harder until he tasted blood. The sharp pain in his lip kept him quiet, even when he heard slow footsteps coming in his direction.

"You catch a slug? You bleedin' out on me? Let me help you."

Jerome clutched the rock like it was a lifeline. When he heard the footsteps stop, he acted. He came to his knees and flung the rock with all his strength. The stone smashed into Franklin's chest and knocked the man backward. He caught his heel on an exposed tree root and flopped down hard.

Jerome swarmed over the log and dived onto the outlaw. He crushed the man, knocking the wind from his lungs. With powerful punches he hammered Franklin's temples, knocking his head from one side to the other. Jerome looked down when he felt something wet on his leg. The sight of blood made him recoil.

"Hurts so bad," Franklin gasped out. "My belly, oh!"

Jerome saw his knee had opened the outlaw's stomach wound. He leaned forward and shook Franklin by the shoulders.

"What are the Benjamins up to? What do they intend to rob? The train? A stage? When? Where?"

Franklin lay limp under him. Jerome rocked back and stared at the man's pasty white face. All blood had drained from it.

Jerome held up his fists and stared at them. He had beaten a man to death. His skinned knuckles oozed blood.

"I only wanted to find out what they intended to do," he said numbly.

He swung his leg off the body and started to stand. Movement gave him a fraction-of-a-second warning.

He had played possum to lure Franklin close enough to attack. The outlaw had done the same thing, only he wrapped his fingers around his fallen rifle and jerked back on the trigger.

Jerome winced as the slug took his derby from his head. He fell away, kicking and trying to disarm Franklin. The man tried to sit up and couldn't. Blood gushed from his belly. That much had been real. He wasn't able to sit up because of his reopened wound. But he didn't have to. He had a rifle. Another round sang along its deadly path. It missed Jerome, too.

Stretching and diving, he landed across the end of the log. He grabbed the six-shooter he had dropped and rolled around to sit hard on the ground, the log at his back. Both hands gripped the six-gun to steady it.

He swung around, ready to continue the fight. Franklin had disappeared.

"I'll get you help. I'll see that the doctor in town fixes you up," Jerome shouted.

His words rang through the forest. Not a sound came back to tell him where Franklin was hiding.

"I don't want to see you dead. You can tell me what the gang's planning. Then I'll let you go. It doesn't matter what laws you've broken. I'll let you go. I'm not a lawman, and I have no desire to be around them."

Jerome dropped to his belly and wiggled like a snake across the camp. Here and there he saw muddy lumps where Franklin had left behind his life's blood to mingle with the dirt. The farther he crawled, the bigger the gory clods were. Throwing caution to the wind, he clambered to his feet and found the outlaw propped against a tree. He hadn't gotten too far in his escape.

"Tell me what I want to know about Henry and Leland," Jerome demanded. He shook Franklin.

The man's eyes slowly opened. Franklin's lips moved, but no sound came out. Then he heaved a shudder and died. Jerome sat back on his heels and stared at the dead body.

He had no idea how to find out the Benjamins' plans now. None.

CHAPTER EIGHTEEN

Jerome rode slowly into town, Franklin's horse trailing him. He had buried the man some distance from the outlaws' camp, hoping the Benjamins wouldn't find the grave. The last thing he wanted was to spook them. He had ridden in the medicine wagon through far too many towns, traveled too many miles, put up with so many fools — he wasn't about to start all over tracking the two brothers. With everything going wrong for the gang, they'd likely pick a spot on the map and ride for it.

Montana. California. Nevada. Alaska.

He was close to meting out justice. Jerome wanted to finish it here and now. He was tired and didn't know how much longer he could continue this life.

The Red Ruby was packed, and Molly was belting out a bawdy song. He smiled, just a little, hearing her voice. Then the small pleasure disappeared when Bear stepped out onto the boardwalk and spotted him.

"Perfesser!" the bounty hunter yelled, waving a log-like arm at him. "Why'd you up and leave me out there?"

Jerome painfully dismounted. He wasn't a horseman and preferred driving his wagon. It wasn't as hard on his legs and hindquarters.

"You headed in the wrong direction," he answered.

"You been out horse thievin'?" Bear examined the horse that had belonged to Franklin.

Jerome quickly explained what he had been through and ended with "If I'm going to find them, it'll take a miracle. When the gang gets back to that camp and Franklin is missing, they'll think he's hightailed it."

"Or is off somewhere turnin' them in for the reward," Bear said, rubbing his bearded chin. "That's the first thing I'd think."

"I got a good look at Franklin's partner but don't know who he is or where he went. For all I know, he's here in Clear Springs. Or galloping away as fast as his horse can take him."

Jerome considered that. The outlaw hadn't looked as if he was headed for the high country. He left, maybe with a destination in mind. And a mission. He was excited maybe, but it was the anticipation of some-thing going right, not wrong.

"Come on into the saloon and you can buy me a drink," Bear said. "It's the least you can do after runnin' out on me."

Jerome was too tired to argue. He had been right; the bounty hunter had been wrong. It was simple enough, and Bear was never going to admit it. Jerome wondered how good a tracker Bear really was. The times they had been on the trail of Benja-mins, he hadn't shown all that much skill. He was a good man to have at your back in a fight, but his skills as a trailsman were lacking.

But someone whose skills weren't lacking performed onstage. Molly switched from singing to dancing. Jerome stood on tiptoe, but the crowd blocked his view. He saw the top of her head bouncing about. He closed his eyes and imagined what she was reveal-ing to the crowd from the way they hooted and hollered.

"Set yourself down. I'll get a bottle. I've worked up a powerful thirst." Bear held out his hand.

It took Jerome a second to realize what the man wanted. He fished out a couple sweat-soaked greenbacks and gave them to the bounty hunter.

While he waited at a table near the door, he stared at the backs of the heads of the crowd. The horde of customers meant the Red Ruby was doing land office business. He wondered who would pocket the money since the owner was dead and the barkeep had loaded up a buckboard with a couple cases of whiskey and probably stuffed his pockets with all the money from the till. It didn't matter to him, but he wanted Molly to get her fair share for generating so much business. Other saloons in town had to be deserted with so many cowboys jammed in here.

"Good booze," Bear said, pulling up a chair.

He put a half full bottle on the table between them and dropped glasses. From the way he slurred his words, he had already started drinking heavily from the bottle.

"Just what I need," Jerome said, knocking back a shot.

He dropped the glass to the table with a click and poured himself another. As he did, he felt a tingle creep up his spine. What caused it became obvious when he caught a reflection in the whiskey bottle.

Turning slightly, he saw Franklin's partner at the back of the crowd. The man hopped onto a chair to get a better look at Molly's show. Jerome felt invisible as long as the lovely woman performed.

"Him," he said softly to Bear. "He's the one who was out in camp. Franklin's partner."

"He got a reward on his head?" Bear squinted as he looked over the back of the crowd. "Which one? They all look like road agents to me."

"I don't know if he has reward on his head, but he can take us to the Benjamins, and they do."

"I'll whup him good and force him to talk." Bear started to stand, but Jerome pulled him back.

"There's another way more likely to work," he said.

His tired brain flared like the morning sun as the idea built. The more he thought on it, the more he liked it.

"Shootin' him down won't do us no good," Bear said. "Besides, it'd interrupt the missus' show."

Jerome blinked. It took a second for him to realize Bear meant Molly. He started to argue the legality of any marriage, then pushed it aside. He needed to focus. He needed to convince Bear to do something insanely dangerous.

"Get in good with him. The gang's hunting for more gunmen. Whatever robbery they're planning needs four or five guns. If you don't recognize that desperado, he's not likely to know who you are."

"Ever'body knows me," Bear said boastfully.

"You've been in the area for a month or two and made a reputation here in Clear Springs."

"As much because of my wife as anything I've done. Pickings have been slim and me and the marshal never got along too good." Bear knocked back another drink and belched. "I know why now. He was as crooked as a dog's hind leg. A thief like Bishop'd know instinctively to hate an honest man like me. Hell, I did his job for him!"

"Cozy up to him. I don't know his name, but if he recognizes you, don't deny it. Tell him you're not making enough off the bounty hunting and want to earn some quick money."

"I'm makin' plenty!" Bear half rose from the chair, furious. "I'm the best bounty hunter in all of North Texas. Maybe all of Texas."

"You're going to go undercover so you can catch them all. The reward on four or five train robbers has to be a lot more than for just one."

"Me, acting? Just like Molly does . . . only I wouldn't be onstage?"

"Yes, that," Jerome said. "Be yourself, get in with the gang. Then we can catch them all. *You* can capture them for the reward."

Bear thought it over. Such heavy cogitation required a couple more shots of tarantula juice. Everything finally came together in his head. He nodded slowly in appreciation of such a fine plan.

"I can do it. I can lie enough to get 'em to trust me. Then!"

He whipped out a Colt, cocked it and started to fire it into the ceiling. Jerome grabbed the bounty hunter's wrist and stopped him. Bear growled, then smiled sheepishly.

"I forgot for a minute. Get in with them first, then start shooting."

"If you have to plug a couple of them, don't hesitate," Jerome said, "but save Henry and Leland Benjamin for me."

His tiredness evaporated, burned off by memory and rage at what they had done to his family. Curtis Benjamin had admitted his part. The Benjamin brothers would confess before he was done with them, too.

"Finding what them varmints is up to will be a chore," Bear said. He slurred his words from too much liquor downed too fast.

Jerome started to keep him from downing another shot, then stopped. Creating a scene now served no purpose, and Bear wasn't one to take kindly to another's suggestion. When it came to sobriety, he'd be even less inclined to agree to being a teetotaler.

"Get to their camp once you've won his confidence," Jerome said. He forced himself not to look at the road agent. "How will you get back to tell me where they are and what they're intending to do?"

"I'm smart. I'll find a way." Bear shoved himself to his feet, grabbed the bottle, which still had a couple fingers' worth of booze in it, and staggered to the outlaw's table.

Again, Jerome forced himself not to look. Bear's broad back blotted out the view of their target. The bounty hunter waved his arms around, took a swig from the bottle, then plunked it down on the table. He sank into a chair and leaned forward to have a more intimate conversation. The raucous cries from Molly's audience made any such talk difficult. Jerome knew they'd leave the saloon soon enough, no matter how successful Bear was.

Either the outlaw bought it that the bounty hunter wanted to throw in with the gang or he saw through the lie. In that case, Bear's body would be found somewhere else. In the alley behind the gin mill, on the trail outside town, somewhere.

Dead.

Jerome didn't want to dwell on the possibility of failure. He left before Bear and headed for the Butterfield office.

He poked his head inside and looked around. Purcell sat propped up with pillows with the telegraph key on the table in front of him. He stared at the device as if it might jump up and run away.

"Are you dead yet?" Jerome asked when the telegrapher didn't acknowledge him standing in the doorway.

"Workin' on it," Leon Purcell said. Only his lips moved.

Jerome leaned on the counter and studied Purcell. The man's pallor had worsened. Before, he had been husky. Now his clothing hung on him like a scarecrow's. When the key began chattering, he reached for a pencil to record the incoming telegram. His hand shook hard.

"Can't the company get you some help?"

"Depot agent, yeah, but nobody else in town knows code. This brings in more money than the stage these days. Won't be long before Clear Springs dries up and blows away."

"Like Chagrin?"

"Like most all towns without a train dumping ash on their heads. I already heard two or three merchants talkin' 'bout moving to San Angelo. Marshal Bishop being such a lowlife hasn't helped matters much, either. There's quite a stigma livin' in a town run by a crook."

"When the bank goes, the town will follow," Jerome said. "Don't go anywhere."

He smiled at the likelihood of Purcell doing more than standing as he went to his medicine wagon and hunted through the herbs and potions in the back. He mixed up some with medicinal value, added a healthy dose of alcohol and shook it up in a bottle.

He started to return to the stage office, then remembered he had to fortify himself some. A swig of his usual potion burned all the way down and joined the rotgut he had swilled in the Red Ruby. Mental fog burned away, and his aches seemed less annoying. Then he found a drawer in a small cabinet where a dozen more knives rested. Transferring the blades to empty sheaths took a while, but he wasn't in any hurry.

Purcell wasn't, either.

Jerome went back into the depot after donning a set of clean clothes and put the bottle of special elixir on the counter.

315

"This'll help build up your blood and make some of your wounds heal a mite faster. It won't cure you, but it'll speed you on the road to recovery."

"You really know these things?" Purcell turned dead eyes in Jerome's direction.

"I do."

He detailed how he had worked as an apothecary. Once he had hit the trail hunting the Benjamin family, he had talked with more than one Indian shaman. When more than one from different tribes agreed on a particular treatment, he investigated their remedies. The consensus rested in the bottle he gave to Purcell.

"I never put much store in the claims of medicine shows," Purcell said. "Didn't stop me from buyin' a bottle or two. My bosses always complained when I drank on duty, but never if I swilled from a bottle filled with a magic potion." Purcell smiled and even laughed a little. It sounded like a death rattle. "Truth is, they sucked up the snake oil themselves in front of customers who disapproved of drinking."

"Those very people likely bought a bottle themselves," Jerome said.

Purcell nodded slowly. He levered himself to his feet, ripped off the top sheet of a notepad and made his way to the counter to try

Jerome's medicine.

"Only a tablespoon's worth at a time," Jerome cautioned. "Every couple hours."

"The way I feel, more medicine than that'd do me in for certain sure." Purcell sampled the liquid and made a face. "Got to work real good. It tastes terrible."

Jerome said nothing about that. He hadn't added bitters to trick people into thinking it was effective medicine. This actually tasted bad and would have been worse without the tincture in it.

"I need to know if there's a big shipment due anytime soon," he asked.

Purcell looked up, startled. "What do you know?"

"The Benjamin brothers are planning a major robbery. They're recruiting gunmen right now for something they can't pull off by themselves."

"I haven't heard a danged thing," Purcell said. "Maybe they're not tellin' me, though. Things haven't gone well in these parts."

He reached for the medicine bottle with his shaking hand. Jerome stopped him and passed over another bottle of the heavily laced alcohol potion.

"Try this between sips of the other. And there's no talk of a payroll or gold or any valuables being shipped?"

Purcell shook his head.

"Thanks," Jerome said. "Anything else I can do for you?"

"Deliver this 'gram," the telegrapher said, pushing the sheet of paper with his crabbed writing on it toward Jerome. "It goes to the bank."

Jerome glanced at it and let out a deep sigh. More proof Clear Springs was slowly dying. The telegram replied to an offer to buy its assets by a San Angelo bank. In a month or two, all the mortgages in the Clear Springs area would belong to an absentee landlord.

"I'll deliver it first thing when the bank opens," Jerome said.

Purcell took both bottles and returned to his post by the telegraph key. In seconds he assumed the posture that looked as if he was more dead than alive.

Jerome stepped out onto the main street and quickly backpedaled, using shadows from the depot to hide him as Bear and his newfound friend rode past. They exchanged lies, neither really hearing what the other said. Jerome took that as a sign the bounty hunter had been accepted as one of the gang.

He felt the itch to follow. But that wasn't part of the plan. Bear would find out what they needed to know and get him the information. Then he'd join the party — the shoot-out.

Jerome worried what might go wrong, then hiked to the Red Ruby to find Molly. She had finished her last show of the night.

CHAPTER NINETEEN

"I've never had this much money before," Molly Davenport said, jiggling a large leather pouch. "It makes me nervous carrying it around. You know the kind of people around Clear Springs as well as I do."

Jerome was sorry he had told her about the telegram he had delivered two days earlier. The bank was in jeopardy of not only being bought out but also having all its assets drained by the purchaser. Jerome had heard of this being done repeatedly when a railroad bypassed a town and left nothing worthwhile behind. The ranches and farms in the area contributed to the Clear Springs bank, but they could as easily work with what was a larger bank in San Angelo.

"If the new owners don't foreclose on them all," he said dourly.

"What are you going on about, Jerome?"

"I've seen it more than once," he told her. "A bank's sold and the new owner sucks it dry, then walks away. Imagine the San Angelo bank foreclosing on all the ranches around here."

"It's time to move on," she said, nodding. "To San Angelo?" Then in a smaller voice, she added, "After we hear from Bear."

He watched the play of emotions on her pretty face. She denied being married to the bounty hunter, but even if she wasn't, she felt something for him.

"If you want to go on, take the wagon. I'll wait for Bear's message."

"I don't cotton much to driving a rig like this. It can get away from a new driver." Molly grasped at straws to keep from taking Jerome's suggestion.

Jerome laughed. "The horse hitched up to the rig's as gentle as they come. Getting it to move at all is harder than stopping it."

"I need to repaint the sign on the side. You said it was too risqué."

" 'Risqué'? Did you dig up that word to describe your act at the Red Ruby?"

"It's a French word. It's classy. And you're the one who told me families'd never buy your potion with such a racy drawing bannered on the side. It'll take me a week maybe to find the paint and decide what to take out. Besides, another week at the saloon will fix us up just fine, no matter where we go."

Jerome started to ask about her using "we" when it came to their next destination. He wasn't sure how he felt having her alongside him in the driver's box.

"Bear can hunt for men with wanted posters just about anywhere," she went on. "He's not very good at it, so what's the difference? If he's made more than a hundred dollars on any crook he's brought in, it'd surprise me. And he's not skilled enough to track down the really bad ones. You've been with him and seen how he follows a trail."

"Or doesn't," Jerome said glumly.

The more Molly rambled on, the less he liked it. He was of two minds about letting her come along with him. Putting up with Bear as well was out of the question.

"Yes, exactly," she said. "He doesn't do a good job of it at all."

She hummed a snippet of a song, then said brightly, "He'd be better off if he worked in a place like Clear Springs as a law dog. Drunks'd take one look at him and surrender. He enjoys a good fight. How much trouble can he get into when the whole town's peaceable?"

Jerome liked this idea. Let Bear preside over a dying town. By the time Clear Springs was nothing more than a saloon and a feed store, Professor J. Frederick Kincannon's Traveling Apothecary and Medicine Show could be a hundred miles away. Farther. Much farther. The notion of going north to Idaho appealed to him because he'd never been there. Or out to the Pacific Ocean. People telling of so much water had to be exaggerating. He wanted to see for himself.

"He said you'd pay me a dollar."

Jerome jerked around, hand going to the holster at his side. The Jenkins boy had walked up on him so quietly, he had never heard so much as a whisper.

"Who're you talking about? Purcell?"

"Not him. Mr. Purcell's got one foot in the grave, even after that fancy medicine you whupped up for him." The boy made a face. "That stuff tasted awful."

"You shouldn't have sampled it," Jerome said. "But if you're not talking about Purcell —"

"Bear!" Molly jumped down from the wagon, grabbed the boy by the shoulders and shook him until his teeth clacked. "Do you have a message from Bear?"

"Who else?" The boy tried to push away from the woman, but she clung to him as if afraid he'd run off. "Stop shaking me. Stop it, Miss Molly. Unless you mean to kiss me again." The boy actually blushed when he

323

said that.

Jerome removed her hands from the Jenkins boy's shoulders and asked, "Where'd you get the message?"

"From him. The bounty hunter. I spotted him skulking around outside town 'fore dawn. He said you'd pay me if I gave you this."

He pulled a stained, tattered scrap of newsprint from his pocket and tried to hold it out of Jerome's reach.

Molly was too quick for him. She snatched it and held the paper up to the light.

"What's it say?" Jerome asked the question but wasn't sure who'd answer.

The Jenkins boy had read it. Not doing so would have violated his personal code of behavior. He prided himself on knowing everything that went on in town. But Molly scowled as she deciphered the smudged lettering.

"Bear can't write. This is printed and not very well. 'He's where you said,' " she told Jerome. "What's that mean? Do you —"

"I know where he means. What else?"

"There's a date —"

"Today," the boy broke in.

"It looks like he wrote 'Big Rock.' I have no idea what that means," Molly said, distraught.

"The Big Rock is a place," the boy said. "I can show you."

"You can tell me," Jerome insisted.

He pulled a silver dollar from his pocket. He moved just far enough to keep the boy from snatching it out of his fingers.

"If I tell you, you won't pay me."

"Yes, he will," Molly said. "I'll make him."

The boy looked at her and pursed his lips as he considered it.

"I promise," Jerome said, feeling time pressing in on him. Bear had written this a day earlier from the look of the article on the torn margin.

"Promise," the boy said. "A deal?"

He spat on his palm and shoved out his hand. Jerome looked at the gob already caked in mud, then duplicated the spit and shook.

"Big Rock is about five miles outside town along the main road. It's off to the south just before you reach that forest. There are three rocks that look like they're stacked on top of one another, only they're stuck together."

"I remember seeing them," Jerome said.

He had ridden past the rock formation on his way back to town. The forest the boy mentioned was the stand of scrub oaks where he had tracked Franklin.

325

"They haven't struck camp," Molly said breathlessly.

The Jenkins boy said nothing. His eyes locked with Jerome's like a hungry snake watching a bird. Those eyes followed the spinning silver arc of the silver dollar. Hands quicker than they had any right to be grabbed the coin and made it disappear.

"Thanks, Professor." The boy started to leave, looked at Molly, then back over his shoulder at Jerome. "If she wasn't here, you would have cheated me, wouldn't you?"

"You figure it out," Jerome said. "Now skedaddle."

The boy laughed and ran off, ducking under the top rail of the Butterfield corral and running to the far side. In seconds he was nowhere to be seen.

"What a confidence man," Molly muttered.

"Bear's alive and something is going to happen at the Big Rock around noon," Jerome said. "It can only be one thing."

He marched into the depot and called to Purcell.

The telegrapher sat in the same position as the last time Jerome had seen him. He turned and smiled slightly. After so much loss of weight, his face looked more like a skull than a living human's, but he had a touch of pink in his cheeks now, and he moved with more assurance.

"I feel better," he said. "That nostrum is fixin' me up slow but sure, Perfesser."

"When does the stage leave today?"

"About the usual time. It'll pull out around eleven. Why're you askin'?"

Jerome performed the numbers in his head. The stage would reach the Big Rock around noon.

"What's the stage carrying? Gold? Something else? Maybe money from the bank being sent to San Angelo?"

"I . . . I don't know anything 'bout any of that," Purcell said. "What aren't you tellin' me?"

"What aren't your bosses telling you?" Jerome countered. "I want to ride along."

"You're plumb loco, Perfesser. This isn't anything to get mixed up in, especially after you talked me into helpin' out with that train robbery. It's not like you're a lawman. I surely am not one." Purcell looked off into space and shook his head. "Then again, you might as well be John Law, you killin' Marshal Bishop and all."

"If I have to, I'll buy a ticket," Jerome said.

"You got no call to do that," Purcell said. "Mix me up more of this medicine and for free you can ride to hell, which is a likely destination." Purcell mumbled something, then said louder, "There's nothin' valuable scheduled to be shipped on that stage, but you'd best think twice if you let Miss Molly go with you."

"She's staying here in town."

"Good. Robbin' everyone of her singin' and dancin' talents would be downright criminal."

Purcell fingered the almost empty bottle of medicine, then held it up to be sure Jerome saw how little remained of the original dose.

Jerome ducked back outside and hopped into the wagon to conjure up more of the medicine. As he worked, he wrote down the ingredients, just in case. He'd expected the elixir to work for Purcell, but not as well as it had. The Butterfield agent was hardly the picture of health after downing most of the first batch, but he had taken a step back from the grave. If he kept improving at this rate, in a week or two, he'd need field glasses to see that grave.

Molly poked her head in from the driver's box. "When you finish whatever you're doing, come over to the saloon. I need some help nailing up the scenery. A corner tore free and makes for a terrible look while I'm performing."

"More medicine for Purcell. It'll take a while longer. Get the new barkeep to help you. From the way he ogles you, he'd walk over broken glass if you asked. I'll be along when I can."

Jerome pointedly focused on his preparations and did not look at Molly. He wanted to get on the stage and be out of town before she realized it.

"What are you going to do about Bear?"

"He can take care of himself."

"Be careful, Jerome. Please." She reached back and lightly touched his arm. Then she slipped away.

He heaved a sigh of relief. She knew where he was going and hadn't made a fuss about it. With a few quick shakes, he dissolved the dried herbs in the tincture and stuffed a cork in the bottle. Then he checked to be sure that his pockets were weighted down with spare ammo and that he carried knives in all the hidden sheaths. He settled the gun belt strapped around his waist.

The sound of a stagecoach out front made him complete his inventory in a hurry.

He raced through the depot, put the medicine on the counter and said, "This will be over soon."

Purcell made a vague gesture. Then Jerome burst outside and jumped to catch the door into the stage compartment as it swung shut. He dropped onto the hard seat and leaned back. No passengers. Just the guard and the driver. And J. Frederick Kincannon. He checked his six-shooter and patted the spots where sheaths held his knives to reassure himself he was as ready as possible for what was to come.

Almost a year had passed, and now the moment of truth was at hand. The Benjamin brothers, the pair remaining, would be brought to justice. *He* would bring them to justice.

Jerome bounced around in the passenger compartment for almost an hour, the anticipation unbearable by the time the stage struggled up a steep hill. Then the driver called out, "Whoa!"

Jerome drew his six-shooter and prepared to fight.

"Stay inside," the guard called down. "There's somethin' strange ahead."

"We're going to be held up," Jerome said. "I got word that it'll be near the Big Rock. Are we close?"

"To Big Rock? Reckon so, but that ain't what's spooking us."

Jerome stood on the coach step and studied the terrain for any sign of attack. This stretch looked familiar. The Benjamins' camp wasn't more than two miles off.

"What do you see?" he called to the guard.

"I ain't gonna go no closer," the man vowed. "There's coyote tracks all over the place. That means something's died and not too long ago."

Jerome stepped from the compartment and cocked his six-gun. The guard looked ahead and to the right off the road. Jerome started walking slowly, every sense straining. He heard nothing and saw only treetops until he found a spot that gave him the elevation to look far enough ahead to see it.

It. What had been a man. He forced himself to look away from the crucified body. The outlaws wanted him to stare so his attention wasn't focused on an ambush. But the area around the cross erected beside the road was barren of life.

"You stay away," the driver called.

"If anything moves out there, take a shot at it," Jerome said. He worried the guard might shoot him in the back, but he had to get closer.

As if he mounted a gallows for his own hanging, he walked the twenty yards off the road to stand at the base of the wooden cross where Bear hung, arms outstretched. Jerome's gorge rose. He held back enough to keep from vomiting. The bounty hunter had been skinned and then lashed to the cross member. Crows had been at work. And the guard's eyes had been sharp to spot all the coyote tracks at the base of the cross.

All that had saved Bear from further dismemberment was the height above the ground. Coyotes weren't able to jump and take a nip of the man's flesh above his knees.

"They're sending a powerful message," the guard said, standing beside Jerome now. "I got through a dozen skirmishes with the Comanche and never saw anything to equal this."

"There's nothing valuable on the stage, is there?" he asked.

"We was told to be a decoy. Whatever's being sent up to San Angelo's in the back of a buckboard and left a couple hours before us along a different road." The guard spat. "I would never have come along if I'd knowed I'd see something like this."

"Decoyed," Jerome said. "That's what they did to me. Lured me out here."

He hunted for any sign they had intended an ambush. He knew if he hiked far enough into the woods and found the gang's camp, it'd be abandoned.

"Can't leave him danglin' that way," the guard said, "but there's no way we're takin' him back to town. Or ahead to San Angelo.

Ain't no way I'm touchin' that body."

Jerome understood the man's reluctance and worked by himself to dig a grave in the loamy ground behind the cross. The ground was soft, but all he had to dig with were a stick and a flat stone. Eventually he completed the task. Together he and the two Butterfield employees upended the cross and let it fall backward toward the grave. Jerome cut Bear's body free and rolled him into the grave. The other two men helped fill it back in, anxious to be done with the distasteful chore and eager to get on their way.

"We should put a marker on the grave," the driver said. "It's only fitting."

Jerome dragged the cross where Bear had hung for hours and laid it atop the earthen mound.

"That'll do him just fine."

"Seems fitting, I suppose," the guard said.

Then he and the driver started arguing about where to go as they walked back to the stagecoach. The driver wanted to return to Clear Springs and the guard insisted that they press on. From the way he spoke, he intended to quit when they got to San Angelo.

Jerome stared down at the grave. He hadn't much liked Bear, but the bounty hunter had deserved better. Almost running, he overtook the two and put in his vote to return to Clear Springs.

CHAPTER TWENTY

Jerome sat on the drop-down stage and stared at . . . nothing. He had chased off the Jenkins boy and refused to talk to Purcell. In some dark corner of his brain, he realized the Butterfield agent was recovering well and didn't need any more of his expert medicinal concoctions. The agent walked around with a sure step and had color in his cheeks. A few extra pounds would round out his gaunt features, but none of this made Jerome feel one whit better.

He had ridden back with the stage driver and guard. The two had spent close to an hour with Purcell, sending off telegrams to the regional office and every lawman they knew within a hundred-mile radius. Jerome wasn't the least bit curious what they had put in those reports.

Bear was dead. His death was grisly and exactly the reason the Benjamin brothers had to be brought to justice.

"Killed," he muttered to himself.

Nothing less would do. There wasn't a marshal in town anymore and going all the way to San Angelo to report what had happened to Bishop was only going to frustrate him more. Purcell had suggested a telegram to the nearest company of Texas Rangers. Jerome knew the Benjamin gang would be long gone by the time a Ranger could be sent. Such a request had to be approved by the governor. There wasn't even a sheriff in the county to enlist.

Both driver and guard had looked at him as if he'd been in the sun too long when he suggested organizing a posse. No one in Clear Springs had cared that much for Bear. He had been loud and obnoxious and a bully. As guilty as Jerome felt about sending Bear into that den of rattlers, he felt even more guilt because he wasn't all that sorry to see him go.

"Just not like that."

"Like what?"

Molly Davenport came up and stared at him. She had been crying. Tears running down her cheeks had left streaks in her thick stage makeup.

"It wasn't supposed to work out like this," he said. He held back his own tears. Then anger burned away the drops welling in his eyes. "He was supposed to get word to me, and we were going to take down the gang together."

"He was a loudmouth," Molly said, her voice cracking with emotion. "He said something that gave him away."

"Or maybe they recognized him for what he was and knew he was interested only in the rewards on them," Jerome said.

He didn't discount the possibility that they had known his real intentions from the instant Bear sat down in the saloon.

Molly fished around in a clutch purse and pulled out a thick wad of paper. She thrust it out. He took it hesitantly, then leafed through the pages. He blinked in surprise.

"There *were* posters out on them," he said. "Bishop lied." He sagged. "Of course he lied. He was in cahoots with them. If he had told me about the wanted posters, he'd have been ratting out his partners."

"I found the posters in his top desk drawer. Bishop hid them away so nobody ever saw them."

"Franklin was recruited in town. The one who rode out with Bear was, too. The Benjamins probably came and went as they pleased. Nobody noticed because the marshal shielded them."

"They cut a wide swath through the countryside," Molly said. "Yorick's place must have been where they stopped to do serious drinking rather than hang out in Clear Springs, maybe because Bear was here."

Jerome clenched his fists. Curtis Benjamin had died because of what he had done out at Yorick's Outpost. If only Henry and Leland had been with him, all three would have been pushing up daisies now.

"I'm sorry, Molly," he said. "I should have gone instead of Bear."

"It'd be you buried out there," she said. Her tone hardened. "It was a foolish plan. There wasn't any way to ever pull the wool over the eyes of suspicious, evil men like them."

She swung her hand in a wide arc. The wanted posters scattered all around. She started to say something more, but Purcell called from the depot.

"I'll be right back," Jerome said, "after I find what he wants. For him to come fetch me, it must be important."

"Important," Molly sighed. "Go on. You do what you have to do, and I will, too."

Jerome started to ask what she meant by that, but Purcell became more insistent. With a hop, he hit the ground and went to talk with the Butterfield agent.

"I got a 'gram for you. Come on. You got to read it."

Purcell tugged on his coat sleeve. Jerome relented and followed him into the depot office filled with its noxious vapors.

"What is it?"

Jerome felt torn between listening to what Purcell had to say and trying to find the words to comfort Molly. She knew exactly what Bear had been and somehow still felt an attachment to him. They hadn't been married nor did Jerome think she loved the bounty hunter, but there was something more than tolerance or even friendship there.

"While you were out decoying the gang, they hit the real shipment. The bank's closing for good and transferred all its assets to San Angelo on a secret wagon."

"It was stolen," Jerome said, scanning down the page Purcell had handed him.

"My boss wants to know if you are one of the gang. It surely does look as if you kept two of our employees occupied so they weren't able to support the secret shipment."

"Bear had been killed hours before we got there. He did something to make them suspicious. If he hadn't, catching them in their camp would have ended all the thievery."

"Well, now, Perfesser, the district Butterfield director is filing a report with the Rangers sayin' you was in on the robbery. If I was you, I'd hightail it out of Clear Springs and head for the tall and uncut."

"Anywhere else but here," Jerome said, disconsolate.

"That's the way I see it."

"Running off will make me look even guiltier."

Jerome crumpled the telegram and savagely threw it as hard as he could. Like everything else he tried, this was only partly successful. The telegram sailed a few feet, caught a breeze and fluttered fitfully to the floor. Even slamming a wad of paper against the wall was denied him.

"Better lookin' guilty than standin' trial and bein' found guilty. You've done right by me, Perfesser. You really have. In spite of you bein' the one what got me all shot up, you're the only soul who's tried to bring those owlhoots to bay."

"If I had succeeded, I'd be richer by the rewards offered for them." Jerome remembered the wanted posters Molly had flashed in front of him. "Close to a thousand dollars each."

"That much? They have been busy boys," Purcell said. "I got to sit down. My legs aren't up to holdin' me upright like they used to be."

He hooked a foot around a chair leg and pulled it under him as he collapsed in front of the telegraph key. Before he said any more, the dots and dashes of a new message filled the office.

Jerome left Purcell to his work and stepped out back. Molly was nowhere to be seen. His heart jumped into his throat. He scrambled into the rear of the wagon. All her belongings were gone. Jerome felt as empty inside as the drawers and compartments of the medicine wagon where she had stored her clothing.

He left the wagon and headed for the only place the woman would have gone. At midday the Red Ruby was almost entirely empty. A few merchants finished their lunches before heading back to work. Jerome's belly flip-flopped at the sight of the tough beef sandwiches and pigs' knuckles that had been served today. Not even the beer appealed to him at the moment.

With quick twists he made his way through the closely spaced tables to the stage. Before he jumped up, the barkeep called out, "She doesn't want to see you."

"I need to talk to her."

Jerome froze when he heard the metallic click of a hammer being drawn back. The echo in the vast, empty room magnified until he conjured up the image of a weapon with a bore the size of a howitzer being aimed at him. Jerome turned slowly. The barkeep had a double-barreled shotgun trained on him.

"I don't want to pull the triggers, but she told me to let you have it with both barrels if you bothered her."

"She's in the back?"

"There's a room where she's staying now. It makes things convenient. She doesn't have to go back to your wagon to change for her show." The barkeep hefted the shotgun to his shoulder. "You need to leave, Professor."

Jerome's feet turned to lead. He stared down the bores of the shotgun. If he'd been trapped in a train tunnel with an approaching locomotive, it would have felt the same.

"Git. Now!" The barkeep hoisted the shotgun and discharged one barrel into the ceiling. A rain of wood and plaster cascaded down.

Jerome should have used the momentary dust cloud to duck behind the curtain and poke around backstage to find Molly. But his feet. And his legs. They were as numb as his brain.

"The next one's for you, Professor. Don't make me shoot. I don't want to clean up the mess you'd make all splattered on the back wall."

The practicality of that lament jarred Jerome enough to shuffle out of the Red Ruby. He felt the weapon trained on him all the way into the street. When a puff of air from inside carried the heavy smoke outward around him, he came out of his daze. He took a deep whiff of the gun smoke from the single discharge and choked. A grim resolve filled him. He marched back to his medicine wagon and began working on a new concoction.

By dawn Jerome had two large glass bottles filled with a greenish gas. He tapped the sides and assured himself the glass walls were thin enough to break unless he was especially careful. With quick, sure movements, he wrapped both bottles in strips torn from a wool blanket and settled them, one on each side, in his coat pockets.

He touched his six-gun resting in its holster, then pushed it away. Five knives rested in their hiding places along his forearms, fitted into the tails of his coat and one in a sheath depended around his neck to press against his spine.

The sun poked above the horizon when he entered the Butterfield office. Purcell slept, head resting on his arms beside the telegraph key. Jerome rapped on the counter loudly enough to awaken the agent.

Purcell stared at him wide-eyed, then said, "You're not part of my nightmare. Well, you are, but I'm not dreamin' now, am I?"

"I want a ticket on the next stage fixing to leave."

Jerome glanced out the front door. The team nervously tugged against the harnesses, making the driver work to keep them calm.

"There's nothin' but a couple passengers on the stage."

From the way Purcell spoke, Jerome knew he lied. Something more valuable was in the driver's box. He didn't call the agent on the untruth.

"I'm leaving town."

Purcell swallowed hard. "Maybe you could take a different stage. One tomorrow?"

"Are you selling me the ticket?"

"Go on, Perfesser. Compliments of Butterfield. I'll settle accounts with the driver."

Jerome nodded curtly, then went out front. Two men already sat inside the compartment. He sized them up fast enough.

One was a gambler he had seen several times plying his trade at the Red Ruby. The other was well enough dressed but obviously a cowboy. Jerome figured he was a rancher heading to San Angelo now that the local bank had closed.

"Gentlemen," he said, climbing in. He settled down next to the rancher, facing the gambler.

"You created quite a stir, sir, if I may say so," the gambler said. "The whole town's abuzz with your . . . departure. It surprises me you chose this stage rather than driving your wagon."

"I sold it," Jerome said. "It's time for me to find other pursuits."

"From gossip that raged all night long, that is wise. Tracking down such dangerous outlaws is a job for a seasoned lawman, not a —"

"Snake oil peddler," Jerome finished for him. "I'm not offended. That is, after all, what I did for the past year."

"That and get a snootful of booze," the rancher said.

Jerome looked at him but said nothing.

"You were off drinking away your sorrow last night, weren't you? Your gal friend spurned you and your best friend died because of your ridiculous scheme." The gambler sounded smug, full of himself and certain he knew everything bedeviling Jerome.

"You heard all that last night?"

The gambler nodded and preened, smoothing out the errant hairs in his mustache.

"I must say you look in good shape for a man who spent the night on a solitary bender," the rancher said with some distaste.

"Practice makes perfect," Jerome said.

He was tossed about as the driver snapped his whip and the stage rolled away from the Butterfield depot. Talking over the rattle of the wheels was hard. Jerome crossed his arms and put his chin on his chest, feigning sleep. Not listening to all his supposed failings suited him fine, in spite of being bounced about like a rock in a Mason jar.

Jerome actually dozed in spite of the rough ride but came awake instantly when the driver snapped his whip repeatedly to spur the team to a full gallop. He pushed aside the leather curtain and looked across the Texas prairie. He craned his neck and caught sight of three riders waving six-shooters around as they pursued the stage.

"We're being robbed," Jerome said. For a moment, he regretted leaving his six-gun back in the medicine wagon.

"We shoulda thrown him out back in town," the rancher grumbled. "He's nothing but bad luck."

Jerome watched the man draw his six-gun and check to be sure it was loaded. The gambler stuck his arm out straight. A spring mechanism snapped a derringer into his grip.

"We can outrun them," the gambler said with some confidence. "If it comes to shooting it out, we have enough firepower." He scowled when he saw that Jerome wasn't packing an iron. "Or maybe not. It seems it's three against two. That gives the road agents an edge."

"The guard's on our side," the rancher said. "We can —"

A thunder of gunfire sounded. Jerome caught his breath as the guard tumbled past the window and then was left far behind.

The driver began slowing the team's headlong rush. He was surrendering.

That suited Jerome just fine. It was what he wanted. All he had to do was live long enough to face the outlaws.

To face the Benjamin brothers and have it out with them once and for all.

CHAPTER TWENTY-ONE

"Don't," Jerome snapped at the two men preparing to fight. "You'll get yourselves killed."

"You mean you're scared of getting all shot up," the gambler said, sneering at what he thought was cowardice.

Before Jerome could stop him, the man kicked open the door and leaped out. He swung his derringer about wildly, got off a round, then died in a storm of bullets.

"Anyone else in there wanting to taste our lead? Your lives ain't worth a few dollars. And if you think they are, we're willin' to oblige."

To emphasize his point, the road agent blasted a round through the compartment, barely missing Jerome's head.

Jerome switched to the seat opposite the rancher. The man had gone pale under his weather-beaten hide. He touched his six-gun with a shaking hand, then sagged like all his courage had fled. The bullet had done more to convince him of the futility of resisting than anything Jerome said.

"We're coming out. Don't shoot! I'm not armed," Jerome called.

He paused to be certain the rancher left his pistol resting in its holster. When the man dropped his hands to his sides in surrender, Jerome kicked open the door.

"Do it real slow. We got no call to shoot more of you than we already have."

Jerome chanced a look out. Both driver and guard were stretched out on the ground. Since he hadn't heard any more gunfire after the last single shot into the compartment or the multiple shots that had taken the gambler's life, Jerome figured the man had surrendered. Only the passengers presented an obstacle to a quick and bloodless robbery, and the road agents showed that spilling blood was second nature.

He climbed out slowly, keeping his hands in plain sight.

"That one's tellin' the truth, Leland, 'less he has a hideout gun."

Jerome's pulse quickened. The man on horseback in front of him was Leland Benjamin. It had to be! He looked around. A small man with a bandanna mask half pulled down on his face had climbed into the driver's box to keep the team under control. He was too short and scrawny to be one of the Benjamin brothers. That meant the other rider on a sturdy paint might be Henry.

The rancher made his way from the compartment and stood, hands in the air.

"I'll pluck this one's fangs," Leland Benjamin said, riding over and bending down from horseback.

"You be sure the other one's not hiding a gun," Henry Benjamin said. "He looks sneaky."

"I don't have a gun," Jerome said loudly enough for the man in the driver's box to hear. "But I got something real valuable in my coat pockets."

"They are bulgin'," Leland Benjamin said. He was satisfied with tossing the rancher's pistol under the stage out of the way. "Must be something real valuable in there."

As the outlaw reached for the indicated pocket, Jerome acted. He took a deep breath and slammed his hand down hard. Glass shattered and a cloud of oily, noxious yellow-green gas billowed forth. It caught on a breeze and blew into the desperado's face. The mask protected him from sucking much of the gas into his lungs, but it burned at his eyes like acid.

Leland Benjamin screamed and flinched away. Jerome pulled the other bottle from his pocket and threw it at the hooves of Henry Benjamin's horse. A new pillar of poison gas rose and engulfed the horse and its rider. The horse reared, forcing Henry Benjamin to fight to keep his seat.

Eyes watering from the gas and lungs about ready to explode, Jerome jumped at the mounted Leland Benjamin and swung a clumsy haymaker. The blow missed because the road agent shied away, retching and clawing at his eyes. Scrambling to keep his position partly draped over the horse, Jerome punched again. The blow grazed Leland Benjamin's head, knocked off his hat and sent the outlaw reeling.

His horse bucked hard because of the gas and the commotion. Jerome landed hard on the ground, staring up at flashing hooves only inches from his face.

"What's goin' on?" the road agent atop the stage called.

The rancher let out a yelp and fumbled about for the gun Leland had tossed under the stage. He groped about, found it and tried to shoot, but he was blinded by Jerome's gas. Two rounds sailed off into the air, never coming close to a worthwhile target.

Jerome blinked furiously to make his eyes water and rid them of the gas. He reached behind, found his coattails with the sheathed knives, drew and threw, left- and right-handed. The knife from his right hand went astray and stuck in the side of the coach. The left-handed toss found its target. The knife drove into the scrawny outlaw's neck, the steel blade sneaking up under his bandanna and plunging deep into his throat.

Jerome dived for cover around the side of the stage when Henry Benjamin began firing. The gas hadn't entirely blinded him. The killer cursed and fired and came ever closer to plugging Jerome.

"You're not getting away with this!" The blinded rancher turned toward the sound of the outlaw's gun and fired. And missed.

Amid more cursing, the mounted outlaw emptied his pistol into the rancher's chest. The man fell face forward onto the ground. Jerome acted fast. He dived to skid alongside the felled rancher, hunting for the dropped six-gun. It took him a split second to realize the rancher had fallen on the gun. Jerome awkwardly grabbed the man's coat and belt. With a heave he rolled him over to reveal the gun pressed down into the dirt.

Two more bullets came his way. The rancher's body shielded him. The man grunted, gave a small kick and finally died. Jerome had no time to regret the death. The man had given his life for a good cause.

The Benjamin brothers were about to meet their own well-deserved fate. The six-shooter filled Jerome's fist. He turned toward Henry Benjamin, but the man still fought his bucking horse. And Jerome remembered the man's six-shooter had come up empty. As much as he wanted to end the man's vile life, he wasn't as big a threat as his brother.

Using the rancher as a barricade, he swung around and fired at Leland Benjamin. The outlaw stiffened and clutched at his belly before slumping forward. As if dipped in molasses, he fell from horseback and landed with a thud. He was severely wounded but not done for yet. With a loud groan, he rose onto his knees.

Jerome got to his feet and took careful aim at the road agent — and almost died when Henry Benjamin spurred his horse directly at Jerome. The heavy hooves passed so close to Jerome's head, he felt the heat radiating from the steel horseshoes. He flung himself backward and crashed into the stage. The impact dazed him and let Henry Benjamin pass within inches of him without doing any harm.

It should have been an easy shot. It wasn't. Jerome failed to swing the pistol upward in time. Henry Benjamin galloped off.

Jerome stared after the retreating murderer. There wasn't any chance of making a shot. He jerked at a loud crack of another report, then felt a wave of pain passing through him, radiating in both directions from his midsection. In his desire to take out Henry, he had ignored his brother. Jerome collapsed, wincing at the pain. Using the back stagecoach wheel for support, he turned and found his assailant.

Leland Benjamin screamed at him at the top of his lungs. The outlaw took aim and fired. The slug whined off the wheel's metal rim. Jerome was more measured with his shot. He knocked the outlaw down. A killing shot wasn't in the cards, though. The hammer fell on a spent chamber. Jerome kept firing and kept finding . . . nothing.

With a roar, he rose, stifled the pain from the gunshot wound and charged like an angry bull. Benjamin worked frantically to reload. Jerome came within ten feet of him when the outlaw lifted his gun and trained it on his adversary.

"You're the snake oil salesman. You been goin' to a lot of trouble to make life uneasy for us. I don't know why you've been doin' that, but it ends here and now." A wide grin crossed Leland Benjamin's face as he sighted in and pulled back the hammer.

Jerome shifted left, moved right and drew both knives sheathed along his forearms. His first cast missed. The second drove through the outlaw's eye. Leland Benjamin's head snapped back. For an instant he looked up at the sky, then toppled backward. On a slope, he began rolling down into a shallow ravine.

Jerome felt no satisfaction in watching each spin drive the knife deeper into the man's brain.

"Two down and one to go," he said, his breath coming in huge gasps.

"You surely did save us, mister."

Jerome whirled about at the words. The driver stood a bit uphill from him and brushed himself off.

"They plugged Ole Reston, but he'll be fine when we get to town so a sawbones can patch him up. If they'd marooned us out here, he'd have bleed to death for sure."

"A horse," Jerome said. "There're two horses around somewhere."

"The ones them varmints rode on? One of them's in front of the team. Misery loves company maybe. It —"

Jerome lit out at a dead run. The driver hadn't been exaggerating. A saddled horse pressed against the team's lead animal as if for comfort. Grabbing the reins, Jerome pulled the horse away and vaulted into the saddle. Henry Benjamin had ridden south. Jerome galloped after him.

After only a few minutes, the pain from his gunshot wound filled him to overflowing. He had been shot in the buttocks and sitting astride the horse caused the wound to bleed more freely. He stood in the stirrups and looked down. Blood soaked into the saddle. Seeing it fueled new determination to find Henry Benjamin and bring his reign of lawlessness to an end.

A dead end.

Just when he began to think he lacked the strength to ride one more foot, he spotted his quarry. Benjamin stood beside his horse, examining a front hoof. The paint had either thrown a show or had pulled up lame. Whichever it was ended the chase — and began the fight to the death.

Benjamin dropped the horse's hoof and stepped back, squaring his stance and resting his hand on the side of his holster. His expression was dark and deadly.

Jerome hit the ground running, stumbled and went to one knee. His wound took its toll on the strength in his leg. He got to his feet and faced the outlaw.

"You're at the end of the road," he called out. "If you surrender, I'll see that you get a fair trial before they hang you."

"Who *are* you?" Benjamin scowled. "You're a grifter peddling bogus cures. What do you have against me?"

"We've never met face-to-face," Jerome said, his voice breaking with strain, "but we know each other."

"That big fellow was your friend, wasn't he — the one calling himself Bear? Well, that bounty hunter got what he deserved."

"No man should be skinned like that."

"Skinned him alive," Benjamin said, his lip curling. "He cried out for his mama. Imagine a hulk of a man like that sobbing like a baby. He said you put him up to lying to us. You're not a bounty hunter. You sure as hell ain't no lawman. What's your game?"

"A year back, outside Fort Smith. You and your brothers killed my family."

"We did? I don't recollect."

Jerome's fury blazed forth. "My wife, Marcie, my son — you burned the house down. You hightailed it before I got home!"

"That sounds like something we'd do, but I don't recall the exact house or family. Did we rape your woman before killing her? Or did we just burn down the house around her ears?"

"I saw Curtis die from a shotgun blast to his ugly face. And back at the stagecoach, I killed Leland. Now I'm going to kill you!"

Jerome's hand moved as if he were frozen in a block of ice. The world crept by. He saw all the small things become important. A horsefly flying slowly, too slowly. The horse hobbling away. Slow as a snail.

And Henry Benjamin's hand went for his six-shooter. That wasn't caught up in the curious slowness afflicting the rest of the world. Jerome grabbed for his gun and barely touched it by the time Benjamin had cleared leather, pointed the Colt in his direction and begun fanning the hammer.

Nothing happened. Death wasn't spat from the gun. Dull clicks told Jerome the outlaw hadn't reloaded after shooting at him so many times back at the robbery.

Although much slower, Jerome pulled the rancher's six-gun from his waistband. His aim was perfect, but his gun was also empty. Every time he pulled back on the trigger, he matched the dull clicks already heard from Benjamin's weapon.

The world snapped back around him. Both he and Benjamin once more moved at normal speed. Jerome didn't have any bullets. Benjamin was fumbling at the back of his gun belt to pull out more rounds to reload. With a rebel yell, Jerome charged. His arms wrapped around the outlaw and bowled him over. They hit the ground together, Benjamin taking Jerome's full weight. Stunned, he lay gasping for breath and not struggling.

Jerome went berserk. He hammered at the road agent's face, every blow leaving a bruise. He slammed the heel of his hand down and broke Benjamin's nose. Blood spurted everywhere. Rather than driving all the spirit from him, the broken nose spurred Benjamin on. He arched his back and twisted hard.

Jerome went flying under the powerful move. He rolled over and over until he hit a rocky patch. Stopped by the hard wall of stone, he kicked out, winced at the pain, then came to his feet in a crouch, ready to continue the fight.

"Where'd you run, Benjamin? Come back and let's fight?"

He heard boots pounding against the rocky terrain and lit out after the man who had murdered his family.

He proved faster than the outlaw and tackled him. They hit the ground and rolled. Benjamin kicked out and dragged a rowel across Jerome's face. A three-inch gash on his cheek began spurting blood. In seconds he was as drenched with blood as his opponent. The fury he'd felt before faded some, but not much.

He swung hard and landed a punch to Benjamin's breadbasket. The power was robbed by the outlaw stumbling backward, but it still slowed him more. Jerome stood over him, fists balled. Before he could continue the attack, Benjamin kicked out and caught him on the knee. Jerome's foot didn't move. Everything above his knee did. He screeched in pain and twisted to the side. He hit the ground hard.

Trying to get back in the fight, he probed his knee. The kneecap had been dislodged. He pushed it back into place, but by the time he got to his feet, Benjamin was a dozen feet away.

"I'm not quitting. I'll track you down to the ends of the earth. You'll pay. I swear it. You'll —"

The outlaw slammed a cartridge into his Colt and closed the loading gate.

Benjamin faced Jerome with a loaded gun. His face caked in blood, broken nose askew, the outlaw still grinned in triumph.

"You're gonna see your whore and bastard kid. Think they're in the promised land or maybe they're in hell? You're going to find out." Benjamin lifted his pistol, then lowered it. "I don't want this to be over too fast. I'll give you a fair chance. See if you can outrun my bullet."

Henry Benjamin slipped his six-shooter into the holster and once more went into a gunfighter's stance. A wide grin showed a broken tooth in front. But the eyes revealed his true character. Jerome had never seen such arctic eyes totally lacking in humanity. If there had ever been any doubt about Henry Benjamin being a cold-blooded killer, those eyes erased it.

"I'm going to enjoy shooting you down like an animal."

Benjamin widened his stance a bit more; he drummed his fingers against the holster and rolled his shoulders in preparation of drawing.

"You killed my family. And you don't even remember them."

"You're right. No matter how much you try to jog my memory, I don't remember. There've been too many. Besides," Benjamin said, "it might have been Curtis or Leland what killed them. Or one of my cousins. A half dozen of those no-accounts have ridden with us over the past couple years."

"You'd shoot an unarmed man?" Jerome slowly raised his hands until they were head high.

"Doesn't matter to me. And it won't matter to the worms eatin' your flesh how you died." Benjamin placed his hand on the butt of his six-gun.

Jerome reacted. His right hand went for the knife sheathed at the back of his neck. He thrust his left out to the side and waggled his fingers about. Benjamin hesitated for an instant, his eyes darting toward Jerome's distracting left hand.

The knife slid free. Jerome turned, putting his entire body behind the throw. The dull thud as it sank into Benjamin's chest sounded an instant before the gunman pulled the trigger on his still holstered six-shooter.

Henry Benjamin stared down at the knife protruding from his chest. A quivering hand reached up to touch the handle, but he lacked the strength to pull out the blade. He made a liquid gurgling sound an instant before blood leaked from the corner of his mouth. Those cold, hate-filled eyes shifted from the knife to Jerome. Then he died.

Frozen to the spot, J. Frederick Kincannon stared at the dead outlaw. Then the paralysis passed, and he could once again breathe. He turned his back on the last of the Benjamin gang and limped away.

CHAPTER TWENTY-TWO

Every uneven step the paint took sent a new
jolt of pain into Jerome's body. After a few
miles, he found that, while he could not
ignore the agony, it diminished somewhat.

"I need a good jolt of my own elixir," he
muttered as he rode into Clear Springs.

It was going on twilight and the townsfolk
had closed most of their stores and gone
home for dinner. The Red Ruby showed
some activity as he rode past, but no one
took notice of him.

More than once Jerome had to reach back
and haul Henry Benjamin's body back over
the horse's hindquarters. He had lashed the
corpse down but hadn't done a good job of
it. After some consideration, he rode on to
the undertaker's office. The man had closed
up shop for the night. Jerome dismounted,
wrestled Benjamin's body around and put it
in a chair by the front door. If there had
been a marshal, he would have dumped the

killer's body at the jailhouse to see about collecting a reward.

He tugged on the paint's reins and got it walking toward the Butterfield office. If anyone in town was still at work, it'd be the station agent. Purcell never strayed far from the telegraph key and the news it spewed out from the rest of the world. Jerome poked his head in. To his surprise Purcell was nowhere to be seen.

Bone-tired, Jerome went around back to the comfortable sight of his medicine wagon. He put the horse into the Butterfield corral, then tried to climb up into the wagon and found he couldn't. The bullet wound in his hindquarters had totally robbed his leg of strength. Using only his arms, he dragged himself up and flopped across the driver's seat. Exhaustion overpowered him.

Jerome came awake when somebody shook him hard enough to rattle his teeth.

"What's it? Who?" He rubbed blurry eyes and saw Purcell bending over him.

"I was beginnin' to think you'd played your last card, Perfesser. I poured dang near a bottle of your miracle potion down your gullet. I'm glad that it finally revived you, just like the medicine you gave me perked me right up."

"Glad you're doing better. Now let me die."

Jerome tried to push away and found himself wrapped in a blanket so that he could hardly move.

"The doc's done left Clear Springs and went up to San Angelo, so I did what I could to patch up your gunshot." Purcell snickered. "You was lucky and unlucky. Lucky that you got shot in the ass and unlucky that you got shot where you have to sit."

"You bandaged me? There?"

Jerome wasn't sure if he felt mortification or if gratitude was more appropriate.

"First off, I did. Haven't been able to since that first night."

Jerome sat up. The tightness in his buttock was noticeable but not painful any longer. Bright sunlight filtered through the cracks in the wagon's sides.

"How long?"

"Two days. Been a lot goin' on in them, too." Purcell fumbled in his coat pocket and pulled out a bulging envelope. "This here's your reward money."

"For Benjamin?" His pulse sped up. "For the privilege of removing such scum from the face of the earth, I ought to pay them." He frowned. "Who's coughing up this

366

money?"

"Ain't for any of the robbers. This is from the US Army. You saved their payroll. And Butterfield's payin' a tidy sum for savin' Reston's life."

"The guard on the stage," Jerome remembered.

"He's right as rain, though it hardly ever rains out here. More like it floods, and then —"

"I didn't know the Army had a payroll on the stage."

"Nobody knew. They tried to sneak it past the road agents. Turns out, Henry Benjamin had an informant in the paymaster's office up in Fort Worth that tipped off the gang. Rootin' him out's also included in the reward money." Purcell licked his lips and stared at the bulging envelope. "There's close to five hunnerd dollars here."

Jerome took the envelope and peeled off half. He handed it to the station agent and said, "For rental on looking after my wagon. And I must owe you for a telegram or two, but I don't rightly recollect."

Purcell licked his lips and accepted the money.

"Perfesser, you're one generous fellow. Thank you." He looked up from the wad of greenbacks. "There's something more. The folks all got together when it got around how you'd wiped out the entire Benjamin gang and voted you in as marshal."

"What? Me? A lawman?" Jerome laughed until it ached. "That's rich. I don't know the first thing about being a law dog."

"You gotta be better than the last one we had." Purcell looked thoughtful. "Truth is, you brought Marshal Bishop to justice, too. We all agree you're more likable than him."

"I'm not cut out for that," Jerome said.

He remembered how he had felt when he killed the outlaws and when he'd had to take aim at another living, breathing human. The memory of what it felt like to skewer someone with a knife and —

"No," he said firmly. "That's not what I do."

"Then set up shop next to the saloon. You can whip up potions to your heart's content. Since we don't have a sawbones here anymore, you'd have what they call a monopoly on healing."

"No."

Purcell worked his way from the wagon. The back door stood open and the stage had been lowered. He sat on the edge and looked back at Jerome.

"I suppose I can't blame you too much for wantin' to get out of Clear Springs. This place is dyin'. No bank, no doctor, only a ripsnortin', rip-roarin' saloon. There's no place like it in San Angelo or anyplace this side of Fort Worth's Hell's Half Acre."

"How long are you going to stay here?" Jerome asked.

He gingerly made his way out of the wagon and sat beside Purcell, legs dangling off the stage.

"As long as Butterfield pays me and I get a few dollars extra listenin' to the telegraph key rattle and clank." Purcell sighed. "It won't be long until the stage line is shut down, though. The train's killed off most of the profitable routes. Maybe I should get a job with the railroad. They run telegraph wires alongside the tracks."

Jerome hopped down and took a few tentative steps. He was healing fast if it had only been a couple days. He rubbed his buttock, and it didn't hurt hardly at all.

"That's my job, sir."

Jerome spun. Molly Davenport came bustling up. She handed a carpetbag to Purcell.

"Stow it if you will."

Jerome watched Purcell toss the bag into the rear of the wagon, then close the doors and push up the stage before securing it.

"Have a good trip, wherever you're

headed."

Purcell pumped Jerome's hand, looked hesitantly at Molly, then grinned broadly when she gave him a hug. He shuffled back a pace, then vanished into the depot office.

"Why'd you put your bag into the wagon?" Jerome looked up and saw the canvas scenery rolled up and tied to the roof of the wagon.

"If we are going to get on the road, we'd best do so while it's still light." She held out her arm. When he didn't take it, she said, "You don't think Purcell patched you up, do you? That's quite a wound." She twisted around as if studying his rear end. "Quite a wound, indeed, and I stitched it up nicely. I'm quite a good seamstress. Now, are we staying or are we going to San Angelo?"

"What if I intend to head somewhere else?"

"Back to Arkansas?" She faced him squarely. "There's nothing but old memories for you there. Make new ones." Molly held out her arm again.

Jerome took it and escorted her around to the driver's box. She had to help him up as much as he helped her, but they soon settled down on the hard bench seat. He took the reins in hand and got the horse pulling the wagon. It'd be lighter without the heavy roll of scenery, but they could discuss that matter when they reached their destination.

Wherever that was going to be.

ABOUT THE AUTHORS

Ralph Compton stood six foot eight without his boots. He worked as a musician, a radio announcer, a songwriter, and a newspaper columnist. His first novel, *The Goodnight Trail,* was a finalist for the Western Writers of America Medicine Pipe Bearer Award for best debut novel. He was the *USA Today* bestselling author of the Trail of the Gunfighter series, the Border Empire series, the Sundown Riders series, and the Trail Drive series, among others.

Jackson Lowry is the western pen name for Robert E. Vardeman, author of more than three hundred novels. Nominated for multiple awards, Vardeman received the 2017 Western Fictioneers Lifetime Achievement Award. His Western titles include *Sonora Noose, Great West Detective Agency,* and the weird Western trilogy Punished. He was born in Texas and has lived in the wilds of New Mexico most of his life.

The employees of Thorndike Press hope you have enjoyed this Large Print book. All our Thorndike, Wheeler, and Kennebec Large Print titles are designed for easy reading, and all our books are made to last. Other Thorndike Press Large Print books are available at your library, through selected bookstores, or directly from us.

For information about titles, please call:
  (800) 223-1244

or visit our website at:
  gale.com/thorndike

To share your comments, please write:
  Publisher
  Thorndike Press
  10 Water St., Suite 310
  Waterville, ME 04901